PRAISE FOR THE SPI FILES NOVELS

"Fresh and exciting, humorous and action-packed . . . urban fantasy at its best."
—Ilona Andrews, #1 *New York Times* bestselling author of the Kate Daniels series

"Nonstop action, hilarious klutziness, romance, and lethal Lotharios everywhere. What could be better?"
—Rob Thurman, *New York Times* bestselling author of the Cal Leandros series

"Makenna Fraser brings Southern sass, smarts, and charm to the mean streets of Manhattan as she battles monsters and other magical beings."
—Jennifer Estep, *New York Times* bestselling author of the Elemental Assassin series

"An absolute must-read. Shearin's incredible ability to combine the scary and the wacky is why she is a star on the rise!"
—*RT Book Reviews*

"One heck of a series that is not to be missed."
—A Book Obsession

"A wonderfully adventurous series, pairing dangerous mystery-solving with the bizarre and supernatural."
—That's What I'm Talking About

"*The X-Files* meets *Men in Black* . . . Snappy and entertaining."
The BiblioSanctum

"Shearin is a fabulous writer who draws the reader into her world."
—Fresh Fiction

Ace Books by Lisa Shearin

The SPI Files Novels

THE GRENDEL AFFAIR
THE DRAGON CONSPIRACY
THE BRIMSTONE DECEPTION
THE GHOUL VENDETTA

The Raine Benares Novels

MAGIC LOST, TROUBLE FOUND
ARMED & MAGICAL
THE TROUBLE WITH DEMONS
BEWITCHED & BETRAYED
CON & CONJURE
ALL SPELL BREAKS LOOSE

THE
GHOUL
VENDETTA

A SPI Files Novel

LISA SHEARIN

ACE
New York

ACE
Published by Berkley
An imprint of Penguin Random House LLC
375 Hudson Street, New York, New York 10014

Copyright © 2017 by Lisa Shearin
Penguin Random House supports copyright. Copyright fuels creativity, encourages
diverse voices, promotes free speech, and creates a vibrant culture. Thank you for buying
an authorized edition of this book and for complying with copyright laws by not
reproducing, scanning, or distributing any part of it in any form without permission.
You are supporting writers and allowing Penguin Random House to continue to
publish books for every reader.

ACE is a registered trademark and the A colophon is a trademark of
Penguin Random House LLC.

ISBN: 9781101989401

First Edition: February 2017

Printed in the United States of America
1 3 5 7 9 10 8 6 4 2

Cover illustration by Julie Dillon
Cover design by Judith Lagerman
Book design by Kelly Lipovich

As always, for Derek,
my happily ever after

ACKNOWLEDGMENTS

To Kristin Nelson, my agent. I'm so incredibly grateful for all that you do.

To Anne Sowards, my editor. It's a joy and privilege to craft Mac and Ian's adventures with you.

To Julie Dillon, my cover artist. Your amazing talent continues to blow me away.

To Logan Hyatt, my assistant. I don't know what I'd ever do without you. You rock!

I was on a date, on a yacht, surrounded by New York's glitterati.

It felt downright surreal. What would the folks back home think if they could see me now?

Being on a date with Rake Danescu was getting to be a regular thing for me, but being part of a floating A-list gathering was a first. Usually when I got to go somewhere this fancy, it was entirely work related. Tonight was only slightly about my job. Rake was the one here on business. I was here mostly for fun, partly in case Rake's business became SPI's business.

My name is Makenna Fraser, and I work for SPI. That's Supernatural Protection & Investigations, to the world's paranormal community. Humans had police, FBI, CIA, Homeland Security, and Interpol. Paranormals had SPI. We were all of the above rolled into one. SPI was a worldwide organization, headquartered here in New York. I was one of five seers in the entire agency.

Criminals, supernatural and otherwise, often used disguises. Supernatural bad guys and gals used more advanced means of going undetected. "Advanced" as in magic. Any paranormal criminal worthy of his, her, or its rap sheet had an arsenal of wards, glamours, veils, shields, and various and sundry spells that helped them go undetected. A good seer could see through any and all of them. It was a talent that made us popular with supernatural law enforcement organizations—and a target of supernatural crime syndicates.

There were high-ranking representatives of some of the latter here tonight. It was my job to know their faces without letting them know mine. But these weren't the people who committed the crimes. Their hands were clean and their reputations pristine. Organized crime most definitely paid, and the ladies and gentlemen at the top of those organizations were especially keen to spread goodwill through philanthropy. In fact, that was the reason for tonight's gathering on a hundred-and-fifty-foot yacht cruising the Hudson River on a balmy evening in late June.

Some of the oldest people on board looked the youngest, and it wasn't due to plastic surgery. Their fountain of youth was an endless series of throats and the blood that flowed through them.

The yacht's owner was a vampire. Bela Báthory was the nephew and presumed heir of Ambrus Báthory, the head of the most powerful vampire crime family on the East Coast.

The yacht's name was the *Persephone*. A little dose of vampire irony there. *Demeter* was the name of the ship that had brought Dracula to England. Persephone was Demeter's daughter.

The men were in black tie, and the majority of the women were wearing high heels and even higher hemlines, or flowing gowns with slits up to there. The yacht was big, but it wasn't big enough to be stable enough for me to walk around on high-heel-elevated-tippy-toes. For me, it was lower heels, lower hemline, and Dramamine, with no alcohol. Dramamine plus drinking would equal me falling overboard. A midnight swim was not in my plans for this evening.

Rake made sure that I could hear him walking up behind me. He didn't want to go for a swim, either. Now that I was duly forewarned, Rake slid a hand, then his arm around my waist. My pulse kicked up for a few beats. A normal man wouldn't have felt it. Rake wasn't a normal man. In a satisfied response, he tightened his hold ever so slightly. When it came to Rake, my pulse—and hormones—refused to go along with my better judgment, which dictated extreme caution. They were more along the lines of tossing caution to the wind—along with my undies. For now, my better judgment was in the driver's seat.

Rake and I stood together gazing out across the river to the lights of Manhattan's Upper West Side.

"What did he say?" I asked.

"He was receptive to my offer," Rake said. "My cards are on the table. The next move is his. Now, I wait."

Rake's seemingly impromptu meeting at one of the yacht's bars had been with a private investment banker. Rake was representing a group of entrepreneurial businessmen looking for capital. At least that's what it was on the surface. In actuality, Rake represented his government's intelligence agency looking to get a foothold in a new technology before the competition.

However, none of the parties involved were human.

Rake Danescu was a goblin. The competition was, is, and probably would always be the elves. They hadn't been at war for several centuries, but that didn't mean they played nice, especially not on our world.

SPI didn't get involved in goblin/elf politics. That being

said, we'd found it prudent to know what was going on. Very often what was considered by goblin and elven governments to be a "private matter" spilled over into criminal activity affecting others. Then it became SPI's business. Rake didn't let us in on every aspect of his business dealings, but he had agreed to bring us into the loop when his business was about to cross the streams with our job—namely keeping the peace between supernaturals, and keeping the supernatural world secret from humans.

The streams had been crossing an awful lot lately.

Rake's business was booming. Unfortunately, so was ours. Some of it was a direct result of goblin/elf dealings, but most of it was not.

I'd been appointed by my boss, Vivienne Sagadraco, as the official go-between. She knew that Rake and I were seeing each other, so "SPI/goblin intelligence liaison" had been added to my job description—at least, as long as Rake and I were dating. If our relationship ever went down the drain, we'd reevaluate my additional responsibilities at that time. Even my boss—who was a multi-millennia-old dragon in the guise of a fierce businesswoman who reminded me a bit of Judy Dench—recognized the awkwardness of continuing to professionally liaise when a liaison of a more personal nature had gone south.

One of the few things I'd actually managed to learn about the mysterious Rake Danescu was that you never knew which way things were going to go. Goblins were like that.

The motives of mortal men were difficult enough to figure out. Goblins—whether involved in politics, business, or interpersonal relations—made Machiavelli look like an intrigue dilettante. When it came to supernatural beings, but especially goblins, very little was actually as it seemed.

Like Rake Danescu's motives when it came to me. I didn't know what they were. Okay, I take that back. I knew exactly what they were. Him, me, horizontal. Or vertical. I didn't think Rake was picky about the particulars.

Rake was gorgeous, rich, brilliant, and could charm anything off of anyone regardless of sex, race, or supernatural species. I was from a small town in the mountains of North Carolina. I was human, average height, blond hair, green eyes, and I'd been told that I looked about as threatening as a declawed kitty cat. My grandma Fraser had always told me I had "little dog syndrome"—small size, big attitude, delusions of toughness. I made enough money at SPI to keep a nice East Village roof over my head, and I was pretty much immune to charm. Though that last characteristic was probably due to an excess of caution and suspicion in my nature rather than actual immunity.

Rake was a dark mage, which meant he was absurdly talented in a type of magic most sane people wouldn't mess with. Rake wasn't most people, or even most goblins. Though as far as I'd been able to determine in the time that we'd known each other, he was sane, at least most of the time. He was also cunning, crafty, and conniving. In short, Rake Danescu was a perfect goblin. Anyone who looked at him— and there were plenty of those right now, both women and men—would see a tall, dark, and unwholesomely handsome man.

As a seer, I saw past Rake's human glamour to his pale gray skin, pointed ears, and—a goblin's most distinguishing feature—his fangs. He was still breathtakingly beautiful, albeit in an exotic way. Unlike the vampires on board, Rake didn't use his fangs for feeding, just defense, offense, and making women crazy. He'd slowly grazed the back of my neck once, so I could attest to that last point from personal experience. The tingles hadn't stopped for days.

It hadn't gone beyond that. Yet.

All I wanted was a nice guy. At least I used to think I

did. Now I wasn't so sure. There was a lot to be said about a brilliant, fascinating, inter-dimensional goblin spy of mystery with tingle-inducing fangs.

I was being cautious. Rake was being respectful of my caution. So, that was where we were. Also, we'd both been busy. Time together hadn't been easy to come by. And SPI had been busier than normal since the first of the year, and we thought it had everything to do with what had happened a couple of weeks before Christmas, when an enterprising demon lord and his elf dark mage partner had come entirely too close to creating a direct flight from Hell to New York.

Some people would argue that it already existed. The demon-and-elf diabolical duo had opened a Hellpit directly under Bacchanalia, which had been the crown jewel of Rake's business and spy empire and the city's most exclusive sex club. Yes, I said "had been," as in past tense. Bacchanalia didn't exist anymore. It had collapsed into the sinkhole created when we essentially slammed the gate to Hell.

Yep, Rake had run a sex club. In fact, that was where we had met on my first night on the job—at SPI, not Bacchanalia.

Never one to lament losing one of his crown jewels, Rake had thrown himself into rebuilding the intelligence-gathering web the demon lord and elf dark mage's activity had damaged, and was playing catch-up with a vengeance.

The yacht had been moving at a leisurely cruising speed up the Hudson—then it wasn't.

The engines had stopped.

I glanced at a now frowning Rake. "Are we supposed to stop?"

"No."

The yacht slowed its forward motion, but didn't come to a complete stop. The Hudson was a tidal river, or to be more exact, an estuary. The Hudson had two high and two low tides within each twenty-four-hour time frame. The tide's rise and fall actually changed the direction of the flow. Not that we needed to worry about that. At least I didn't think we did.

That thought had no sooner crossed my mind when the yacht shuddered beneath our feet. It didn't simply stop, it was jerked to a stop, and I was grateful not to be wearing high heels. I grabbed the railing. Rake grabbed the railing with one hand and tightened his grip on me with the other.

Then the lights went out, immediately followed by screams and shouts.

Rake pulled me away from the railing, but not before I saw a long, dark shape knife through the water.

I'd been out on deck long enough that my eyes were already adjusted to the dark. Those inside the salon had gone from bright light to no light. Those below decks were in total darkness until the emergency lights kicked in. Even the vampires and goblins would need time for their night vision to adjust.

It stayed dark.

Rake pulled us over against the salon windows to keep us from being trampled by panicked passengers.

I tried to further flatten myself. "Doesn't this thing have emergency lights?"

"Yes."

That one word told me what I didn't want to know.

This was no accident. And when your host was near the top of the supernatural crime food chain, any non-accident could be very bad for anyone unlucky enough to be around him. I had no intention of going from party guest to collateral damage.

A dark column as big around as a power pole and nearly as long rose out of the water and fell across the railing not twenty feet from where we stood. The tapered tip crashed through a salon window, then withdrew and flailed blindly until it found the railing and coiled around it, getting a good grip.

Power poles weren't in the middle of rivers, and they definitely didn't have suction cups.

It was a giant tentacle.

2

THIS was one of those times when even I doubted what I was seeing. I felt like I'd just been dropped into the middle of a B movie creature feature from the 1950s.

Part of my agent training when I started working for SPI included watching more than a few of those movies for educational purposes. You'd be surprised at what some of those low-budget Hollywood filmmakers got right. Still, I couldn't believe what was less than twenty feet from us.

"Is that what I—?"

"Kraken," Rake confirmed. In one smooth move, he released me, raised his now red-glowing hands, and launched an incendiary spell.

Other than giving us a better look at what was about to drag the yacht to the bottom of the Hudson River, the spell did nothing.

"Well, I'll be damned," Rake said mildly.

"I think we all are."

As a seer, my job was to point out the supernatural bad

guys, then get the heck out of the way so they could either be taken into custody or, if necessary, taken out. I was presently on track to become SPI's longest surviving seer. My three predecessors had met with on-the-job accidents that had turned out to be not so accidental. Some unknown entity was trying to keep SPI without a seer. I was trying to live long enough to qualify for retirement. Lately, I'd been glad just to survive until my next paycheck.

All that being said, I had a gun, I'd been trained, and I almost had the confidence to use it. Though suddenly, I went from having one target to what SPI's shooting instructor called a "target-rich environment."

We were being boarded. It wasn't by pirates, and unfortunately none of them looked like Johnny Depp. If I had to assign a movie to the things that were slithering entirely too fast up the side of the yacht and over the rail, it would be *Creature from the Black Lagoon*. The kraken was holding the *Persephone* still while the creatures swarmed over the sides. Screams from the other side of the ship suggested the starboard guests were getting their share of attention. The humans on board were probably the ones doing the screaming—the non-clued-in ones, that is. Thankfully, my training kicked in before my vocal cords could.

But call me picky. I liked to be sure that the bad guys were actually bad before attempting to fill them with holes. Seconds later, one of the creatures lashed out with a webbed hand tipped with hooked claws and ripped the throat out of one of the crewmen trying to fend it off. Dark blood sprayed the yacht's windows.

Bad guy. Check. I opened fire.

Magic was great, but sometimes there was no substitute for lead and silver.

If it had worked.

Not only did hollow points infused with silver not kill it, the thing wasn't even inconvenienced. That was bad.

There was now no one between us and two targets that were close enough for me to see the gills flexing on the sides of their necks. Too close. I squeezed off two more shots: one hit, one miss. I forced myself to relax the two-handed death grip I had on my gun.

Rake was the poster boy for cool as he readied another spell. "Aim for the eyes."

I had been aiming for the eyes; that part was easy. The things were glowing yellow and were the only light on the boat, or at least the corner we were trapped on. Killing them was the hard part. My bullets might as well have been gnats—minimal annoyance, no damage.

Rake launched a different spell. In my deep knowledge of magic, I knew it was different because it was blue and not red. This one picked up the creature in question and hurled it off the side of the yacht and out over the river at a distance the Yankees would have envied. Rake followed that up with doing the same to the next six boarders.

He was panting with exertion, but sounded pleased with himself. "If I can't destroy, disperse."

Rake was winded, but all the creatures had to do was swim back to the yacht, their trip across the river having merely pissed them off.

In the next instant, darkness covered everything as if a black, smothering blanket had been dropped on top of the entire yacht. I could not see my hand in front of my face. My breathing became labored, and the screams sounded unnaturally distant. As far as my ears were concerned, turning down the volume on dozens of panicked people was a good thing, but nothing else was.

I no longer sensed Rake next to me, or even near me.

He was gone.

Or had been taken.

"Rake?" I didn't want to shout and earn the undivided attention of any remaining swamp things, but I wanted Rake to hear me.

No response.

I replaced my gun with a knife.

A hand grabbed my arm, and I slashed out. Another hand grabbed my wrist. The grip was like iron, but it didn't smell fishy.

"It's me!" Rake hissed.

"Why didn't you say something?"

"Why did you yell? I was right here."

"I didn't yell, and I can't see anything," I snapped. Rake was a goblin. Cats were blind as bats compared to goblins. "Can you see?"

"Not much. It's black magic."

With an emphasis on black. And silent, at least on our side of the yacht. The screaming escalated on the other side.

"Old World, ancient, and black magic." Rake sounded concerned. If my badass, dark mage, goblin superspy, maybe boyfriend was concerned, I should be terrified.

"Can you make light?" I whispered.

"Maybe, but I shouldn't."

"Maybe?"

"Light isn't all that's being smothered here."

My blood went cold. When a mage at Rake's level couldn't use his magic, the situation was officially FUBAR. Many of the guests were either mage-level talents or supernatural beings like vampires, whose magic was part of what they were. That someone had tossed a metaphorical blanket over their magic to keep them from fighting back or even defending themselves was beyond terrifying.

No power—either engines, lights, or magic.

And suddenly no deck beneath our feet.

The yacht groaned like a living thing as the kraken pulled it nearly on its side. Rake and I slid down the deck and into the water. I made a grab for the railing, which was now in the water, but missed. I went under, swallowing what felt like a double-lungful of the Hudson.

I fought my way to the surface, coughing and gasping for what air I could find. My feet were now bare, my shoes probably sinking to the bottom of the river. Better them than me. Rake surfaced next to me, smoothly treading water. He got an arm around my shoulders and held my head above water while I coughed and sputtered.

I looked to where the yacht had been. All I could see was a yacht-sized blackness, and all I could hear were screams. We were outside the smothering darkness—if that was better than being in the water with a kraken, a horde of swamp creatures, and who knew what else.

Until tonight, I didn't think vampires could cross running water, and I had no clue what would happen if one took an involuntary swim in a river. I saw one of the vampire guests bobbing nearby, doing a decent job of treading water, meaning vampires didn't melt when they got wet. Though come to think of it, that was the Wicked Witch of the West.

The last swim Rake and I had taken together had been in a Hellpit full of molten brimstone. Rake's magic had been all that'd been between us and instant flash frying.

Whatever brushed past my legs just then felt big enough to make the shark in *Jaws* look like a guppy. I knew the Hudson had some salt water in it, but I'd never heard of sharks coming this far upriver. Though compared to the kraken, I think I'd prefer it to be "only a shark," regardless of size.

The whatever-it-was brushed my legs again, and I shrieked and kicked out.

Rake swore and bobbed under the water, nearly dragging me with him.

"You felt it, too?" I asked when he surfaced.

"Yes, you kicked me."

"Sorry."

Then Rake's eyes went wide. Seemed I wasn't the only one who'd just had a close encounter.

"I really don't want to stay here for a second pass." My teeth were beginning to chatter. I was chalking it up to cold water and night air rather than terror, but if I could get away from the things now circling us, anyone could call it anything they wanted.

"I wasn't going to suggest it. I will, however, make us unappetizing." Rake took a deep breath and gazed down into the water. I didn't feel any less potentially tasty, but several large splashes and sudden shifts in the water beneath us said our new acquaintances abruptly took their attentions elsewhere.

The shouts and screams didn't lessen; but over that, and getting closer, was a sound I wanted to hear. Sirens. The captain must have gotten off a mayday before the power was cut.

Let's hear it for the Coast Guard.

Rake raised his eyes to mine. "Let's hope that spell holds."

"What did you do?"

"Made us scarier to them than they are to us."

"That's some serious scary."

"And it's just an illusion."

At this point, I'd gladly take it.

The blanket, curtain, whatever parted just long enough to show me the *Persephone* on its side, with a pair of swamp creatures carrying a slumped figure between them. They slid off the yacht and into the river with their prisoner.

The kraken released the *Persephone*, but instead of its

tentacles sliding off into the water, it actually righted the yacht, as though it had gotten what it came for and put its tub toy back the way it had found it, before vanishing into the depths.

The water was flowing again as it usually did, as if a kraken hadn't just tossed around a hundred-and-fifty-foot yacht like a buoy. The moon came out from behind the clouds, shining down on nothing but water—no kraken, no swamp creatures.

It was just another date as usual with Rake Danescu.

3

THE NYPD was definitely on top of their "protect and serve" game tonight.

A crime had been committed on board the *Persephone* tonight, and the damaged mega yacht—aka floating crime scene—that belonged to the obscenely wealthy kidnap victim—aka a powerful and influential tax payer—was being escorted back to port. The *Persephone* was full of witnesses, some injured, others traumatized, who were also powerful and influential, though not to Bela Báthory's level. It was enough that we were going to get treatment reserved for royalty or heads of state—after we had given our statements.

The police weren't going to get much from anyone on the yacht. Most of the guests were supernaturals, and by necessity were very adept at explaining the impossible with the mundane. The kraken became an underwater cable that must have come loose from its moorings and the fish men became SEAL-type kidnappers in high-tech dive gear. The supernaturals had gotten their story together before the Harbor Patrol had arrived, leaving the panicked mundanes raving about sea monsters.

After hearing the more rational explanation, the humans began doubting what they had seen, or what they thought they had seen. A couple of vampiric hypnotic suggestions, a reminder about how dark it was after the kidnappers had cut the power to the ship, and the humans admitted that they couldn't possibly have seen what they thought they saw.

As a result, the police were focused on the kidnapping of Bela Báthory.

The Báthorys were a known criminal family. That the heir apparent to the family's "business empire" had been taken from the deck of a yacht in an elaborate kidnapping plot was completely believable.

When one of New York's wealthiest and most notorious citizens gets snatched off a yacht in the middle of the Hudson River, the media will get wind of it and be swarming worse than mosquitoes in July. While plenty of press and more than a few satellite trucks were waiting when we arrived at the South Street Seaport, one reporter stood out.

I recognized him. He knew Rake.

Rake hadn't gotten a chance to kill any of those swamp creatures. The snarl he didn't even try to hide said he'd like nothing better than to satisfy those urges on the person of one Baxter Clayton.

Baxter was an investigative reporter for a local TV station. He was tall, handsome, and immaculately groomed with blond hair that gale-force winds couldn't have budged.

Baxter Clayton was also a Grade-A asshat.

Last year, he'd stalked Rake for an exposé he'd been doing on New York's upper-class sex industry. And as the owner of the most exclusive sex club in Manhattan, Rake was on Baxter the Bastard's radar. Bacchanalia was gone, but Baxter's radar was always sweeping the city for the next big, ratings-grabbing story. A mob boss's nephew kidnapped off his own yacht amidst a who's who of New York's society. It was right up Baxter's alley. And within minutes, he would get the unparalleled satisfaction of seeing Rake Danescu among the guests. And no doubt that satisfaction would increase tenfold when he saw that Rake was wrapped in a foil blanket and dripping like a wet cat.

"Do you want to jump overboard again?" I asked him. "I wouldn't blame you in the least."

"Not unless I can take Mr. Clayton with me."

"If you did, you'd win the instant undying gratitude of every man and woman on board, both living and undead."

"If we weren't surrounded by representatives of no less than three law enforcement agencies, I would seriously consider it," Rake said. "There are many people here who I would love to have owing me favors."

I spotted our salvation—or at least our getaway car.

Yasha's black Suburban.

I didn't bother asking myself how my coworkers had found out what had happened. If it happened in New York and involved supernaturals, SPI would know minutes later.

I was grateful for it.

Even if it meant explaining to my partner, Ian Byrne, what had happened. It wasn't that once again I'd ended up involved in what was likely to be our next big case; it was who I was with. Rake had absolutely nothing to do with what had happened tonight, but that wouldn't stop my partner from dropping the blame right at Rake's designer-shod feet.

The passenger side door opened and Ian got out. He and Rake locked eyes.

I did not need this.

Ian's blame dropping wasn't logical, but neither was his big-brother protectiveness. It was about feelings. For me. Feelings that caused him to do anything he had to do to keep me safe. It was hard to be mad about that, or at least hard to stay mad for long.

My partner was SPI's number one producing agent, which meant if he went after a perp, he got them—one way or another. He was inhumanly qualified to bag his bad guy in every way, even though he was human. A career in a branch of the military that he either wouldn't— or couldn't—talk about had been followed by a stint as a homicide detective with the NYPD.

Ian's time as one of New York's finest came to an abrupt and brutal end one night in a high-end pawn shop that specialized in unique and estate pieces. There had been a string of robberies and murders linking stores selling high-priced estate jewelry. Ian would have been better off not investigating that particular store on that night—because Ian's partner wouldn't have been eaten by the gang of ghouls responsible for the string of crimes.

That'd been Ian's first encounter with the supernatural; and when Vivienne Sagadraco had offered him a job going after creatures like the things that'd killed his partner, Ian had turned in his NYPD badge and accepted SPI's.

Vivienne Sagadraco had assigned Ian to be my partner my first day on the job. Three of my predecessors had met violent ends on the job that hadn't had a thing to do with bad luck but everything to do with someone with a lot of power and a lot of pull wanting, for some still-unknown reason, to keep SPI from having a seer in its headquarters' office.

Ian had been deemed most qualified to keep SPI's newest seer from becoming its latest casualty.

To me, it felt more like glorified babysitting; and initially, Ian agreed with my assessment. But the big boss had given him a job to do, and he was going to do it, even if he didn't like it—or me, for that matter.

It didn't take long for that to change—the him liking me part. What can I say? I grow on people.

Now my problem wasn't that Ian didn't like me; it was that he was overprotective, like big-brother overprotective.

As a Southern girl from the North Carolina mountains, I knew my way around guns. However, that knowledge only extended to target shooting and some halfhearted hunting back home. It did not include returning fire at someone or something hunting me. That was an adjustment I was still making. I appreciated Ian's training efforts in that area as well as hand-to-hand combat, but I'd pretty much gotten as good as I was going to get, though I kept trying, and Ian kept teaching.

However, criminal creatures that went bump in the night weren't all that Ian had deemed me needing protection from. He'd extended his attentions to the men in my life—more specifically to the goblin in my life.

Ian didn't like Rake. Rake wasn't particularly fond of Ian. Though in my opinion, the vast majority of their animosity was a direct result of two alpha males locking horns.

Over me.

I think Rake kind of enjoyed Ian's reaction, though even a goblin dark mage knew when teasing was liable to get his ass kicked by Ian and his butt kicked to the curb by me. Rake most definitely wasn't stupid. Quite the opposite. He knew when to back off.

Rake also knew that where that black Suburban was, Yasha Kazakov would be behind the wheel. Yasha was one of SPI's drivers. In a city where there were more paranormal perps than parking spaces, having a good drop-off and pick-up guy was crucial. And even better was a driver who'd never hesitated to go above and beyond his job description to keep the streets of his adopted city clean and law-abiding. Yasha broke most of the city's traffic laws on a daily basis so that those same streets would be safe for humans and supernaturals alike.

Yasha was a werewolf and considered me and Ian part of his pack. So if Ian didn't like Rake, Yasha didn't like Rake either, and both for the same reason—protecting me.

The Suburban's rear passenger door opened and Alain Moreau got out.

Oh crap.

I shouldn't have been surprised to find Ian, Yasha, and Alain Moreau waiting when the *Persephone*, with its police and Harbor Patrol escort, limped back to the South Street Seaport.

There were quite a few supernaturals working for the NYPD and the city's municipal agencies. Many of them were SPI's eyes in the mundane world. Cases involving supernatural criminals seldom remained separate from the mundane world. Having people on the inside was invaluable for keeping mortal police involvement in supernatural affairs to a minimum.

Having Alain Moreau show up at the scene of yet another awkward situation I'd found myself in the middle of—by no fault of my own, may I add—still put a knot in my stomach.

Alain Moreau was my manager at SPI. Normal people got a hitch in their breathing when their manager asked them to step into their office or a nearby conference room. I'll admit to that giving me a bout of butterflies, too. But most of the time it was because I'd developed an unwanted knack for landing in the middle of what would become New York's next paranormal crisis du jour.

It also didn't help my nerves that my manager was a vampire. He reminded me of a really pale Anderson Cooper, which meant he was as cute as he could be, but that didn't change the fact that humans were food and I was human. I knew I didn't need to worry about that, but sometimes your lizard brain outvoted your logic.

I didn't know exactly how old Alain Moreau was, but I suspected he'd been around longer than America had been a country. The first time I'd found myself in trouble with the boss was when a shapeshifter had disguised itself as me to gain access to SPI headquarters and wreak havoc. My innocence had been proven by surveillance footage showing me and my evil twin at the same time, but in separate places in our headquarters compound—with one notable difference. The shapeshifter had copied the clothes I was wearing that day, but it didn't replicate one important accessory—powdered sugar. It'd been the week before Christmas and I'd been eating cookies and wearing some of the powdered sugar they'd been rolled in.

Saved by my sweet tooth.

Before I'd been cleared of wrongdoing, I had been afraid of losing my job. I liked my job. Heck, now I loved it. I was good at it, and lives were saved as a result. There weren't many places where you could get that kind of job satisfaction. Alain Moreau had assured me that my continued employment at SPI as well as my continued survival were important to the agency.

All that being said, my vampire manager didn't look happy. He didn't look pissed, but he definitely wasn't amused.

He and Ian made a nicely matched set.

And Alain Moreau was in charge of SPI for the next three weeks. Vivienne Sagadraco was taking her first vacation in over a century. Everyone needed time off, and a multi-millennia-old, fire-breathing dragon in charge of a world-wide supernatural protection organization needed it even more.

The press was left cooling their heels outside of a very impressive police barrier. As guests finished giving their statements, they were escorted to where their cars and drivers waited to take them home.

Rake had driven us himself in one of his cars, an older model Range Rover. It wasn't what one would expect a rich spy master/sex club owner would tour about town in. Unfortunately, it was also parked outside of where the police had set up their no-media-allowed barricade. We'd have to walk right past Baxter Clayton to get there.

I saw Rake's eyes go from Baxter to his car and back again.

I smiled sweetly. "Give you a lift?"

Yasha had parked inside the police barrier.

Rake glanced from Baxter to where Ian and Alain Moreau stood next to the Suburban, arms crossed over their chests, expressions set on disapproving scowl, and sighed.

Ian and my vampire manager had just been declared the lesser evil.

I linked my arm through his. "See? Now you don't have to get a microphone shoved in your face. Your evening's looking up."

"That's open for debate."

4

IF you wanted to kidnap a master vampire, you needed to break out the big guns.

A kraken and a couple dozen swamp creatures had done the trick.

"Sounds like they went a bit overboard," Ian noted. "No pun intended."

"None taken," I said. "Even though quite a few of us did go for a swim."

My partner definitely hadn't made a pun, intentional or otherwise. He would have had to have been in a joking mood for that, and Ian Byrne most definitely was not in a joking mood. By now my hair had more or less dried, and so had my dress, but dry didn't get rid of the eau du river aroma I was presently wafting in all directions.

"This is getting to be a habit," Ian noted, glancing over to where Rake was "answering a few final questions" from the police, that were neither few nor probably final.

"Hey, ninety-five percent of our dates haven't had the

police involved," I reminded him, "and none of them were Rake's fault."

"He just happens to be places where all hell breaks loose."

I gave my partner an arch look. "May I remind you that two of those three times, you were there as well?"

The first time was my and Rake's first date. By what was an authentic coincidence, Ian and Kylie O'Hara, SPI's director of media and public relations, were at the same restaurant, having their first date as well. Needless to say, that arrangement was awkward. Then the occasion took a hop, skip, and a jump from awkward to downright bizarre as a man there for a business lunch had a drug-induced freak-out and was suddenly able to see every supernatural being in the restaurant. The situation went to Hades in a handbasket from there, ending with the restaurant burning to the ground.

The second time involved a gang of drunk teenage werewolves who decided that their wolf cousins at the Bronx Zoo needed to be set free. Their attempted jailbreak had unfortunately coincided with the zoo's largest annual fundraising event. I'd been there with Rake. Ian had been there with Kylie. Chaos happened.

"Best of all, we didn't have to lie," I told Ian. "We just left out the little details the police wouldn't believe anyway. That kind of honesty will get you sedated and sent to the hospital for psych evaluation. To paraphrase Jack Nicholson, 'They can't handle the truth.'"

A few of the police on the scene had recognized Ian from his time on the force. He'd honestly answered their questions about how he had been and where he was working—he was doing great, and was working for a private security firm. All were true, while not being the whole truth.

A few minutes later, Rake made his way over to us, looking neither left nor right, not rushing but not dragging his feet, either. The press had spotted him and were shouting to get his attention. My date was a center of near-Zen calm as he pretended that none of them existed, especially Baxter Clayton. All I can say is that it was a good thing there was a police-guarded barricade or Rake would have been mobbed, and that would not have ended well. Goblins were rather like cats: neat, fastidious, mostly aloof, with an intense dislike of being dunked in water. If you did anything to them that they considered to be degrading or annoying, you'd better prepare to be shredded.

Rake Danescu was wet, his tuxedo was likely ruined, and though his expression was carefully blank, I knew that inside he made Grumpy Cat look like a cheerleader. But when he got close enough to us, he did at least acknowledge Ian.

The goblin inclined his head. "Ian."

"Rake."

There was no handshake, and definitely no bro hug, but no one ended up injured and requiring hospitalization. Considering how Ian and Rake felt about each other, the use of a first-name greeting rather than fists meant they were starting to get downright friendly.

Rake repeated the gesture to Moreau. "Alain."

"Lord Danescu."

The use of Rake's goblin court title didn't indicate dislike, at least not necessarily, but instead was due to Alain Moreau being many centuries old and French. Moreau's body was undead, but not his sense of etiquette. Those same exquisite manners helped smooth over the next awkwardness.

"May we drive you home?" Moreau asked Rake.

The goblin glanced to his Land Rover and the swarm of media types that were smack-dab in between. A growl vibrated low in Rake's chest. "Yes, if it wouldn't be too much trouble."

"None at all, I assure you."

It would also give Moreau the benefit of time to get the answers to his questions. Rake knew it, he didn't like it, but like I said: lesser of two evils.

Yasha was driving, Moreau was in the front passenger seat, Rake and me were in the middle seats, with Ian right behind us on the third row. I had no doubt Ian arranged it that way to make Rake uncomfortable. If it did bother Rake, he gave no sign.

Rake and I told them everything that happened—and what the police had been told.

"At least that's the story everyone seemed to be going with," I ended.

"Your professional opinion?" Moreau asked.

"As a seer, everything was exactly what it looked like, even though I didn't know what they were."

"The Creatures from the Black Lagoon?" Yasha asked.

"Those were the ones."

My Russian werewolf friend loved classic horror movies— and classic musicals. I caught a flash of a grin in the rearview mirror with a nod that said "cool" loud and clear.

"I'll have the archivists pull everything we have that is bipedal and aquatic," Moreau said.

"That kraken was aquatic," I told him, "but it certainly wasn't bipedal."

"Are you sure it was a kraken?" Ian asked.

"Uh, a tentacle the size of a power pole?"

"It was a kraken," Rake said from beside me. "In my world we have a similar creature. However, that creature would not have stopped once it began attacking a ship. It would drag it under, crushing it, then consume anything edible that tried to escape from the wreckage, or any bodies that floated away. The one we encountered tonight not only ceased its attack, but seemed to stop on command."

"Did you sense a mage in the area?" Moreau asked.

Rake shook his head. "Other than those who were guests on the *Persephone* using their magic to defend themselves, no."

"So we've got kidnappers out of a bad horror movie—" Ian began.

"*Creature from the Black Lagoon* is classic," Yasha objected.

"Excuse me, kidnappers out of a campy, cult horror *classic*, who grabbed the nephew of the head of the most powerful vampire family on the East Coast, using a kraken that was trained like an attack dog."

I nodded. "That pretty much covers it. Though that seems like an awful lot of trouble to go to for a kidnapping. Wouldn't there be an easier way to get Bela Báthory?"

"His uncle, Ambrus, is notoriously private," Moreau said, "and seldom leaves his family compound on Long Island. When he does leave, he's surrounded by enough security to make it impossible to even get close to him, let alone abduct him."

"Unless you have a trained kraken at your disposal, who plays fetch with a hundred-and-fifty-foot yacht," I noted. "Whoever has him, they went to a lot of trouble. The next question is why."

Alain Moreau almost snorted, but it sounded elegant coming from him. "That list is as long as Ambrus Báthory's life, Agent Fraser. One of his family's many enemies is very happy tonight."

5

WE dropped Rake off at one of the buildings he owned in Lower Manhattan where he conveniently kept a car in its parking deck. I guess free parking was one of the perks of owning real estate in New York. Then Yasha drove to my apartment in the East Village, and Ian insisted on walking me up the stairs to the fifth floor.

I didn't say a word to try to change his mind. Ian hadn't been there to protect me tonight and it was bothering him. I think it bothered him even more than Rake being there instead of him. My partner and I had had the talk more than once about me being a big girl who could take care of herself against the Big Bad Wolf that was Rake Danescu. I think deep down, Ian believed me when I said that, but he also believed that when it came to keeping me safe against who or whatever had been responsible for the deaths of three of SPI's seers, he could do a better job than even a goblin dark mage.

When we'd slammed that Hellgate and unfortunately

turned Bacchanalia into a crumbled crater cookie, Ian and Rake had made a great team.

I thought it prudent to keep that opinion to myself. One of these days (or years) they'd either come to the same conclusion or kill each other, but I'd let them figure it out on their own.

I unlocked my door, then stepped aside so Ian could do his thing, which was to thoroughly check my apartment to ensure that no one or nothing was there, had been there, or would stand a snowball's chance in hell of ever being there.

While Ian conducted his security ritual, I stood beside the now closed and locked door and waited for him to finish.

The same elf dark mage who'd opened the Hellgate had planted demon eggs in my apartment's ductwork that had subsequently hatched and would have attacked and eaten me in my sleep. Ian and I had eradicated the infestation using an assortment of weapons including guns, a machete, a baseball bat, and a can of Raid.

Yeah, there'd been quite a mess to clean up.

After that I'd given serious consideration to finding another place to live. Rake had offered me a rent-free apartment in his building on Central Park West, with no strings or obligations of any kind attached. I'd thought about it, but ultimately had turned him down. Call me old-fashioned, but I simply couldn't do it. Besides, this was my home, and I wasn't going to let an elf dark mage's baby demon minions run me out of it, even if it had meant sleeping with a small armory around my bed for the first few months.

And it had.

"All clear?" I asked Ian when he finished his patrol. It hadn't taken long; it wasn't like there was a lot of area to check out.

"All clear."

Neither of us had really expected any different. In addition to paying for the repairs, Vivienne Sagadraco had two of the agency's mages put down a serious layering of wards and spells that would not only keep anyone or anything out, they'd also let me know if anyone had tried. So far, so good.

But Ian hadn't been on the *Persephone* tonight to do his guard thing, so I let him do it now by checking my apartment.

"They weren't after me," I said quietly.

"That's not the point. You could've just as easily been collateral damage."

"I, or anyone else in this city, could be collateral damage by a cab jumping the curb."

"You aren't anyone else."

Rake had told me the same thing once, when he was trying to convince me that he wanted me for me, not some ulterior motive involving me being a talented seer. I had believed it from Rake then, and I believed it from Ian now. I also knew what was coming next.

"Rake shouldn't have taken you there. It wasn't safe."

"Because of a kraken. It's not like anyone could've predicted that."

"You know what I mean."

I did. We'd also discussed it before. Though "discussed" made it seem like we'd reached some sort of an agreement. We hadn't.

"It was on Bela Báthory's yacht," Ian said.

Now we were getting to the real reason.

"Báthory has security out the wazoo," I reminded him, even though Ian knew that only too well.

"That's not the point," Ian said.

"He invited some of the most influential people in the city to his little soiree," I said. "It wouldn't be in his best interests to let anything happen to any of them."

"Getting that many wealthy people together in one place creates a target."

Time to cut to the chase. "And as long as I'm seeing a wealthy man, *I'll* be a target."

"I didn't say that."

"You didn't have to."

Silence.

Yasha and Alain Moreau were waiting downstairs. Ian couldn't stay much longer and he knew it. I didn't want to leave this unresolved. It was Friday night. I wouldn't see Ian again until Monday morning. I didn't want this to fester. Whether you're married or just work partners: never go to bed angry.

"Ian, I took good care of myself tonight. I nailed two of those fish guys right through their beady yellow eyes. Unfortunately, it didn't kill them, but that doesn't change the fact that I made killing shots, under pressure, while keeping my balance on a deck being tilted by a kraken." I gave my partner a little smile. "Not too shabby, if I do say so myself. And it was you who taught me all of that." I broadened the smile. "Good job, partner."

Ian's breath went out of him in a rush and he nodded tightly. He still didn't like the circumstances behind what had happened tonight, but what I'd just said had made him feel better.

It wasn't a resolution, but it was one more step in the right direction.

6

IT started out as a typical Monday morning in the office. It's amazing how quickly things can go to crap.

In the U.S., it's not in the least bit unusual to flip to any of the cable news channels at any time of the day or night and be able to watch a crime or disaster live as it's happening. Unfortunately, that was becoming the new normal, a normal that didn't make anyone look twice or think much about what they were seeing, let alone surprise or shock them.

This morning's crime du jour was different. Oh boy, was it different.

A gang of ghouls had robbed a bank last night. We knew about it because the security footage was being played live on CNN.

The anchor was amazed at how realistic the robbers' makeup looked.

I wasn't.

With that, I knew the Báthory kidnapping had just been

booted from the top spot on our caseload. The bank that'd been hit wasn't just any bank. Their customers were the cream on top of the one percent, and a lot of that cream was supernatural.

The ghouls had been caught on the bank's surveillance cameras; though saying they had been caught would imply that they'd tried to hide. They hadn't.

I, for one, really wished they would've made the effort.

I recognized the gang's leader as the same creature who had nearly killed Ian on two occasions. The first time had been five years ago when Ian and his then NYPD partner had responded to a robbery. The leader had killed and eaten Ian's partner, and had put Ian in the hospital for a month. The most recent attempt had been two years ago in a subway tunnel below Times Square on New Year's Eve.

We had hoped we'd seen the last of him.

It sucked when hope got squashed flat.

I'd come in early this morning. Ian wasn't here yet. I hurried toward the elevator. If I was lucky, I could catch him before he got here and caught sight of what was playing on every monitor in the bull pen. That is, if he hadn't already seen—

The elevator doors opened.

It was Ian and two other agents. The agents barely waited for the doors to open all the way before they scrambled out.

I didn't blame them.

One look at Ian told me he'd already seen the news.

Well, crap.

Barely controlled rage was rolling off my partner in waves. He had it under control because the creature he wanted to unleash it on was on every TV, not standing where Ian could get his hands on him. Most of SPI's agents were psychically sensitive. In a contained environment such as an elevator, strong emotions would be magnified tenfold. If

I hadn't known what had set Ian off, I'd have wanted to get out of his way, too.

I caught my partner's eye and jerked my head toward a nearby conference room. It was too early for meetings, so we'd have it all to ourselves. Very few people at SPI knew Ian's history with that ghoul, and that was the way Ian wanted to keep it.

Ian went in first. I followed, and shut the door.

Ian spat his favorite four-letter word and looked around for something he could punch and not break. Finding nothing that met that requirement, he started pacing. The room was small, so all pacing did was add to his frustration.

"You wanna go down to the gym and work out on the big bag?" I asked. "We can find Yasha to hold for you, cause I'm sure not gonna do it. I like my ribs where they are."

In response, Ian dropped into a chair and repeated the same cuss word, but with less emphasis and no looking for something to hit. That was a good sign.

"Want to talk about it?" I asked. "Using more than one word? Though if you need to put that one on repeat, go for it. I wouldn't blame you a bit."

Ian stared straight ahead. "The video's everywhere. TV, online —"

I half shrugged. "Cannibalistic bank robbers made up like ghouls are ratings gold. Problem is they're real ghouls."

With that, I had Ian's full, complete, and undivided attention. "Cannibalistic? That wasn't on the news."

"Thank God. It wasn't caught on the surveillance cameras, but the NYPD and our agents got to see the aftermath in living color." I paused and winced. "So to speak."

One of the bank guards who had been on duty last night had been unfortunate enough to have walked in on the robbery. Ghouls did what ghouls do—they ate him. That hadn't been caught on camera. I'd never be ready to actually watch ghouls eat a human.

"The ghouls didn't enter or exit through any of the bank's doors," said Alain Moreau from the now-open conference room door. "That means there was a portal in the Gotham Bank & Trust Company."

And our morning just kept getting better. A portal was a doorway to another world, dimension, or just another part of town. As SPI's newest seer of portals, that meant I'd be paying the crime scene a visit. And Ian had become just as obsessed with hunting down and taking out the gang's leader, who wasn't actually a ghoul. We didn't know what he was aside from being incredibly ancient, and able to shapeshift between forms and species at will. The last time he and Ian had crossed paths, Ian had barely escaped with his life. I knew he wanted nothing more than another shot as this thing—and the thing wanted another chance at Ian. I didn't want them on the same side of the planet as each other.

Moreau knew Ian's history with the ghoul, and he still wanted us to go.

"You want us to go to the bank," I said with a distinct lack of enthusiasm.

Moreau nodded once. "The sooner, the better."

When it rained, it poured.

The Gotham Bank & Trust Company looked like any other Midtown Manhattan financial institution—more like a fortress than a city building, and seemingly made from a block of granite. Though to a gang of ghouls with a portal at their beck and call, it might as well have been made out of Play-Doh.

"The bigger they are, the harder they fall," I murmured, gazing around the marble lobby.

Ian was talking with the NYPD detective in charge of the investigation. They knew each other. Not from Ian's time in the NYPD, but from the NYPD's previous joint work with SPI.

Yes, mortal and supernatural law enforcement worked together—and both had been grateful for it on more than one occasion. That cooperation was under the radar as far as the majority of the NYPD was concerned; but just as SPI had human agents, the NYPD had supernaturals all the way up the ranks. The NYPD couldn't openly acknowledge SPI's existence, but when criminals and victims fell on both sides of the law enforcement spectrum, it helped that all the good guys traded information that helped bring down the former, and protect and defend the latter.

The detective in charge was also in the know regarding SPI, and knew that there were supernatural perps and robbery victims, so we'd be granted just as much access to the crime scene as mortal law enforcement. Officially, we were consultants, which covered a lot of ground in any organization or industry.

Every camera on every door leading into and out of Gotham Bank & Trust was in perfect working order. None had shown the ghouls entering or leaving the building, which was baffling the heck out of the NYPD—at least those who weren't clued in. Those who were had to be some of the most frustrated people on the planet. They knew the supernatural world existed, but they couldn't tell anyone about it, and they had to find a way to solve cases in a way that kept the woo-woo to a minimum.

We knew monsters existed. Lucky us. Portals also existed, and people who could open and close them were very popular with the criminal classes. I couldn't open or close them, but I could see them.

It was a new ability for me, and it'd turned out to be a

good thing. If I hadn't been able to see portals, Earth would have become Hell on Earth by now, as in overrun by the population of Hell. I didn't know how I'd picked up my new talent, but I suspected I really didn't want to know, considering it could have been a combination of a momentary mind link with an ancient, megalomaniacal, psychotic Russian dragon/crime lord and a power surge from touching a clutch of magical diamonds activated by the most powerful ley line on the East Coast. I'd taken a wallop of power that night that could have activated a dormant ability. Seeing portals ranked right up there with being a seer, making me even more of a target of supernatural bad guys.

It'd only been a couple of hours since the robbery and murder, so if a portal had been opened here I would be able to sense it, if not actually see the magical leftovers. While the portal could be anywhere in the building, it made more sense for it to be closer to where the ghouls would have been doing most of their work.

The safe deposit box vault.

The area outside of Gotham Bank & Trust's vault looked like a C-level office suite at a Fortune 100 company. I'd never been in one of those before, but I imagined this is what one would look like—if it had been armor-plated. There was a pair of fire doors that had to be three inches thick at the head of the short stairway leading down to the vault area. They were standing open.

Gotham Bank & Trust would want their most valued customers to feel the love while waiting for their personal banker to bring their protected preciouses out to them. There were four small offices on either side of the posh sitting area—with doors that locked from the inside, where clients could commune with their valuables in private.

The inside of the vault was pristine. The ghouls had removed the five boxes that they'd wanted to rob, lined them up on a small, steel table bolted to the floor in the center of the vault, opened them, and scooped out the contents.

Ian and I weren't the first SPI agents on-site. Two mages from SPI's evidence collection department were intent on the five empty boxes. Well, a mage and his top apprentice. Kirby was a nice kid and absurdly talented. He glanced up and gave me a quick nod instead of the big grin and high five I was greeted with in the halls at headquarters. Orson Rogerson was our top forensic mage and was notorious for not breaking a smile and expecting the same from his apprentices. Orson was the best, and he was tough but fair.

Ian and I remained just outside the vault. Orson didn't have to say a word; we knew better than to step one foot onto his crime scene. And yes, until Orson declared it otherwise, it was his.

The vault had been sealed, five safe deposit boxes lined up on the steel table in the center, standing open, contents gone. I glanced at the boxes again, then squatted just outside the vault door so I could see them at table level. Not just neat, perfectly aligned, like they wanted us to give them Brownie points for being tidy robbers. That or they were totally OCD.

The last time we'd come across a locked door, there had been a dead body inside and we'd ended up dealing with high-ranking demons and a portal to Hell. Yeah, capital "H," home to fire, brimstone, and torment. This time I smelled no brimstone, which meant no direct connection to Hell, though I was sure the bank guard during his final minutes would have disagreed.

Dead was bad enough. Dead because he'd been eaten alive was as bad as it got.

I jerked my mind away from that image and firmly back to solving this case and finding the things that'd done the killing. "So I'm confused," I said to Ian.

"How so?"

"They got in and out without setting off any alarms, stole what they'd come for, but left the boxes sitting out. They weren't rushed, so they could just as easily have put the boxes back. Until one of the owners came to check on their stuff, they wouldn't even know they'd been robbed. Instead they went out of their way to be obvious."

"We have the latest in security technology as well as level 12 wards," said a voice from behind us.

A man wearing what I'd learned from being around Rake was a very expensive suit stood by the vault door regarding us with barely disguised animosity. Whether it was aimed at the apparently worthless level 12 wards or at me for pointing out that they were worthless, I didn't know.

"No one," he continued, "mage or mundane, should have been able to gain unauthorized access to this building, let alone this vault. I'm Richard Carlton Winthrop, vice president of customer relations." He made no move to shake either my or Ian's hand, instead giving us both a quick glance, up and down, and not appearing to be particularly impressed with what he saw. "I'd been informed by Lieutenant Vane that they would be bringing in special consultants."

He looked as though he'd steeled himself for an inquisition, though that might have been more from having a robbery and murder happen on his watch. If he wasn't just being paranoid, it was a good thing we were talking to him before he wasn't vice president anymore. Considering that many of the bank's clients were long-lived supernaturals who had accumulated their wealth over many human lifetimes, the man might have more to worry about than just being fired.

"We are," Ian told him. "I'm Special Agent Byrne, and this is Special Agent Fraser." Ian didn't make any move to shake Winthrop's hand, either. So there.

We wore our badges at our belts, and they looked almost

exactly like the ones the FBI carried. Ian hadn't claimed that we were FBI; however, we were agents, and my mom had always told me I was special. No lies, therefore no foul.

I didn't feel like being nice, but I could be professional. "I understand, Mr. Winthrop. I didn't mean to imply that the bank hadn't taken every precaution to protect their clients' valuables. Could the contents of more boxes be missing?"

In response—and without looking at me—Winthrop flipped a switch by the vault door. A thin, pale blue glow outlined each of the boxes, except for the five outlined in bright red.

"The wards are intact on all of the others," he explained.

"I can see that. Nice work."

Winthrop frowned in profound disapproval at the red outlines. "We certainly paid enough for it."

It sounded like the mages who built those wards were going to be getting a highly irate call from *their* customer, namely one Richard Carlton Winthrop. Though if he didn't change his attitude, Winthrop could find himself in worse shape than his wards. You watched your words around mages with enough power under the hood to construct level 12s.

"Who owns those boxes?" Ian asked him.

"I cannot divulge the names of the boxes' owners, or the contents of the boxes themselves. The latter because we do not know what our clients keep in their boxes. It is a private matter."

The contents of the safe deposit boxes weren't safe from thieves, but the names of the owners and what they'd kept in those boxes were safe from us. That made all kinds of sense.

"Okay, let me see if I have this straight, Mr. Winthrop," Ian began. "There was a robbery, or at least there are five empty safe deposit boxes sitting on a table in a vault that had been locked. You called us to investigate the robbery, but we do not know what was stolen or who the stolen items even belong to because of client confidentiality."

We found ourselves on the receiving end of an actual smile. "Yes, so good of you to understand."

"No, I don't understand. We are here to investigate. We can't do that." Ian's jaw tightened. "Nor can we find who ate your guard—unless we know what was taken. I'm certain that your customers whose valuables were stolen want them returned. We can't get them back unless we know what we're looking for. I do understand your customers not wanting their confidential information shared with just anyone. We're not just anyone. A little cooperation would go a long way right now toward finding who or what butchered your guard." My partner's eyes narrowed. "You do care about your own people, don't you?"

"Of course, but—"

"If it's 'of course,' then there is no 'but.' The family of that man needs and deserves closure, your valued clients want their valuables back, and I want to do my job to see that both happen."

The banker swallowed audibly. "I will see what I can do."

"I would appreciate that."

I waited until Winthrop had left and my partner's shoulders had relaxed before saying anything. "I love the smell of cooperative bureaucrat in the morning," I quipped to lessen the tension hanging in the air.

Ian sighed, though it sounded more like a pressure release valve. "Judging from his determination to be as uncooperative as possible, I believe the owners of those empty safe deposit boxes are a particularly dangerous and long-lived breed of supernatural."

"Vampires."

"Yes."

"How do you figure that?"

"Gotham Bank & Trust is exclusively for one percent of the one percent. Aside from dragons, only vampires live long enough to amass that kind of wealth. A dragon's valuables wouldn't fit in one of those little boxes. They hide their hoards themselves, and provide their own security."

I looked to where Winthrop had shut himself in his office. Hopefully to get the information we needed. Probably to call his lawyer and make sure his will was up-to-date once his vampire clients found out their goodies were gone.

7

NOW it was my turn to work hard for the money.

With every door locked, five safe deposit boxes empty, and one dead security guard, there had been a portal opened somewhere in the Gotham Bank & Trust Company.

It was my job to find it. Now. The bank wasn't all that large, at least not in terms of a football field, but it wasn't exactly a neighborhood branch office, either. Considering that my last encounter with portals had involved a demon lord, a sadistic elf dark mage, and a yellow brick road of brimstone leading to a Hellpit, I should have felt at least marginally better about the one I was looking for now.

I didn't.

This one had been used by ghouls. Ghouls that were led by the ghoul—or whatever form he was taking now—that had killed and eaten Ian's NYPD partner, and had tried to do the same to Ian.

Logic said the portal would be near the vault. But if the

portal was near the vault, why was the dead body of the guard upstairs?

I knew from experience that a portal could be opened anywhere, even if the other side of the wall was packed dirt or solid rock. Those ghouls hadn't wanted to escape to whatever was on the other side of the wall where the portal had opened. I knew that stepping through that portal could have put them a block from the bank, hundreds of miles away, or in an entirely different dimension.

I opened my senses to any magic in the building, willing myself to be receptive to anything that gave me the heebie-jeebies.

It didn't take me long to find it. A bloody handprint on a white wall on the main floor was pretty much impossible to miss.

So was the dead body surrounded by bright lights and a forensic team a few feet away.

"I don't know whether to be glad for the assist," I muttered, "or insulted that the head ghoul thought I needed it."

Ian scowled. "I'll add it to the list of things I'm going to take out of his hide."

That sounded disturbingly similar to what the ghoul wanted to do to Ian. I didn't point it out. Besides, Ian wasn't the one who'd killed and eaten a guard. That was plenty enough difference for me.

"So you're sure this is it?" Ian asked.

"Oh yeah. I don't need a snootful of brimstone for confirmation. The wall's flat, but it's like I'm wearing 3-D glasses. That handprint is smack-dab in the middle of a ghoul-sized and indented section of wall." I blinked rapidly and had to look away. "And all wavy-like and more than a mite quease inducing."

Even more nauseating was the thought of what we had

to do next. The guard's body—or what was left of it—had not yet been taken away. I recognized the medical examiner who crouched over the body, using tweezers to extract something I thankfully couldn't see from the ruin of the man's chest.

Dr. Anika Van Daal was the medical examiner. She was also a vampire and mage who had arrived in the city soon after it had been taken from the Dutch by the British and the name changed from New Amsterdam to New York. That'd been in 1625. At that time, two-thirds of the island had still been wilderness.

She'd begun her career as a midwife, and had become the first licensed female doctor in the city. Every few decades, she "retired" from one position and took another. She'd been in her mid-twenties when she'd been turned so she didn't stand out when she went back to school after a "retirement" to catch up on the latest medical advances. She'd learned to glamour and glamour well. As a result, she'd never had problems blending in or with being found out.

Vivienne Sagadraco had a lot of pull in this town, and one of the ways she used it was getting supernaturals placed in strategic jobs. In addition to supernaturals in the NYPD, there were mages who, like Dr. Van Daal, could place a glamour on a dead supernatural and hold it there until the body was turned over to the family. Or if no one claimed the body, until it was cremated or buried by the city. These mages were in homicide divisions, the medical examiner's office, and CSI teams.

The boss had covered all the bases she could, but occasionally a corpse tried to steal home. When that happened, there was a lot of scrambling and improvising by whichever agents were closest.

No one had needed to scramble today.

This victim was human.

He hadn't stood a chance against ghouls—especially when one of those ghouls was something far worse.

Ian took a long breath, quickly exhaled, and walked over to where Dr. Van Daal was working over the remains of the dead bank guard.

She glanced up, then returned to tweezing something out that I had no desire to see up close.

"Agent Byrne, I've been expecting you."

That was a surprise. Ian had said that a handful of people at SPI knew his background. It appeared that Dr. Anika Van Daal was one of them.

"Was he alive?" Ian asked quietly.

"Not for long. He was dead long before he bled out. He's wearing a med alert bracelet for heart disease. Most of the bites and cuts were post-mortem. I won't know for certain until I get him back to the lab, but I would say that he died of a heart attack before most of the wounds were inflicted."

My stomach turned. The cause of death may have been a heart attack, but the poor guy had a heart attack because ghouls were eating him alive.

Ian didn't flinch away from any of it. He'd been special ops in the military and then a homicide detective in the NYPD. My partner had seen death in all its forms. He was studying the guard's remains to memorize what had been done to him. Ian planned to see to it that each of those ghouls paid the ultimate price for every bite and slice. Ian hadn't known the guard personally, but he wasn't going to let that stop him from avenging his death.

Dr. Van Daal lowered the guard's arm to the floor from where it had been folded over his chest. His hand was clenched into a fist, but a glint of metal gleamed from between his fingers.

Ian knelt beside the body. "What's that?"

Dr. Van Daal used her gloved hand to straighten two of the fingers, and a pendant on a chain dropped onto the floor.

"It's a St. Michael medal." My partner was white as a sheet. "Anika, turn it over."

I moved closer and leaned over Ian's shoulder to try to see. "I can't read it, does—"

"It says, 'To Peter, all love, M.' And there's a date." Ian sounded as if he were about to be sick. "If you'll excuse us, Dr. Van Daal, we'll let you get back to your work."

Ian stood and was halfway across the room before I could even scramble to my feet.

Just because Ian had kept his reaction off of his face didn't mean he'd been able to keep his heart rate under control. Though that was probably some kind of anti-interrogation technique he'd learned in the Rangers. Anika Van Daal was a vampire, and an old one at that. She could hear a human heartbeat without using a stethoscope, which no doubt came in handy being a doctor. But even I had noticed Ian's reaction.

He wasn't waiting for me, but that was okay, I was fully capable of catching up. "You've seen that medal before."

Silence.

"Ian, it's me. That medal didn't belong to that guard, and you recognized it, meaning that ghoul left it for you to find."

"Nice deductive reasoning," Ian said as he kept walking. "You're getting better."

"I was taught by the best. The best also happens to be my partner, who is also holding out on me."

He slowed. A little. "Not from you. Moreau."

"That makes all kind of nonsense."

Ian blew out his breath and stopped. We were in the bank lobby and out of anyone's hearing. He pulled me aside.

"What you don't know, you can't tell Moreau."

"If it's that important that he not know, I won't tell him." I gave him the eye. "Unless it's something he *needs* to know."

Ian's silence told me the answer to that one.

"Okay, perhaps a better question would be why you don't *want* Moreau to know."

"Because he will pull me off of this case."

"I won't tell Moreau," I said. "But I want you to tell me. Who is Peter?" As soon as the name was out of my mouth, I froze and remembered. "Your partner, Pete."

Ian nodded. "The medal wasn't found on his body. It was a gift from his wife, Meg, when he graduated from the academy. The date was the day he graduated."

I felt sick. And a fat lot of protection that medal had given Pete.

"St. Michael is the patron saint of the police and the military," Ian continued. "A lot of cops and soldiers wear those medals."

"They believe in an archangel's protection, but not in ghouls and other monsters."

"Yeah."

"And that ghoul took it as a souvenir."

"Right."

"He knew you'd come, so he left it for you."

Ian nodded once.

I connected the rest of the dots. "So that you would come after him. Ian, that thing's baiting a hook and he wants you on the other end of it." I let a little silence grow between us. "I won't tell Moreau, but I think you should, because if you don't, Van Daal will. If you're up front with him now, he'll be more inclined to believe you when you tell him you're not going to go off on your own and do something stupid."

The muscles in his jaw clenched. "I'll tell him."

The words said one thing; the jaw told me he'd tell Moreau about the medal, but he wouldn't like it. I didn't care if he liked it, I cared about him. If it took an order from Alain Moreau for Ian to keep his promise, so be it.

A bank robbery by a gang of ghouls was one thing. A bank robbery by a gang of ghouls led by the same being that had eaten Ian's partner was worse. But that he left Ian's dead partner's St. Michael medal for Ian to find clutched in the dead fist of his latest meal/victim?

That was as bad as it could possibly be.

8

DR. Van Daal would bag the St. Michael's medal for the lab. I didn't hold out hope of it yielding any evidence. Things like that ghoul didn't leave fingerprints; and if they did, they wouldn't be in any database, including ours. The SPI lab would call it evidence. I called it what it was—a sick greeting card for Ian. I don't know what that ghoul wanted with the contents of five safe deposit boxes, or even what those contents were, but he'd obviously decided to mix some sadistic pleasure with his business.

The ride back to SPI was quiet. Yasha sensed Ian's mood and didn't try to engage him in conversation. Ian also didn't tell Yasha what we'd found. That worried me. Maybe Ian didn't want to talk about it yet. I could certainly understand that. That didn't allay my suspicion that Ian wasn't telling Yasha because he knew Yasha would sit on him for as long as it took someone else to find and take down that ghoul. Bottom line was that Ian didn't tell Yasha because he hadn't ruled out independent action. Come to think of it, Ian had merely said he'd tell Moreau about the St. Michael's medal. He hadn't promised anything in regard to not going rogue on that ghoul if the opportunity presented itself.

Neither the NYPD nor SPI had any leads on Bela Báthory's whereabouts. There was no trace of the nephew of the East Coast's most powerful vampire crime family. House Báthory was one of the top two most powerful vampire families in North America and one of the top five in Europe.

As a vampire, Bela Báthory didn't need to breathe, so those swamp creatures could have taken him underwater to another yacht, boat, or ship far enough from the *Persephone* so as not to be seen. One of the more elaborate police theories had the kidnappers doing the same thing, but with an oxygen supply for their victim, which aside from being unnecessary for a vampire, smacked of a James Bond villain evil master plan.

The NYPD couldn't exactly put the Hudson River and New York Harbor on lockdown, but they continued to search and investigate as best they could.

Nothing.

However, SPI had access to witnesses who had probably seen both the kraken attack on the *Persephone* and the kidnapping of Bela Báthory. Witnesses who the NYPD not only hadn't interviewed, but didn't even know existed.

New York's merpeople population.

Around Halloween last year, Ian had had a productive chat with a mermaid. He'd called, she'd answered. She'd also confirmed Ian's questions about where the bad guys had been headed. We might have been able to have found out that information without the mermaid's help, but by then it would have been too late to have saved the lives of every supernatural being in the tristate area.

So yeah, merpeople were good people.

True to his word, Ian had told Alain Moreau about the medal. In turn, Moreau was allowing Ian to remain on the case provided that basically he use his investigative powers for good, and not evil. He was not, under any circumstances, to take on or attempt to take down the ghoul alone. Now that Ian had a trail to follow and work to do, other than pushing papers at his desk, I felt a lot better about my partner's promise of cooperation. That being said, once we ran the ghoul to ground, Ian had made it abundantly clear to everyone at SPI who might be involved in the actual take-down that when the time came, that ghoul was his.

No one had objected to that.

And I hadn't objected when Ian said he was going to question the merpeople as potential witnesses. He was looking for answers, not a ghoul.

We took one of SPI's boats out on the Hudson, and Ian opened it up and headed north. When we'd passed where the *Persephone* had been attacked, I spoke up. Actually, I had to yell over the wind and motor.

"We've passed where the *Persephone* was attacked."

"I know," he shouted back.

"Then what are—"

"We're going to see Sirene."

"Sirene?"

Ian cut back on the throttle a little so we didn't have to continue to scream at each other. "The merpeople don't have titles, but if Sirene did, the closest to what humans have would be queen."

"The mermaid queen."

Ian shrugged. "Merpeople are a matriarchal society. The females hold all positions of power."

I nodded in approval. "As it should be. I like Queen Sirene already."

"If Sirene wasn't a witness, some of her people must have

been, and they would have reported to her everything that happened."

About ten minutes later, we reached the northernmost tip of Manhattan where the Harlem River emptied into the Hudson. I think the neighborhood was Inwood, which was being touted as New York's next gentrifying neighborhood. They'd get there a lot faster if they knew a mermaid queen lived offshore.

"I would have expected merfolk to live closer to the open ocean," I said.

"They winter in the ocean, taking the Gulf Stream south. They summer here."

I grinned. "Two-legged Northerners do that, too."

Ian pulled a long chain from under his T-shirt and lifted it over his head. He'd used it before to call a mermaid source for information.

I leaned forward to get a better look at the pendant. It was a silver oval with what looked to have once been intricate engravings, now worn with age. "You say you don't have any psychic abilities, but you can dip a necklace in the water and telepathically talk to mermaids. I'd call that pretty danged psychic."

Ian shrugged as if it was no big deal. "My grandad gave it to me. His father gave it to him. He was a fisherman back in Ireland. Grandad said his father told him he could use it to call the merfolk. Grandad didn't put much stock in fairy tales as he called them, but it's been in the family at least as far back as four generations, so he wanted me to have it."

"And when you came to work for SPI, you realized that fairy tales were fairy fact."

"That's right."

"Cool."

Ian leaned over the edge of the boat and submerged the pendant on the end as I'd seen him do before. It wasn't dark yet, but it was close enough to make the water look more than a little ominous, especially considering what had happened Friday night. I winced and held my breath, fully expecting a kraken tentacle or a Creature from the Black Lagoon to drag Ian over the side. I didn't like that Yasha hadn't been able to come with us, and neither had he. Merpeople were nervous around many supernaturals, including werewolves.

A head broke the surface a few feet from where Ian leaned over the side. Long hair flowed over slender shoulders and down into the water. The features indicated that it was female, and all of the above seemed to be more or less human—except for the green skin.

Or at least it looked green from what I could see.

Her large eyes were solid, dark orbs. Orbs that stared over Ian's shoulders to where I sat. She looked familiar. More than familiar, she was identical to the mermaid who had come when Ian had called that night on the edge of the East River. I wondered if all mermaids looked alike, or whether even asking that question would be extremely offensive. I opted to keep my mouth shut and let Ian do the talking, telepathy, or whatever.

The mermaid submerged completely.

Seconds later, she surfaced right under where Ian's hand held the chain and pendant stretched over and into the water. My partner didn't move as a long-fingered, webbed hand reached up to him. Ian lowered his hand and she closed her definitely green, webbed fingers around his.

She gazed up into his eyes and they stayed like that for a good two minutes. Then she simply released his hand and sank back into the darkening river without leaving even a ripple as a sign she'd ever been there.

Ian removed the pendant from the water and dried it on a towel before putting the chain over his head and tucking the pendant under his T-shirt. He turned toward me with a crooked smile. "The queen will see us now."

I didn't necessarily expect a crown of seashells or coral, but I did expect the queen of New York's merpeople to have differentiated herself from her subjects in some way. Since only her head and shoulders were above the water and it was night by now, I thought maybe her fish-like tail was fancier or sported some kind of aquatic-themed bling. Her features did look more regal than those of the mermaid Ian had initially made contact with, but aside from that, there was no outward indication of rank.

However, four long and sleek forms swam just beneath the surface around our boat and the queen. They were broader of shoulder and carried trident-like spears.

Guards. Male.

Once again there was no speaking, only telepathy between the queen and Ian, and it lasted less than five minutes.

When she'd finished communicating, the queen smoothly sank below the surface and disappeared, her guards along with her.

I leaned forward in my seat. "Well?"

"We have a witness. Dozens, actually."

"Good. Now we're getting somewhere."

"Not exactly."

"What do you mean, not exactly?"

"They saw what happened to the *Persephone*, acknowledge the invaders to be a threat, but they don't have a name for them. Yasha's black lagoon things, not the kraken. They know what the kraken was. Sirene will try to get more information for us on the black lagoon guys. Her people reported that Bela Báthory was taken farther up the Hudson."

"They took him up the Hudson past Manhattan?"

"Without a doubt."

"So much for the swamp creatures being hired fins for one of the other vampire families."

"I asked Sirene if she had any plans to have her people

scout farther up the river. She tried that, but pulled them back. There's a pair of hydras where the river gets deeper just past Yonkers."

I blinked. "There's hydras in Yonkers?"

"Sirene said they showed up around the same time as the kraken and the others."

"I'd pull my people back, too. So what's up the Hudson past Yonkers?"

"About three hundred miles of river."

"How much of that is brackish water?"

"From New York Harbor all the way up to the Federal Dam in Troy, about a hundred and fifty miles."

"So . . . Creatures from the Black Lagoon and their kraken buddy kidnap the nephew of a vampire crime lord and then post hydras off Yonkers to keep anyone from following them." I just sat there waiting for that scenario to sink in. It didn't. "This is the trippiest case ever."

Ian started pulling up the anchor. "You'll get no argument from me."

9

THE ghoul gang had robbed another bank.

Ian and I were at our desks in the agents' cube farm—known as the bull pen—watching the action unfold on two of the flat screen TVs mounted on sections of wall.

An agent nearby muttered a word that would've gotten my mouth washed out with soap back home. I agreed with my coworker's word choice, and silently added a few of my own.

I glanced at Ian out of the corner of my eye.

My partner was the embodiment of stoic—eyes on the monitor, face set on neutral. It was his cop face, his soldier face, the face that said he could handle this, that he was handling this. Nothing to see here, move along.

I was his partner and I was close enough to see the pulse in his neck, a pulse rate that was at odds with the emotionless mask he was wearing.

The Prime Bank's surveillance cameras started to show what no one wanted to see—unless they were into snuff films. I knew what was coming. Thankfully, CNN cut away from the footage at that point, but they did tell their millions of viewers what had happened to the two bank guards. We all knew it was only a matter of time until a pirated version of that footage made it online. Then anyone who was sick enough or had a strong enough stomach could watch the ghouls eat those guards alive to their hearts' content.

SPI's Media and Public Relations department was in full-blown crisis mode. They specialized in working behind the scenes to explain the unexplainable, turning actual encounters and sightings into simple hoaxes by those looking for their fifteen minutes of fame, or exposing them as elaborate cover-ups by any number of shadowy government agencies that were ripe for the blaming. No one made direct accusations, of course; their information was usually based on "a source close to the investigation speaking on condition of anonymity because they weren't authorized to discuss the investigation publically."

And not all people in SPI's Media and PR department worked from headquarters. They had people in the highest levels at TV networks, cable news, all across/over/throughout the web, and even in the increasingly archaic print media. Influence had been bought, paid for, and was being well used—except today apparently.

CNN had already interviewed the department director, Kylie O'Hara. SPI was her real job, but the world at large didn't know that. Her cover job was being a world-renowned debunker of anything and everything that smacked of the supernatural, which was ironic as all get-out considering she wasn't even human. Kylie was a dryad, which meant she was gorgeous. Her real name was something unpronounceable with way too many apostrophes. The shortened version of her first name was similar enough to Kylie, and she used O'Hara because it was the name of the state forest near the shore of Lake Ontario in Upstate New York where she was born. And people thought her green eyes and last name meant she was Irish.

Kylie was also front and center on TV and radio talk shows, and was accepted by respected journalists as an expert on the exposé. Heck, Syfy had been after her for years to do a series. Kylie had explained away the latest robbery with movie-quality makeup, and the cannibalism part with sick bastards—my words, not hers.

When more than a few agents' phones started beeping or buzzing with incoming texts, we knew exactly where we'd be going next without even looking at our screens.

The war room.

SPI had conference rooms of all sizes, but the war room was one of the largest. It seated over a hundred, and was reserved for all-hands-on-deck emergencies. Ghoul bank robbers eating bank guards being reported on CNN certainly qualified as an agency-wide emergency. No one said a word as we filed in.

Alain Moreau was standing at the front of the room, waiting for everyone to get in and get a seat. If he was cursing the day Vivienne Sagadraco had told him she was taking her first vacation in a century, you'd never know it to look at him.

Yasha was already there. Normally that would be a surprise. Briefings were usually for agents only. To me and Ian, Yasha was much more than a driver. But if he was here, then Moreau had invited him. I didn't need to be told why. Any case that involved the ghoul involved Ian, and if it involved Ian, then as our driver, Yasha needed to be involved.

To keep Ian out of trouble.

Yasha had saved two seats for us. He said nothing to either one of us, but gave Ian a solemn nod, which I took to be werewolf/manspeak for "I've got your back."

Alain Moreau picked up a remote from the podium. "Agent

Foyle? If you'll close the door, please. Ladies and gentlemen, last night seven ghouls entered the Prime Bank on Madison Avenue and its vault via a portal. The method of entry and exit is unconfirmed, but seeing as no alarms were triggered, and all doors were locked, we'll operate under that assumption. The ghouls took the contents of two safe deposit boxes, and rather than exit the vault with no one being the wiser until this morning when the vault was opened . . ." He turned to the screen mounted on the front wall and clicked the remote he held.

The security footage showed the closed vault door. Slowly, the wheel in the center of the massive steel door began to turn, then deadbolts—I didn't know what else to call them the size of my upper arm slid smoothly from the vault's wall. No one was outside the vault; it was being unlocked from the inside, by ghouls. It was one of the creepiest things I'd ever witnessed in my life.

The screen split to show two security guards at their desk, watching the monitors. The eyes of one man widened as he leaned closer to be sure he wasn't imagining what he was seeing. I wanted to scream for them to run out the front door and keep running, don't go downstairs. For God's sake, don't go downstairs. They went downstairs.

By the time the two guards got there, the ghouls had the door open and were waiting for them, the safe deposit boxes they'd emptied again sitting on the table in the center of the vault. They'd taken care of business; now they wanted some pleasure—and to be seen doing it. Once they began feeding, the six ghouls didn't look up, but their leader stood to the side of the butchery, arms crossed over his chest, smiling up at the camera, knowing he was being watched—knowing Ian was watching.

Ian's expression never changed and his breathing remained even, the consummate professional objectively viewing evidence of the most gruesome crime I'd ever seen—though not that I'd ever heard of. Both humans and supernaturals were endlessly creative in finding new ways to kill each other.

It took nearly three minutes for one of the guards to stop screaming.

Some agents looked away, others took quick glances, and a few fled the room, retching.

Ian didn't so much as blink.

The other agents had never watched ghouls eat a human. Ian had lived it.

I glanced down at my hands, clenched into fists in my lap, willing the contents of my stomach to stay put. I glanced over at where Ian's hands calmly held his phone, his text screen visible. It was Moreau's summons—but he'd sent Ian more. He'd told Ian that he'd be showing the entire tape, what was on it, and that Ian didn't need to attend, he would brief him afterward.

And here Ian sat.

Alain Moreau had offered Ian a way out of watching it, if he wanted to take it.

I knew my partner, and Moreau did, too. If the rest of the agents had to sit through this, Ian would, too. Moreau knew Ian would refuse, but he'd still offered.

On the screen, the lead ghoul unfolded his arms, and in his hands was what looked like a long, triangular spearhead. The video was in black and white, and while clear, it wasn't close enough to see details. The ghoul stepped over to the dead guard closest to him and sank the spearhead halfway up its length in the man's chest. Then he looked back at the camera and smiled. He snapped his fingers and the ghouls stopped eating, went back into the vault, and no doubt out through the same portal they'd used to gain access.

Alain Moreau stood and clicked the remote to end the televised nightmare, the one we'd all be having later.

"That, ladies and gentlemen, is what we're up against and what we must find. As you saw, those ghouls knew where those cameras were and they made no effort to conceal themselves—or alter their appearance."

I raised my hand to ask what Ian had to be thinking. That spearhead had to be another message for him.

Moreau nodded in my direction. "Agent Fraser?"

"Do we have access to that spearhead; and if not, can we get better resolution on that image?"

"Yes, to both. Unfortunately, the first police on the scene were not our people inside the NYPD. However, we are working with our higher ranking contacts there to get access to the evidence, including the spearhead. Agent Hayashi is presently working on cleaning up the video image until we can obtain the copies of the forensics photography. As the medical examiner on the first murder, Dr. Van Daal will have access to the victims in this robbery, as well as all evidence and reports."

"What are the mortal police saying?" an elven agent asked.

"They know even less than we do concerning the robbers' motives. The two safe deposit boxes that were emptied belonged to Hunter Enterprises. The authorities know the CEO of that company as Gabriel Frontino. We know Monsieur Frontino as the head of New York's second most powerful vampire crime family, next to the Báthorys. Like Gotham Bank & Trust, the Prime Bank was founded by and largely caters to supernaturals. When one has an extended lifespan, it's less awkward and more convenient to bank where you don't have to pretend to die every ninety years."

Roy Benoit, commander of one of SPI's two commando teams, raised his hand and Moreau acknowledged him with a nod. "Even if they used a portal, a bank of that caliber should have wards that would have alerted not only the guards on-site, but off-site security as well. What happened to those?"

"They do have wards," Moreau replied. "Or they did. The mortal security measures were bypassed, and the wards and magical shields were simply destroyed. Though I highly doubt there was anything simple about the way it was done. What we have is a mage—or mages—of the highest power who wanted what was in those safe deposit boxes badly. And discovery not only wasn't a concern, it was desirable."

Roy sat back and crossed his arms over his broad chest. "Why? Other than to make more work for us, and especially for Director O'Hara and her people."

"Unknown," Moreau said. "However, we have several leads we are pursuing."

Which was a polite way to say that Moreau wasn't sharing any of them at the moment, because that reason was my partner.

"And we now know the owners' names of the safe deposit boxes burglarized two nights ago," Moreau continued. "There were five boxes and three owners: Anton Tepes, Charles Ruthven—and interestingly enough, Ambrus Báthory, the uncle of Bela Báthory who was abducted from his yacht on Friday night. Neither Tepes, Ruthven, nor Báthory are cooperating with us or the mortal authorities as to the contents of their boxes. However, my efforts are ongoing."

10

AFTER the meeting, Ian was deep in thought. That was hardly surprising.

Once we were out in the hallway, Yasha pulled us aside.

"I have a friend who can help," he said. "He is a bodyguard for vampire families. He has worked for Báthorys in the past. They talk; he is there to hear. If he has information, he will help."

Ian snapped out of his reverie, and clapped the big Russian on the shoulder. "Then lead on, buddy."

We went to see Yasha's friend—a Czechoslovakian vampire named Vlad. No, I'm not kidding.

We met Vladimir Cervenka at a bar down by the Lower East Side docks. It was mid-morning on a sunny day, and the vampire was sitting in a corner booth with a steaming mug of something on the table in front of him. The booth was made to fit two people, but it barely fit one Vlad. Yasha had warned us not to make jokes about his name. After getting a look at this guy, I wouldn't have dared. Not to mention, he had to be closing in on a thousand years old if he could be out and about after dawn.

He stood when we approached. Whoa, Vlad was a seriously big boy. He engulfed Yasha in a hug that looked more like a polar bear attack.

He had shoulder-length white blond hair, ice blue eyes, rugged and actually ruddy features. Either he'd just fed, was feeding (or at least snacking, judging from the mug), or he'd spent a lot of time outside before he'd been turned—or all of the above.

Yasha introduced us and there were handshakes all around. Considering that my hand was completely wrapped in Vlad's massive paw, I was almost surprised to get it back.

Normally werewolves kept to themselves, and vampires did likewise, but Yasha wasn't like most werewolves. He chose his friends because he liked and trusted them, not because they went all fanged and furry every full moon. I hadn't met that many vampires in my time, but I sure as heck hadn't met one that looked more like a mountain man.

Who was smoking a cigar impaled on his left fang.

That was an eyebrow raiser.

Vlad noticed and laughed, a laugh that was just as big as he was.

"I enjoyed many things when I was alive," he said. "Good food and drink, and the pleasure of fine tobacco. Now I can only drink blood, and I no longer breathe." He grinned in a flash of strong white teeth and two seriously imposing—and scary—fangs. "I can make myself inhale." He proceeded to give us a demonstration, dragging the smoke into his lungs, the cigar's tip glowing bright, and as he exhaled through his nostrils, I was reminded of a fire-breathing dragon of my acquaintance.

"When you are dead, you take your enjoyment where you can find it. Though there is an advantage to death, I can smoke as much as I like." The Czech vampire took the cigar between his fingers and carefully ground the flame out against the brick wall beside him. "However, I am considerate of those less dead than myself."

I smiled. Yasha had good taste in friends. I liked him, too. "Thank you."

Vlad inclined his head in acknowledgment. "Yasha tells me you need information about some of my clients."

"We do," Ian said. "Though some of our questions may be what your clients consider to be confidential information."

Vlad grinned crookedly. "I am paid for my muscle. I am, how do you say, a deterrent."

"If you were guarding something," I said, "I'd sure be deterred from trying to take it."

Vlad cheerfully spread his hands. "Then my job would be done." His expression became serious, or as serious as this man probably got. "If a client tells me, 'Forget you are seeing this,' I forget it—unless it is needed. The laws of mortals do not matter to me, but I have lines that I will not cross for any amount. I will not violate my personal honor. I am the last of my family, so I owe no loyalty to those who hire me. I will keep the secrets of their House—unless it would bring harm to others. From what Yasha has told me, the problem you are having would qualify."

"We believe so, yes," Ian said. "You've heard about the robberies?"

"I have."

"And of course, Bela Báthory's abduction."

Vlad gave us a single, dry chuckle. "That one will not be missed, even by his own family." Another chuckle. "*Especially* by his own family."

"Do you think they might have had something to do with it?" I asked.

"Giant octopus and fish men?" Vlad shook his shaggy head. "Too complicated, for any of the Houses. While many would enjoy seeing Bela Báthory permanently dead—and watching him suffer while getting that way—that is far too much trouble to go to. Vampires are more direct."

"The heads of the Houses aren't talking," Ian told him. "Those inner circles are some of the few places where SPI doesn't have contacts."

"And I have been on the inside many times." He paused. "And have heard many things."

"There are advantages to being treated like furniture," Yasha said. "I have been treated same way."

I glanced from one to the other. That was some seriously big furniture to ignore.

"It's more like an attack dog," Vlad noted. "Until it's needed, it's ignored." He nodded to Ian. "Yes, I have heard things lately. For the past eight months, I have been working for Ambrus Báthory." He flashed a grin. "Today is my day off."

"What do you do for Mr. Báthory?" I asked.

"He has personal bodyguards who are members of his family, though in my opinion, it is not in his best interests to trust them with his life. Other heads of vampire Houses do the same. I guess the old man feels safer keeping his enemies close. If so, he is doing a fine job. He hired me to keep watch over his enemies in his own family, and to oversee security when he leaves his compound. I am not of his House, so Ambrus knows I have no ties, loyalties, or obligations to those who want him gone. But most of all, he knows I cannot be bought or successfully threatened." One side of Vlad's mouth curled in a crooked half smile. "Sometimes he has even been known to take my advice."

I glanced at Ian and Yasha. They seemed to get the logic of what Vlad had just said. I didn't. "Why would members of your own family want to kill you . . . permanently?"

"Vampires live to be very old. Those of us who choose our risks wisely can live even longer. Those who are not in power can have a long time to wait to be in power—unless they take matters into their own hands."

I nodded in understanding. "And hurry things along."

"Exactly."

"But then you'd be in the same position as the guy you just conspired to bump off—constantly looking over your shoulder and trusting no one."

Vlad shrugged. "It is the game they play. I choose not to play. A long life can mean much boredom. The games can make your time more interesting." He smiled. "I don't have that problem since I am a simple man and more easily amused."

I seriously doubted either one. Vladimir Cervenka was playing a dangerous game right now, especially if Ambrus Báthory found out he'd been talking to us. Though Vlad seemed like the type who had successfully taken care of himself for a long time.

"What would anyone gain by kidnapping Bela?" I asked.

"Ambrus had tapped Bela to be his heir. There is much jealousy in the old man's inner circle, and throughout the family. Bela is not popular."

Rake had told me as much before the party Friday night. I'd just put Bela in the same category as many young, rich, and power-hungry men—mortal or immortal. Such men made enemies almost as quickly as they accumulated wealth. However, when the only way to get rid of them was a stake through the heart and decapitation, impatience and frustration was bound to build up.

"Has there been any communication from the kidnappers?" Ian asked. "Ransom demands?"

Vlad shook his head. "And I don't think there will be. Even if there was, Ambrus would not pay. He is not exactly grieving for the loss of his nephew."

Now I really was confused. "But you said he'd made Bela his heir."

"Only to keep his most dangerous enemy closest of all. Bela wants—or *wanted*, if his head has now parted ways with his shoulders—his uncle out of the way. Permanently. You must understand that Ambrus Báthory comes from the Old World, and sees no need to change for modern times. Nor does he believe the time has come for him to step down in favor of Bela. The young one has long been a fang at the old man's throat. I'm surprised he has not killed Bela himself."

"So why would anyone kidnap Bela?" I asked.

"He knows things. Things the old man wanted to keep secret."

"Like what Ambrus keeps in his safe deposit boxes?" Ian asked.

"When you are constantly surrounded by your enemies, it would be best to keep the possessions you value the most away from you. This way you would only need to protect yourself. Whatever it was young Bela had discovered, last night the old man swore to snap Bela's head from his body if he doesn't keep his mouth shut."

"Okay, on Friday night, Bela Báthory was taken from his yacht by a team of swamp creature commandos," I said. "During the early hours of Monday morning, Ambrus's safe deposit boxes at the Gotham Bank & Trust were robbed by ghouls. The kidnap/robbery angle doesn't sound like a coincidence. As to the kidnappers and the robbers, I can't imagine what swamp creature commandos have in common with ghoul bank robbers." I opted to leave out that said robbers

were led by an ancient being obsessed with having my partner for its next meal.

Vlad shrugged his massive shoulders. "I'm merely a paid
attack dog, but Ambrus trusts me—to a point. I will test
where that point is and try to dig something up for you."

11

MOREAU had been true to his word. By the time we got back to headquarters, he had the photos of the Prime Bank crime scene in our e-mail inboxes. Ian had Kenji Hayashi's enhanced image of the spearhead on his screen. He was leaning back in his desk chair, arms crossed over his chest, brow furrowed in intense concentration.

I pushed my feet on the floor to roll my chair over next to his.

"Recognize it?" I asked.

"No . . . and yes."

"Uh, care to clarify that, partner?"

"I've never seen this spearhead before, but he left it for me, I'm sure of it."

I was pretty convinced of that myself.

Ian slouched down farther in his chair, scowling. "But yet, it's familiar somehow."

"Could you have seen it in a book somewhere? Or was it used in a murder you investigated?"

"No and no. If I'd seen it in a book, it would have been here. The researchers don't have any record of such a weapon in any book in SPI's library."

"How about a date when it was made? With all that Celtic-looking scrollwork, it looks old, and is that real gold?" I didn't want to call a spearhead sticking out of a dead man's chest beautiful, but this weapon was. The detailing was incredible.

"Dr. Van Daal managed to get it for us, at least long enough to run some tests. It's up in the lab now. It appears to be bronze decorated with gold, of Irish make, and dated from approximately 200 B.C."

"Okay," I said, drawing out the word. I leaned back in my chair in a mirror image of my partner. He seemed to think this was a good angle at which to receive enlightenment, so I'd try the same. Or at least, we could be utterly baffled together. I believed in supporting my partner in all things.

"Well," I said after nearly a minute of silence. "You are Irish; at least your ancestors were. Other than that . . . I got nothing."

Ian pushed back his chair and stood.

"Where you going?"

"To the lab to see that thing up close and personal."

I followed.

SPI's labs were equipped to handle, contain, and analyze virtually anything.

When you could be asked to determine the acid content of Brazilian basilisk spit, the ratio of magic to mortal poison in the ink of a late-Renaissance grimoire, or something as simple as determining the gold content in a 200 B.C. Celtic spearhead, our white-lab-coated folks were ready for it.

SPI's labs were separated by a hallway on the third level

of the headquarters complex. One lab dealt with organic materials, the other with inorganic. Though in our line of work, those lines got blurred, a lot. Large, long windows allowed an unobstructed view into both labs from the hallway. I didn't know what the windows were made of but it sure as heck wasn't glass. It was rare that an experiment or subject being analyzed got out of control, but those windows had to ensure that what happened in the lab stayed in the lab. The clear view was so when anything did go wrong, and if a tech couldn't reach an alarm, there'd be witnesses to call for reinforcements. That was mostly an issue in the organic lab, but not always. SPI was a very interesting workplace.

Things were relatively quiet today, and I didn't think the presence of an itty-bitty spearhead would change that, regardless of how old it was, or who had last used it—and what it had been used for. At least I hoped not.

Ian and I weren't the first to visit the lab looking for more information on the spearhead.

Alain Moreau was already there, intently studying the spearhead. It was lying on a square piece of white cloth that bore a disturbing resemblance to a formal dinner napkin.

At least someone had cleaned the dead bank guard's blood off of the blade. The NYPD's lab must have gotten all the evidence they could from the blood, or more to the point, what might have been underneath it that could help determine the identities of those who had handled it, or where the spearhead had come from or had last been stored.

Standing next to Moreau was Dr. Noel Tierney. Him being here wasn't a surprise, but he wasn't acting in his primary job as SPI's chief psychologist. Dr. Tierney was here because of one of his secondary gifts.

When you fought creatures most people not only didn't believe in, but thought you were nuts if you saw, mental gymnastics were often called for to keep your mental health on an even keel. Dr. Tierney looked like a lot of the guys I'd seen in photos of my mom's college days in the 1970s, where she'd done just as much protesting as studying. At least that's the way it appeared from her photo albums and newspaper clippings. Most college kids were proud of the first "A" they got in their hardest class. Mom was most proud of the first time she ever got arrested. Now she was the mayor of our hometown—re-elected three times—and her sister was the chief of police.

Go figure.

Noel Tierney had multiple psychology and psychology-related degrees from the best schools. His work clothes were khakis, crisply pressed button-downs, and God help us all, bow ties. He had a themed collection. It was a bright, summer day, so today's tie had tiny daisies on it. One of his most memorable was his Thanksgiving tie, yellow and spotted with itty-bitty cooked turkeys. But other than the ties, Tierney wore doctor clothes at their most proper. However, I'd seen him several times on days off, and he'd been in jeans, environmental T-shirt du jour, round sunglasses, and Birkenstocks. So regardless of what he wore in the office, that was what I saw when I looked at him—a walking flower-child cliché.

I knew he wasn't in the lab because the spearhead had been emotionally traumatized by being driven into a dead man's chest.

Dr. Noel Tierney was a psychologist *and* a psychometric. He would know the entire history of that spearhead simply by touching it. By the looks of him right now, not only did he not want to touch it, he didn't want to be in the same room with it. That meant it was a seriously nasty knife. He was also an artist, and occasionally could get clear enough images from an object or a person to be able to draw what he'd seen. That'd come in handy on more than one occasion.

Tierney glanced up when Ian and I came in and gave us a nod and as much of a smile as he could, given what he was standing over.

He knew us and we knew him. Vivienne Sagadraco believed in her agents being sound in mind and body. To that end, after the conclusion of particularly bad cases, each agent was required to have at least one session with Dr. Tierney to work out any trauma they may have experienced as a result. It also gave Tierney a psychological baseline on every agent should any big issues come up. He knew all of our strengths and weaknesses. In an organization whose employees hunted monsters, his appointment calendar stayed full.

Dr. Tierney gave a resigned sigh. "I can feel the static from here. I believe I'll need a chair for this one."

One of the lab techs rushed to comply, rolling a desk chair over to him.

Yep, he knew this was one nasty blade. It must have been giving off evil vibes with a capital "E."

He sat, and a gloved Dr. Clare Cheban, SPI's lab director, put the spearhead—with its dinner napkin—on a metal tray and held it out to Tierney.

The psychometrist gave her a half smile. "Don't take the tray away, Clare. I have a feeling I'll want to get rid of it quickly."

Tierney picked up the spearhead with his bare hand, careful to keep it directly over the tray, wrapped his fingers around the spearhead's base, and closed his eyes.

Everyone in the room waited in complete silence.

Within seconds, Tierney dropped the spearhead to the tray with a clank and kicked back with his feet to propel his chair as far away from it as possible. The back of the chair slammed into a lab table. Tierney didn't even seem to notice. His eyes were open, but he was still seeing what touching the spearhead had shown him. He squeezed his eyes shut, leaned over with elbows on knees, and did some deep breathing, smooth exhaling. When he sat up, he was definitely seeing us, but he looked really confused.

Moreau was the first to speak. "Dr. Tierney?"

"Yeah, I'm here. Give me a minute."

More silence.

"First," Tierney began, "I would say that it's definitely old, at least as old as the tests showed, possibly older."

"What makes you think it could be older?" Dr. Cheban asked.

"This wasn't forged by humans. It just appears that way."

Cheban blinked. "And you can tell this how?"

"The hands I sense making and then wielding this weapon don't belong to any human."

No, that wasn't in the least bit creepy. I resisted the urge to back up a step.

"This individual is something more, much more."

"We just passed creepy, and went straight into spooky," I muttered.

Tierney nodded. "I agree completely, Mac."

"What has it been used for?" Ian asked tightly.

"War and killing, both with great enthusiasm." He paused. "I said 'enthusiasm,' didn't I?"

"Yes, you did."

Tierney's full attention was now on Ian, intent attention.

"I didn't get that from the spearhead . . . I knew it by looking at you, just now."

Suddenly I wasn't the only one who wanted to leave the room. My partner looked like he wanted nothing more than to be right behind me.

As far as I knew, Ian, Moreau, and I were the only ones in this room who knew about Ian's connection to the St. Michael's medal. Like me, Moreau had to suspect that whatever message the ghoul was trying to send with the spearhead, it'd been intended for Ian. I flicked my eyes to Moreau, and he shook his head almost imperceptibly.

That meant Tierney knew that all by his lonesome. Like I said, spooky. But sometimes, especially around here, spooky turned out to be a good thing. Maybe Tierney could find out what Ian didn't know.

I cleared my throat in Ian's general direction.

Ian was intent on Alain Moreau. "Sir, may I pick up the spearhead?"

Huh?

"I believe the ghoul left it for me, and while I've never seen it before, it's familiar—if that makes any sense."

Tierney chuckled. "This is SPI, Ian. Nothing makes sense here. Is there any history of psychometry in your family?"

"Not that I'm aware of." My partner attempted a little smile. "We're plain, vanilla humans."

"You stopped being plain the day you signed on the dotted line to work here." Then Tierney glanced at Moreau.

"If it's something you feel you need to do," Moreau told Ian.

I drew breath to tell Ian that he might want to sit down, but my partner was too quick.

He picked up the spearhead.

And it glowed as bright as a tiny sun.

— 12

THAT was unexpected.

Ian dropped that spearhead on its tray even faster than Tierney had. And when he did, the spearhead stopped glowing.

I stood perfectly still. "Has anything like that ever happened before?"

Ian likewise wasn't moving. "No."

"Interesting."

"I don't think so."

"I'm sure you don't." I glanced around at SPI's lab-coated brain trust, some of whom had quickly donned protective eyewear against the glow, all of whom looked way too excited by what had just happened. "Any theories or explanations?"

"None," Dr. Cheban said. "Agent Byrne, could you—"

"No."

"But if we could just get a measurement of any electromagnetic—"

"Why?"

Dr. Cheban hesitated, probably thinking "because it would be cool" wouldn't be a very scientific response. "Are you experiencing any reaction to the contact?"

"None."

"Any pain?"

"No."

Dr. Cheban turned to Moreau. "Sir, could you arrange for us to keep the spearhead for a while longer?"

Moreau already had his phone out and was texting. "I'll see what I can do."

Ian now had the same thousand-yard stare as Tierney.

I moved closer. "Ian?"

No response.

I reached out to touch his arm. A faint zap, like static electricity, ran through my hand. My partner was definitely paler than it was good for him to be. I held on to Ian with one hand and pulled over a chair with the other.

"Ian, you need to sit down. Now."

He sat without protest, which made me even more concerned.

"I'm fine," he told me.

Someone, probably Moreau with his text, had called Mike Stephens, SPI's chief medical doctor. The lab techs stood aside as Dr. Stephens came in, bent over, and did that obnoxious thing with a penlight to Ian's eyes.

"I'm fine," Ian repeated, with more emphasis.

Dr. Stephens put away the penlight, but he wasn't giving up. He squatted down next to Ian's chair. "Agent Byrne, I want you to come down the hall for an examin—"

Ian sighed and half rolled his eyes. He put his hands on the arms of the office chair and pushed himself to his feet. "Okay, I'll come and get checked out, though there's nothing . . ."

He took one step and went as white as a sheet.

Dr. Stephens grabbed Ian's arm and missed. He missed,

because my partner was already falling backward. I did what any good partner would do—I let Ian squash me flat when he fainted.

Ten minutes later, the only thing wrong with my partner was an acute case of embarrassment.

"So you passed out," I said for what felt like the umpteenth time. I was careful not to use the "f" word. For some reason, men had a problem being told they'd fainted. Passed out was better. Knocked out was best. It meant you'd probably been engaged in a manly activity like fighting or football when you'd gotten your bell rung.

We were in the same room in SPI's infirmary where I'd spent the night after going one round too many with a squid demon in a parking garage.

Exciting times, and it hadn't even been the weekend.

"Are you all right?" Ian asked, also for what seemed like the umpteenth time.

"I'm. Fine. Nothing got broken or even bent." Though I was going to have one hell of a bruise tomorrow from where my hip had slammed into a desk, but unless I up and decided to come to work tomorrow without pants, no one would see it.

Ian was in a bed, hooked up to a whole mess of machines, most of which I had no clue what they did. My partner glared at the various tubes and wires that ran from him to the machines.

"Hey, at least Dr. Stephens only took your shirt. You could have woken up in one of those gowns that lets your ass hang out."

Ian grunted.

Actually, that'd been my doing. Dr. Stephens had been ready to have Ian stripped. I intervened, asking whether it was really necessary, and couldn't he hook up all his gadgets and leave Ian with a shred of dignity—and at least his pants. Dr. Stephens relented, even though he didn't like what some of the machines were telling him; actually it was more like he didn't understand what they were telling him. He insisted they weren't malfunctioning, which added one more worry to my quickly growing stack.

I believed my partner was going to become a lab rat for the next few hours—or longer.

The door opened and Kylie O'Hara hurried to Ian's side. "What happened? I heard you fai—"

"Got his bell rung but good," I finished before she could.

Kylie didn't get to where she was without being perceptive. She took a sharp left turn into "Are you all right?"

"I'm fine." Ian started to sit up, but Kylie's dainty hand on his shoulder pushed him right back down. Dryads were strong. "I'm better than fine, but try telling that to Dr. Stephens."

I grinned. "When Stephens gets someone new to poke and prod, he likes to hang on to 'em for a while. Smart people get bored easily. Ian touching that spearhead and lighting it up made him downright irresistible to the lab-coat crowd around here. They probably stuck a tracking device somewhere on you in case you try to make a break for it, which has happened a lot around here."

Kylie fixed Ian with her sharp green eyes. "But you're not going to be the latest escapee, are you?"

Ian met her fix and raised her a glare. Kylie didn't back down.

I stepped in. "Ian, if the ghoul left it for you, that means he knew it would react to you the way it did. He knows why. We don't." I paused for emphasis. "We need to know. There's a lot more to this than just a ghoul chasing the one that got away."

"And I need to be out there finding him."

"*All* of our people are on this one, Ian," Kylie told him.

"And since that spearhead is Irish, our Dublin office is involved now. The men and women of this agency admire and respect you. This thing is after you, and it's baiting a trap. They take that personally. If this thing can be caught, they will do it. *We* will do it."

Ian reached out and put his big hand over her tiny one, and suddenly I felt like a third wheel. "Nice try," I told him. "I'm not stepping outside to give you privacy. You ex-special forces guys are sneaky."

Ian grinned, and I was glad to see it. "Would I do that?"

"In a heartbeat."

Kylie extracted her hand, put it over his, and patted it. "While you're here, you can finally get some sleep."

That was news. "You're not sleeping?"

Ian dismissively waved the hand Kylie wasn't holding. "It's nothing."

Kylie harrumphed. "It's something. And it's not just that he's not sleeping; it's the nightmares."

That was news, too. Ian wasn't the type to share any personal issues with anyone, which meant Kylie had been there when said issues had happened. I bit my bottom lip against a smile. They were sleeping together. At least Kylie was sleeping, Ian apparently not so much.

"When did that start?" I asked him. "The nightmares." Not their sleeping together, though I admit I was curious.

Ian shifted uncomfortably. That told me they hadn't been a recent acquisition.

"Perhaps I should ask how long have they been going on?"

"Sleep and I haven't been on speaking terms lately."

I scowled at him. "Dodgy thing, aren't you? Define lately."

"Off and on. Now, mostly on. I had the first one five years ago, when I was in the hospital."

"After the ghoul attack." I didn't ask it as a question. I knew, but I wanted to say it, to get it out there.

Ian nodded. "Every time I see him I start having the dream again."

"The same one."

"Yes."

"And you didn't tell anyone."

"I didn't see a reason to. Besides, I didn't want anyone to worry."

"Maybe some of us should," Kylie said. "You don't seem to." Silence.

"You are worried, aren't you?" I said quietly.

Ian half shrugged. "Sleep dulls the reflexes, slow reflexes can—"

"That's not what I mean and you know it."

Ian took a long breath and let it out. Even that seemed to take too much effort. I wasn't getting worried—I was already there.

"Describe the dream," I told him.

"There's a battle," Ian said. "It's not here, and it sure isn't now."

"Where?"

"Don't know. I know the language in my dream, but not when I wake up." He paused. "And I'm wearing armor. Old-fashioned armor, like medieval. The weapons are swords."

My breath hitched. "And spearheads?"

"Not that spearhead. At least not that I remember. There's a battle going on all around me. I see the armor in flashes of gold and silver. Incredible workmanship. The men wearing that armor are . . . glowing, that's the only way I can describe it. At least their faces are glowing."

"Like that spearhead?"

Ian hesitated, and that gave me my answer right there. "Yeah," he admitted. "Like that spearhead."

"What armor are you wearing?"

"I don't know."

"Don't know or can't see?"

"Yes."

"Huh?"

"I'm wearing a helmet."

"At least your dream self is safety conscious."

"It has a half faceplate, with a slit for the eyes, to see out."

And the tip of a sword blade could get in, I couldn't help but think.

"Who are the enemies?" I asked.

Ian slowly shook his head, his eyes on the wall over my shoulder, but it wasn't beige infirmary paint he was seeing.

"I don't know, but I'm looking for someone. The one I need to kill."

Now we were getting somewhere.

"Is it the ghoul?"

"I don't know. My dream self knows. I don't. So far, I haven't been able to find him."

"So it's a man."

"Male, not man. And no, I don't know what he is," Ian said before I could ask.

The ghoul had been involved in the incident at the Metropolitan Museum of Art last Halloween. And Isidor Silvanus, the elf dark mage responsible for nearly releasing Hell on Earth, had claimed the ghoul was a mutual acquaintance who wanted to "reach out" to Ian in the very near future.

It sounded like the ghoul was keeping his promise—in Ian's dreams and reality.

"Is he in your dreams?" I asked quietly.

Ian nodded, a smooth muscle tightening in his jaw. "I haven't seen him, but I know he's there. I'm starting to think that the night in the jewelry store with Pete wasn't a random event. Whether the ghoul recognized me then, or he'd set me and Pete up, or it still could have been some sick coincidence . . . the ghoul knows me from someplace."

"Or some time," Kylie said quietly.

I was about to take our discussion to a whole new level of strange, and Ian wasn't going to like it. But getting to the bottom of this was more important than my partner's paranormal comfort level.

"Ian, I think you should talk to Dr. Tierney."

My partner didn't look surprised by my suggestion, but I certainly wouldn't have described his expression as happy.

"My psychological health is perfectly—" Ian began.

"I'm not talking about seeing him as a shrink. He also does past-life regressions."

The flat look Ian gave me said loud and clear what he thought of that idea. Some things were too woo-woo even for Ian to accept.

Ian could accept that vampires and werewolves existed just fine. He also had no difficulty accepting that they lived longer than humans—a lot longer. Heck, he wasn't even bothered that our boss was a three-story tall, multi-millennia-old dragon in the guise of a petite human woman.

But that human souls could have lived before in another body?

My partner's normally flexible mind didn't want to wrap itself around that one, especially when it came to himself.

The look I gave him in return conveyed all of that and more.

"Ian, you're best friends with a werewolf, your manager is a vampire, your boss is a dragon, and you're sleeping with a dryad. I mean, come on."

No reaction to the "sleeping with" part from Ian, but Kylie confirmed it with a big ol' grin.

"It's not the idea of past lives that I don't like—" Ian began.

"Don't *like*?" The bulb in my head came on and I was enlightened. "Oh, it's the hypnosis, isn't it?"

My tough as nails partner actually squirmed.

"It *is* the hypnosis." I wanted to laugh, but I wasn't about to actually do it. "Ian, Dr. Tierney is a medical professional. I promise he has no interest in making you cluck like a chicken."

"I'll go under, wake up an hour later, and not know what happened. Would *you* like that, Agent Control Freak?"

"Agent Control—" I put my indignation on pause. "Come to think of it, I probably wouldn't like that."

"*Probably* wouldn't?"

"Okay, definitely wouldn't. But if that ghoul was obsessed with me and this was the only way to find out why . . ."

"I'm not convinced it's the only way."

"Ian, you said it yourself. Your freaky dreams started that night. They'd go away until the next time you two ran into each other. There's obviously a connection. The ghoul is in these dreams, and you know *he's* real. Is it that big a leap to accept that it *is* you in that armor? Okay, not exactly you, an earlier version. Finding out what that dream is and what it means could be the key to discovering why a who-knows-how-old sadistic shapeshifter has picked you to pick on. There has to be a reason." I gave him a look that said arguments and resistance were futile. And just in case I didn't look fierce enough, I added, "Don't make me tell Moreau, because I will, and he'll insist that you do it."

Ian's expression was outfiercing mine.

"We care about you, Ian," Kylie said. "You need to put this behind you, and to do that, we've got to get to the bottom of it. If these dreams are related to the ghoul—and it sounds like they are—Dr. Tierney would be the person who could find out what's going on, or at the very least, provide a few much-needed answers."

My partner lay there for a few moments, motionless, then came my sign of victory—a resigned sigh.

I gave a little internal cheer.

Ian scowled at me. "Don't look so happy."

"I don't look happy."

"Yes, you do."

"No, I don't."

"Mac?"

"Yes?"

"*Never* play poker."

13

KYLIE'S phone beeped with an incoming text. She read it, spat her favorite four-letter word, then glanced from Ian to me and back again, her distress evident.

Concerned, Ian put his other hand on top of hers. "What is it?"

"I have to go. The footage from the second robbery—all of it—was leaked online almost as soon as the networks had it. It's all over the Internet now."

Kylie didn't need to specify what "all of it" meant. Even people who weren't necessarily sick and twisted wouldn't be able to resist at least a peek at what those ghouls had done to those guards. Most people knew that ghouls couldn't possibly be real, but the sight of four men in movie-quality prosthetic makeup eating two men alive had to be sending normally logical and levelheaded people into a panic.

Kylie and her department had their work cut out for them.

"Go," Ian told her. "I'll be fine."

"And I'll be here," I promised.

The door opened and Yasha filled the space.

I smiled. "And right on cue, here's my backup. Ian won't go anywhere he isn't supposed to."

Yasha was never one to hide his feelings, whether affection or violence. His heart was firmly on his sleeve at all times. It was one of the reasons why I loved him so much. Right now, Yasha was worried about the man he considered to be his best friend. If that ghoul put in an appearance anytime soon, he wouldn't stand a chance against an enraged and protective Yasha, regardless of who or what he actually was.

Kylie clearly still didn't want to leave, but she knew she had to.

"We've got this," I assured her.

"I know you do, it's just that—"

Ian pulled on the hand he was holding, bringing Kylie down to him and into a pretty danged passionate kiss. For the duration, I found a fascinating spot on the ceiling to study. Yasha watched, a happy smile on his face that his partner had found someone. Note to self: find Yasha a nice werewolf girl to settle down with.

No sooner had Kylie shut the door behind her than Ian sat up in bed and tossed back the blanket that had covered him from the waist down. He hadn't even glanced underneath before he shucked his covers. Good thing he was still wearing pants.

Yasha stepped in front of the door.

I joined him. "And what, pray tell, do you think you're doing?"

"Leaving." Ian looked around for his shoes. "I've got work to do."

"You're not leaving this room, mister. Not until Dr. Stephens says you can."

The door opened, or at least someone on the other side

tried to open it, but a six-foot-eight Russian made for one heck of a doorstop.

"Excuse me, is someone not decent in there?" Dr. Tierney asked.

"We're all decent," I told him. "And we even have clothes on."

Yasha stepped away from the door, and Tierney opened it the rest of the way. "I was blocking the door."

Tierney had to look up—way up—to look Yasha in the eye. "And a fine job you were doing. I take it Dr. Stephens's patient is losing his patience?"

Ian swung his long legs over the side of the bed. "You take it right."

Dr. Stephens came in and he didn't look happy. He began unhooking Ian's monitors. So much for the cause of the frown; he was losing his lab rat.

"Finally," Ian said. "Thank you."

"Don't thank me," Stephens said. "And you might not want to thank Noel here, either."

Dr. Tierney gave Ian an apologetic smile that didn't look all that remorseful. "You're going from Mike's end of the hall to mine."

Dr. Tierney wanted to talk to Ian. Ian needed to talk to Dr. Tierney. My opinion, not his.

I was Ian's partner, and had been at the site of the first robbery/murder, and had met the ghoul myself on two occasions, so Ian wasn't the only one Dr. Tierney wanted to talk to.

His office was down the hall from the infirmary and medical offices, near a main stairwell. He knew that some of SPI's agents would only come to see him if they could do so privately. His office placement was intentional.

As a psychometric, Dr. Tierney got psychic vibes from

objects, even furniture, especially antique furniture. As a psychiatrist, he needed to keep his concentration on his patients. That explained why all of his office furniture came from Ikea. He even assembled it himself so that the frustration of the people who had to put it together didn't sink into the wood and fabric. I'd heard there'd been a lot of Zen meditation and burning incense involved while Dr. Tierney had assembled the desk, chairs, and bookcases. As a result, his office was a psychic neutral zone, a center of calm for himself and his patients.

On our way to his office, Ian gave Dr. Tierney the shortened version of his dream. Needless to say, with everything that'd happened this afternoon plus the dream as the cherry on top, Tierney cleared his schedule for Ian.

Noel Tierney had furnished his office to put his patients at ease. Low lighting, tabletop water feature, soothing colors, strategically placed boxes of Kleenex, and an honest-to-God crackling and popping fireplace—all to make people feel warm and fuzzy and comforted.

Ian was none of the above.

He was former military, ex-cop, and presently wound tighter than a spring.

"Ian and Mac, go on in," Dr. Tierney said from down the hall. "I'll be right there."

SPI headquarters was completely underground. Dr. Tierney loved plants. Plants loved sunlight. Not to be deterred, he had brought in glow lights. It didn't help. Bless his environmental-loving, nurturing heart, but the man had a black thumb. The only thriving plants were in his drawings that he'd decorated his office with. But to his credit, he never gave up on his plants, and he extended that same determination to his patients.

"Please be seated and make yourselves comfortable," Dr. Tierney said, closing the door behind us.

Ian and I chose chairs. Dr. Tierney sat next to me and across from Ian, leaving the chair between them empty.

Good move.

I half raised my hand. "Dr. Tierney, I have a question."

"You can ask it on one condition."

"What's that?"

"Call me Noel, both of you. Dr. Tierney is my mother."

I smiled. "Done." I inclined my head toward the fireplace. "That. How the heck?"

"The flames are an illusion. One of our mages set it up for me. While it doesn't put off any heat, it also doesn't make any mess or require tending."

"I feel cheated. Our conference room only has folding chairs and a whiteboard."

I was trying to help Ian relax. It was obvious he felt uncomfortable, even though Noel didn't have a notepad, pen, or a file with Ian's psychological profile in front of him.

Noel leaned forward, his hands lightly clasped in front of him.

"Before we discuss the dreams that have been bothering you, tell me more about this creature."

"Where would you like me to start?" Ian asked.

"The beginning is usually a good place."

Ian snorted. "Not for me."

"I understand," Noel said. "What would be helpful for me is whether you recognized this creature—on any level—when you first saw him. A fleeting sense of familiarity, perhaps?"

"Should I have?"

"That is for you to tell me. Did you sense that he knew you?"

"He looked glad to see me, but I thought he was just hungry." Ian was being glib, but his hands were clenched on the chair's wooden arms. They appeared to be sturdy, but were creaking ominously. I hoped Noel had replacements stowed somewhere, because Ian was about to snap them plum off.

"When you first encountered him that night, he was wearing a mask. You thought he was human."

"I did." Ian glanced away from Noel and at a plant in the corner that was far from flourishing. "But plenty of perps have a crazy look in their eye."

Ian told Noel the entire story, including the dreams he'd been having, sparing no detail. He followed that with the encounter we'd had with the ghoul on New Year's Eve in an abandoned subway station beneath Times Square. I told him of my encounter on a snowy street in SoHo several days before that.

Noel sat quietly for a few moments after we'd finished, absorbing and pondering what we'd said. "In my professional opinion—in my studies of the supernatural criminal mind—such a being would not continue pursuit merely to recapture a meal that escaped, if I may be so blunt. Beings that live multiple centuries and millennia view events and time differently than we do."

"The big picture," I said.

"Precisely. And to live for as long as this being theoretically has, that picture is very big indeed. His fixation on Ian is part of that picture. He has robbed two banks and taken the contents of a total of seven safe deposit boxes. Do we know what the contents were?"

"Not yet," Ian replied. "Moreau is working on finding out from the vampires who were renting the boxes."

"Do you think these robberies could have any connection to the robbery five years ago? Ian, you said that this gang had been responsible for a string of robberies at jewelry and high-end pawn shops. What was taken?"

"Various pieces."

"Like what?"

"Necklaces, bracelets, rings, brooches."

"Were they similar?"

"No, different stones, both modern and old settings."

I sat up straight, a theory forming. "How about the size of the stones? Was at least one stone per piece over a certain carat size?"

"I don't know," Ian admitted.

"We might need to find out. Were any of them ever recovered?"

"Initially I tried to trace the ghoul through the stolen jewelry. None of the pieces ever turned up on the market, either broken up or whole."

"Maybe because he kept what he needed and trashed the rest. If you were that old . . . One, would you suddenly decide to become a jewel thief? And two, if you did, wouldn't you go after something bigger and more valuable?" I half smiled as it came together. "Unless . . . he didn't care about the value of the stones, because he planned to keep them, at least the larger ones, because he wanted—no, he *needed*—those *specific* stones."

"What are you thinking?" Noel asked.

"We know the ghoul was at the Met for that opening night gala, when the Dragon Eggs were stolen. We also know that Sebastian du Beckett wasn't the mastermind behind stealing those seven diamonds. Did the jewelers have insurance photos of the stolen pieces? And if so, could you still get them?"

Ian nodded, liking where this was going. After having things out of his control for the past few hours, he had something that he could do. He took out his phone and began texting. "I've got an old friend on the force who's worked in Evidence for years. There were photos of most of the stolen pieces. If he can lay his hands on them, I'm sure he'll e-mail them to me."

"Just because the settings are modern doesn't mean the

stones are," I said. "Some gems are much older than that ghoul. They may have even been recut from larger gems between the time the ghoul last had contact with them and when they were set in the latest pieces of jewelry. They'd still be the stones he was looking for, but just broken into smaller pieces." I flashed a grin. "Just because something is small doesn't mean it doesn't have kick."

"Speaking of kick," Noel said. "I'd like for you to tell me what you felt when you picked up that spearhead."

Ian settled back in his chair, an actual half smile on his face. "I will, if you tell me how you knew by looking at me that it had been used with 'enthusiasm.'"

Noel gave a short laugh. "Fair enough. Over the years, I've done enough consulting with SPI offices and other agencies to determine the background on artifacts, relics, and devices with suspected paranormal qualities—both ancient and of recent make. I, myself, am not qualified to determine the age of an object, but through past experience I've discovered that the more I feel as if I'm spiraling down a bottomless pit, the older and more powerful an object is." He turned his head to the side and flipped his ear forward. He was wearing a scopolamine patch.

I grinned. "Nice to know I'm not the only one around here who gets the woozies."

"When Alain told me he wanted me to have a look at the spearhead, I patched up as a precautionary measure." He winced. "It was a good thing I did—for everyone in that lab. When I picked up that spearhead, I felt its age as well as the violence it had been used for. Though that wasn't unexpected. After all, it's a spearhead, not a knitting needle. As to how I connected that to you personally . . ." Noel paused. He wasn't uncomfortable with what he was about to say, but he knew Ian would be.

"Past life?" I asked.

"It seems like a logical conclusion." Noel glanced at Ian. "An ancient creature that is obsessed with you, a spearhead left for you, the spearhead's reaction when you picked it up . . . and most of all, your reaction to the spearhead. As to my 'enthusiasm' remark, I had a sense of you wielding the full spear with that head attached. Let's just say you had a grim purpose. You felt your opponents needed to die and you took satisfaction in causing their deaths."

Whoa.

"Uh, did you get a sense of whether the spearhead was good or evil?" I asked.

"Neither. Which probably means it could be used for either one."

"That sounds like something we shouldn't send back to the NYPD."

"I agree, and so does Alain. He's having our armory's museum searched for a similar-looking spearhead so the mages upstairs can throw enough mojo on it to make it appear identical." Noel gave Ian an impish smile. "As a former NYPD detective, you didn't hear that."

Ian's brief chuckle was totally without humor. "I end up doing that a lot. But in this instance, I agree."

"Okay, I've told you mine," Noel said. "Tell me yours."

"When I picked it up, I felt powerful. More than that. I felt invincible. I could cut down every opponent who came against me. None survived, I couldn't allow it."

Ian was gazing into the fire, its light making his profile even stronger than usual, harder, colder. I sat perfectly still, not daring to move.

"I wasn't alone," he continued. "Other men and women were fighting by my side and near me, glowing with power. We waged war against things that didn't belong in the same land as the rest of us." Ian's eyes darkened. "Tentacles, not arms. Two heads, not one. Four arms or six, instead of two.

Only one eye. Deformed. Monstrous. They fought with their backs to the sea, and we kept advancing, forcing their retreat, retreat or die, driving them into the sea."

"Would you be willing to allow me to view your dream as you're having it—to help identify your enemies?"

Ian's gaze stayed locked on the flames. "I am willing."

I didn't know who was doing the answering: Ian or the man who had driven the monsters into the sea.

Ian's phone beeped with an incoming call, snapping my partner out of his reverie.

I swore silently at the crappy timing.

14

IT was Ian's evidence contact at the NYPD, and he stepped outside to take the call.

I stuck my head out the door to make sure Yasha was still standing guard to keep Ian from making a run for it. He was, so I ducked back into the office and closed the door, hoping the call would take longer than a few seconds.

"What was *that*?" I blurted at Noel. "Or more to the point, *who* was that?"

"I believe we got a look at an event in the life, if you will, of that spearhead. A very important event."

"That sounded entirely too much like Ian's dream." A dream triggered when Ian had first met the ghoul—and deepened by a spearhead that the ghoul left for Ian. "The ghoul knows who Ian is—or *was*."

"It appears likely."

"It was like pulling eye teeth for me to get Ian to talk about it, but in less than five minutes here—"

"The fireplace isn't only for comfort," Noel said. "Mine

or my patients'. And I confess, it's not entirely a fireplace. The flames flicker at a rate that is very conducive to relaxation. Another touch added by our mages. Anyone seeing a psychiatrist for the first time is understandably nervous. There is nothing more soothing on a deep primal level than a warm and flickering fire. Our distant ancestors gathered around fires for protection against what prowled just out of sight in the darkness—either real or imagined. That need for safety is a part of who we are as humans. It's a need that has never left us. Agent Byrne felt safe here. He was in headquarters, surrounded by his friends, his trusted partner by his side. The fire merely aided what was already there."

"So you didn't hypnotize him," I said rather than asked.

Noel shook his head. "And it's doubtful that it would have worked, given Ian's natural reticence and his distrust of my calling."

"He hypnotized himself."

"In a way. The fire was soothing, and due to his emotional state and lack of sleep, Ian was obviously near exhaustion. It worked because it was on his terms and he was in complete control the entire time. I merely guided his thoughts."

I smiled and nodded in approval. "Slick. You're a smart guy."

A corner of his lips briefly turned up. "That's what my diplomas say. Success is what counts."

"Do you think he knows this thing from a past life?"

"It's my opinion that's what Ian believes."

"What's the next step?"

"If Ian's dreams are indeed a remembrance of a past life, I would like to do a dream link."

"Which is?"

"I have a gift, Mac. Under the right conditions, I will be able to experience Ian's dream as he is having it." Noel's eyes took on a haunted cast. "And I will remember every moment of it."

"How can you be sure he'll have the same dream again?"

"My asking Ian whether he would be willing to have me view his dream as he was having it was more than a question."

"It was a hypnotic suggestion," I realized.

Noel nodded. "But as was the case with the entire session, Ian was in control of the direction our discussion took. He agreed to the link; it was his choice."

"And because it was Ian's choice and he agreed to it, he'll hold himself to it."

Noel smiled. "Agent Byrne is a man of his word, and he will keep that word, even to himself."

Needless to say, once he was out of Noel's office, Ian didn't like the psychiatrist's suggestion.

However, as Noel had predicted, he agreed to it.

"I want that ghoul gone," Ian was saying. "Somehow these robberies are connected to me and men are being butchered. If there's a possibility that letting Tierney inside my head will save even one life, I have to do it."

Since Ian was having trouble getting to sleep, let alone staying that way, Noel prescribed a dose of a drug that'd been developed by SPI's doctors in cooperation with two of the pharmaceutically gifted mages in our Research and Development department. It'd help Ian get to sleep, but it wouldn't interrupt his regularly scheduled dreams.

Ian was sitting on the side of the bed. Noel would be using a nearby reclining chair. My partner only had to shuck his shoes this time, but at least now he was conscious to do it himself. On the downside, he'd be sleeping in a hospital room, hooked up to monitors, with people watching him sleep and studying his brain waves like he was some kind of lab experiment.

Ian had asked if I would stay.

We had been partners for a year and a half. That one request told me that my partner trusted me to have his back. We were in a room in headquarters surrounded by the good guys, not in a dark alley surrounded by monsters. In a situation like that I still didn't think I'd be his first pick to have his back. Yasha during a full moon would be a much better choice. I didn't blame him; I wouldn't want me to have my back, either. None of that changed the fact that he wanted me here with him now.

"We can start whenever you're ready, Agent Byrne." Noel got to keep his shoes on, but as a concession to comfort, he'd taken off his bow tie.

Dr. Stephens was standing by to administer the shot to Ian. An IV would be preferable, but these were nightmares Ian was having, not visions of fluffy unicorns. The human body generally kept itself still during REM sleep, where dreams occurred, but neither Dr. Stephens nor Noel wanted to take a chance that Ian's sleeping self would strike out. And with him dreaming about a battle . . . well, nobody was lining up for a piece of that.

Ian lay back on the bed and shook his head when Dr. Stephens offered him a blanket. My partner had no intention of staying here one minute longer than necessary.

Noel attached the sensors to Ian's temples and on his forehead above his eyes; the doc wore a matching set of sensors. To me they looked like the round sticky patches used to monitor vitals during surgery, but what showed on the monitors looked like nothing I'd ever seen before.

Ian studied them with keen interest. "At least there's something going on in there," he quipped.

"There will be more once you begin dreaming," Noel said. He went to sit in the reclining chair, a sketch pad and pencils in his lap, and Dr. Stephens attached his sensors to the same monitoring machine.

Ian lay back and closed his eyes. The drug must have kicked in quick, because in less than five minutes the monitors started going crazy; at least that's what it looked like to me.

It was mighty interesting to the Drs. Tierney and Stephens as well. Dr. Stephens flipped a switch to what looked like a fancy printer, and Noel settled back in his chair, closed his eyes, and did some kind of yoga breathing.

Apparently it was showtime.

The only indication I could see that anything was happening—other than the impressively patterned light show on the monitors—was Ian's eyes rapidly moving beneath his lids.

Noel sat up and began sketching, his hand moving so quickly it was nearly a blur. I stayed perfectly still, forcing down an almost overwhelming urge to cross the room and stand over Tierney's shoulder to see what he was getting from Ian.

Then Ian's breathing came faster and took on a ragged edge.

Noel smoothly ripped the page from the pad, his pencil flowing over the next page before it'd even hit the floor.

Naturally, it landed facedown. So much for immediate gratification for my curiosity.

I didn't know how long dreams lasted, but Ian's was at least six sketched pages worth. Some of Noel's pages landed faceup, and I really wished they hadn't.

It was a nightmare I wouldn't wish on my worst enemy. Cancel that. The ghoul had caused Ian to have them, so as far as I was concerned, he deserved them right back—with interest.

Ian—or whoever he had been channeling in Noel's office—hadn't been exaggerating when he said the things he'd fought didn't belong here. The creatures in Noel's

sketches looked like a progression of horrific part-human/
part-aquatic hallucinations. On the page that had landed closest to me was a thing I'd seen in person and entirely too up
close.

The squid demon from the parking garage.

I had an unwanted flashback to a thing that had been a
man one minute, and a squid demon less than thirty seconds
later. His two human arms had lengthened and smoothed
into tentacles, and two more pairs of tentacles had sprouted
from his fish-belly-pale torso. The bottom half of his face
had writhed as snake-like tentacles emerged like a fleshy
beard. Putting a bullet between his eyes had only made a
dimple that'd spit that silver-infused bullet right back out.
His six tentacles versus my two arms equaled no contest,
and also no chance for survival on my end. I'd had two knives
which had made the difference between escape and being
dragged through a portal to Hell. The tentacles had been
rubbery, the core tough, and the grip like a python on ste-
roids. I'd had to hack and saw, but my life was worth every
effort. The blood that'd come out of those tentacles had been
black and as slippery as oil. As a result, I now carried knives
with some serious grips. Loose knife, lose life.

The director of SPI's Demonology department, Martin
DiMatteo, had been confused that a squid demon had
appeared so far from open water. Was it a coincidence that
I'd had a nearly fatal encounter with one seven months ago,
and that Ian was having a nightmare with one in a supporting role right now? Ian hadn't seen my squid demon, so this
one was all his.

It was all a little too coincidental for my taste—or nerves.

Ian's hands, which had been resting easily at his sides,
began to twitch. Dr. Stephens wisely put another two steps
between himself and his patient. I didn't blame him. I'd seen
Ian's fists in action on numerous occasions. Though at least

if my partner did slug someone, they'd already be in the right place to get the damage repaired.

Ian's hands were twitching, but Noel was white as a sheet, his breath coming in ragged gasps as if he was about to be sick. I silently nudged the room's trash can with my toe to get it closer to the doc's chair.

As far as I was concerned, it was the proper reaction to being forced to watch a bunch of ancient Irishmen hack and carve sea monsters to bits. Ian had a military background; he'd probably seen it all. The closest Noel had probably come was reading about it.

After a few more minutes, Ian's twitching subsided and his eyes ceased flickering back and forth beneath his lids.

Noel drew a series of shallow breaths, and swallowed with an audible gulp.

It looked like Ian's dream was now Noel's waking nightmare.

Ian was still out. Dr. Stephens had given him enough of the drug to help him sleep for the next several hours. He was still hooked up to the heart and breathing monitors, Dr. Stephens was in the room, and Yasha was sitting in the chair that Noel had used.

Ian had wanted me in the room with him, but seeing Noel's drawings of Ian's dream was more important. Besides, I was still watching over him. The room we were in had an observation window into Ian's room. My partner's features were relaxed, his breathing deep and even. I wouldn't have woken him up for anything in the world.

The conversation we were having definitely would have disturbed him. It was disturbing the hell out of me.

Alain Moreau had joined us. I'd called him two seconds after seeing Noel's drawings, and when Moreau had gotten a look, he immediately called in Amelia Chandler, one of SPI's historians and our expert on classic Greek and Roman mythology, as well as Nordic and Celtic. From what I'd heard around the office, if anyone could tell us what Ian had running around in his head, it would be her. Most folks would say that history and mythology couldn't be more different, but when you worked at SPI, you knew they were the same thing.

However, right before her arrival, Moreau flipped a switch on the wall next to the observation window and the glass went opaque, concealing Ian from view. I didn't know Moreau's motivation for not letting Amelia Chandler see Ian sleeping, but I approved wholeheartedly, even if it meant I couldn't watch over him for the next few minutes. Ian would be safe there. I wouldn't want a parade of people watching me sleep, either.

I recognized two of the creatures from unfortunate personal experience, and I'd assured Moreau that they most definitely were not myths. One was the squid guy.

The other was the Creature from the Black Lagoon.

Ian had two monsters in his dream that I'd seen in my reality. That said many scary and scream-inducing things about everything else in Noel's drawings.

The monsters were only part of it. The others were breathtakingly beautiful.

Noel had just finished filling in some of the detail he hadn't had time to work on while linked to Ian. It was these details that interested Amelia Chandler the most.

The armor looked like nothing from this world during any century. It appeared delicate, but was apparently stronger than any weapon their monstrous opponents could raise against them.

"I've seen two of the sea monsters in person," I told her. "Who are the humans?"

She smiled as though her birthday had come early this year. "None of the beings in these drawings are human, Agent Fraser. This was before humans became the dominant life on this planet."

"Uh, before humans? Wasn't that dinosaurs?"

"Before modern humans, after dinosaurs."

Well, that made it clearer.

"What we are looking at is from the age of the gods. I believe the exquisitely armored ones are the Tuatha Dé Danann, the not-mythical race of deities and heroes that settled in Ireland before the modern Gaels."

"How long ago was that?"

"About four thousand years," she replied without pausing in her study of the drawing with the squid guy and other misshapen mashups of men and sea creatures. "If those are the Tuatha Dé Danann, that would make their opponents none other than the Fomorians, purported to be a race of demons that came from the sea. The name is said by some scholars to come from the Old Irish *fo*, signifying under or beneath, and *mur* (sea), meaning the 'ones from under the sea.' Another interpretation suggests that it comes from *mór* (big/giant), meaning 'the giants from beneath the sea.'" Amelia picked up another sheet. "Collectively these drawings could very well represent the Second Battle of Magh Tuireadh, which was said to have taken place in Connacht in Ireland's west. In it the Tuatha Dé Danann defeated the Fomorians by driving them back into the sea." She set the sheets down. "I have a colleague at the University of Dublin, Dr. Conor Delaney, who—based on the detail Noel has provided—would probably be able to put names to some of these faces. He's worked with our European offices in the past."

"I'm familiar with Dr. Delaney's work," Moreau said. "I agree with your suggestion."

"I would ask where Noel saw them, or *who* he saw them

from, but I recognize 'only on a need to know basis' when I see it." She glanced at the opaque window. "Or don't see it."

"Thank you for your understanding. This is of the very highest sensitivity."

"No need to apologize, Alain." She smiled. "I was never here, and I never saw these."

"There is one more thing," Moreau said, passing three photos of the spearhead, shot from multiple angles, across the table to her.

Amelia's eyes widened. "Is this what was brought in from the Prime Bank?"

"It is."

"Is there any chance I could see this in person?"

"Can you identify it?"

"The condition is incredible. Do you know how rare it is to find an intact weapon in this condition from that age?"

I leaned forward. "What age?"

Amelia nodded toward the stack of drawings. "That age." She didn't seem to be breathing all that well. Hopefully, she wouldn't be joining Ian in the infirmary. "Has Harald seen this?"

I assumed they meant Harald Siggurson, SPI's in-house bladed weapons expert.

"He's examining it now."

"Where?"

"Down the hall in the main lab."

Amelia Chandler, a historian with four degrees, looked like she was about to squee. "Is there any way I could—"

Moreau took out his phone. "I'll call and tell them to let you in."

Amelia jumped out of her chair and was halfway to the door when she stopped and turned. "We're finished here, right?" Her words came out in a rush.

My manager smiled. "Yes, we are."

"Do you need Conor's contact information?"

"I have it. Thank you."

"No, thank *you*." Then she was out the door, her high heels clicking against the linoleum as she ran down the hall to the lab.

15

"WHAT do you mean I'm not on the team?"

Ian was furious. Alain Moreau was standing his ground.

Our manager was the last person who could ever be accused of having his emotions written on his face. But this morning, I knew he had to be hating being in charge of SPI right now. I wondered if vampires took vacations. If Moreau had been a human in this situation, he'd have been thinking that when Vivienne Sagadraco got back, he deserved a bonus at the very least, though a bonus and an extra week of vacation sounded about right.

I did not envy our manager becoming everyone's boss the week the vampire families were at each other's throats *and* Ian's ghoul stalker surfaced in front of the mortal world, and now Ian was being taken off the team that would hunt him down. This was why Ian had joined SPI, and now Moreau was telling him to stand down.

"Agent Byrne, you know the reason."

"Yes, the bastard called me out—and he knows things about me that I don't."

"Which is precisely why you will not be on the team. Your knowledge of this creature will be invaluable to our search, but you will not be going outside of this complex to hunt for him. We have other agents who are just as qualified—"

"Name one," Ian snarled.

"Every senior agent in the bull pen."

Ian inhaled slowly in an attempt to calm down.

It didn't work. The only thing that would make my partner feel better about this would be that ghoul's neck between his hands—or better yet, on the business end of Ian's favorite machete.

"Sir, this thing was the reason I joined SPI."

"We are grateful for that decision," Moreau countered. "You've saved countless lives, and it is my job to keep you alive to save countless more, not let you sacrifice yourself to satisfy your need for revenge."

"I assure you it wouldn't be sacrifice. I have no intention of dying—only killing."

"Agent Byrne . . . Ian, we don't know the reason behind these thefts—and we don't know why you reacted to that spearhead the way you did. Thanks to a lack of cooperation from the vampire families, we don't even know what has been stolen. What we do know is that these crimes have been committed in daylight and in public. SPI would be involved due to the identities of the criminals, but we are doubly involved because they have struck openly in full view of mortals. For now, the media is telling the world that it's elaborate makeup. It won't take much to disprove that." Moreau paused, his pale blue eyes intent on Ian's. "The ghoul wants you to come after him, perhaps so he can finish what he started—perhaps something else, something more. By involving SPI to the degree that he has and then calling you out, he wants to make it irresistible for you to come after him. There is more to this than a desire for escaped prey on his part. There is more at stake, more that he wants, and you are the key to whatever it is. It has been my unfortunate experience, Ian, that when a being as old as this wants something—or someone—it is catastrophic to many if they get it. To prevent that from happening, I will do whatever I must do to keep you from endangering not only yourself but any and all others who may suffer or die as a result of your actions. You are not to leave this compound until the ghoul is in custody. Do I make myself clear, Agent Byrne?"

"As crystal, sir."

"Dismissed."

As the elevator doors closed behind us on the executive suite, I glanced over at my still-silent partner and could virtually see the wheels turning.

"Ian," I said in warning.

"I'm not going anywhere."

"Yet." I took out my phone and started texting.

Ian knew it was about him. "Who?"

"Insurance."

"For what?"

"Good behavior. Yours."

I sent the text, put my phone back in its holster, and it beeped with an incoming almost immediately. Though to be exact, it howled.

Ian scowled. "Yasha."

"Six foot eight of hairy insurance. Moreau's not taking chances with you and neither am I. You merely said you heard him crystal clear; you didn't promise anything." I thought for a moment, reached out, and hit the elevator "STOP" button.

We heard voices complaining from below. "Take the stairs," I bellowed. Then I turned both barrels of my anger at my partner and let him have it.

"Some of us care whether you live or die," I snarled. "Even if you don't."

"I never said—"

I snapped my hand up for silence and got in his face, which was less effective than it could have been considering how much taller he is than me.

"*Yes*, you're the best agent in this place; and *yes*, you're the most qualified to send that ghoul back to the deepest corner of Hell where he came from." I was yelling and I did not care, and I didn't think I could've stopped if I wanted to. I sucked in a double lungful of air and kept going. "That's also why we can't lose you." Tears stung my eyes and I growled because that made me even angrier.

"*I* can't lose you. You might realize that if you thought for one second about someone other than yourself. You *can't* bring your partner back. What happened that night *wasn't* your fault, and from what you've told me about him, if he were here right now, he would *kick your ass*. I'd do it for him if I thought I could, and if it would do any good." My eyes were getting blurry with unshed tears. I swiped the back of my fingers across one eye and kept going. "So don't give me that *bullshit* that you're doing this for him. You're doing it for you and no one else. Yeah, you got away from that ghoul and he can't let it go. Well, neither can you. All you're being is a selfish *bastard*."

I made a fist and punched the button to restart the elevator. It hurt like hell.

When we reached the bottom floor, the elevator doors opened, and no one was waiting. I glared out over the bull pen and I'd never seen so many people trying so hard to look so busy. Under better circumstances, it would have been funny. As far as I was concerned, circumstances couldn't get any crappier than they were right now.

"I need a drink," I spat to no one in particular.

I went straight to my desk and grabbed some quarters out of my top drawer.

There was nothing in the breakroom drink machine except tooth-enamel-eating battery acid. My dentist had told me she had a couple of cops as patients, and they always carried cola in their squad cars in case they needed to clean blood off a crime scene sidewalk.

That was the button I punched. To my teeth, it might be battery acid. But to my taste buds, it was sugary bliss. "Live fast, die young, and leave behind rotten teeth," I muttered.

I heard the breakroom door close quietly behind me. I knew it was Ian, but I didn't turn around. I'd said my piece. If he wanted to talk—or get himself eaten alive by that ghoul—there wasn't a damned thing I could do to stop him. With that happy thought, I tossed back a gulp.

"Go easy on that stuff," he said gently. "You're gonna give yourself the hiccups."

I barked a short laugh—and hiccupped.

"Dammit," I said. I didn't shout or snarl. My throat was raw. "I think I pulled a vocal cord."

Ian's hands came down on my shoulders.

"On the upside, nobody out there will *ever* make the mistake of pissing you off."

"Like you did?" *Hiccup.*

"Like I did," Ian admitted quietly. "I'm sorry. I didn't know you were that—"

"Pissed? Enraged? Livid?"

"Yes."

"Apparently I didn't know, either." *Hiccup.* "I stood there, watching Moreau try to get through that thick head of yours."

Hiccup. "And knowing he'd have been better off talking to a wall for all the good it was doing." *Hiccup.*

Ian got a glass out of the cabinet and poured a glass of water. "Drink this."

I took the glass of water in one hand and still had the can of cola in the other. "Look at me." *Hiccup.* "You're turning me into a two-fisted drinker."

I started drinking the water slowly and continuously while continuing to breathe, also slowly. Then I hiccupped again and damned near choked myself.

Ian went to the table and sat down. I leaned against the drink machine, closed my eyes, and told myself to calm down unless I wanted to hiccup my way through the rest of the workday.

It took a few minutes, but I got rid of them. When I opened my eyes, Ian had a Krispy Kreme cruller on a paper towel at the place next to him.

A sugar-glazed peace offering.

I was suddenly too tired not to take it. Besides, it was a doughnut. I sat down, took a bite, and washed it down—carefully—with a sip of delicious, not nutritious battery acid. I swallowed and my stomach rumbled in gratitude when they both arrived. "Oh yeah, I haven't eaten today."

"Also my fault," Ian said.

I leaned back in my chair. "Well, what are you going to do?"

"I have a choice?"

"You always have a choice. And you know what I think."

Ian smiled, slightly. "Me and every other agent with ears."

I shrugged. "I've never been shy about letting my opinion be known."

Ian leaned forward, serious. "Mac, I'm sorry if I hurt you, upset you, or made you mad."

"Yes to all of the above."

"And you may be right."

Whoa. I raised an eyebrow. Heck, I raised both of them. "About . . .?"

"Why I want to go after the ghoul. But what you said, what you think, is only part of it. I've been talking to Noel, and being honest with myself." Ian looked down at his hands folded on the table. "Mac, I'm afraid of that thing. All my life, I've confronted my fears."

"Confront and defeat."

"Yeah. Though it's more than that. The dreams, the voice. They follow me; they stay with me. If someone else kills this thing . . ."

"The nightmares might still be there," I finished.

"It's not just that. What about the next ghoul, and the next? I'm not a runner, Mac. I'm a fighter. The fear, the not knowing where he'll turn up next, is eating me alive just as surely as if it was his teeth. For it to go away, I have to be the one to make it stop."

"No, you don't. I understand the need to see the body. No body, no death, and all that. I'm sure Sandra or Roy's teams would be glad to haul what's left of the carcass home with them so you can have closure. I'm all about having closure. As to the 'next ghoul' . . ." I coughed out a couple laughs and shook my head. "A shapeshifting monster of undetermined— but definitely ancient—age with an unhealthy obsession with Irish-American SPI agents. Chances are slim to none that there are any more of those running around. I'm sure the rest of your career will have plenty of nasty beasties, but I think the ghoul is a completely original, one-time-only supernatural psycho." I finished the doughnut and sat back, suddenly worn out. A hissy fit worth having really takes it out of a girl. "Just stay put, okay? Can you promise me that?"

"For you, I can promise."

My phone howled. I looked at the screen. "Good, because Yasha's about to, and I quote, 'lock him in Suburban and put both on lift.'"

"That wouldn't be pleasant."

"No, it wouldn't."

16

THE breakroom door opened again. It was Alain Moreau. He looked perplexed.

"It's unnaturally quiet out there," he noted. "And when I asked where the two of you were, no one answered, they just pointed."

Ian and I exchanged a glance and shrugged.

"I came to tell you that Bela Báthory has been found."

Ian sat up straighter. "Alive?"

"Not even in one piece. Dr. Van Daal found signs, and rather obvious ones at that, connecting Bela's kidnapping to the ghouls. I didn't want you leaving this complex, but at the same time, it's critical that we solve this as quickly as possible. You are best qualified to do that, as well as to identify any clues that may have been left for you."

"Clues?"

"We have our official connection between the Báthory kidnapping and the robberies. Bela was eaten by ghouls."

I stood up. "Sir, you said, and I completely agree, that Ian shouldn't—"

Moreau held up a hand. "I will be going with the two of you, as will Agents Miles and Foster as guards. They will be assigned to Agent Byrne for the duration of this case." His pale blue eyes bored into Ian's. "Do not try to lose them, Agent Byrne. I want your word."

Ian stood, raring to go. "You got it."

Calvin Miles was one of SPI's commandos. He'd been instrumental in us taking down the male grendel just before midnight on New Year's Eve. He'd also been on the takedown team for a hydra in a Chelsea apartment building laundry room. Small space, big mess, most of it had been made by the man who now stationed himself protectively behind Ian's right shoulder. He was at least a foot taller than me with biceps the size of my thighs in my fat jeans, bull neck, and bald head. Kind of like Mr. T without the bling or funky facial hair. Calvin had been an army field medic in Iraq, which had come in handy on more than one occasion that I'd been involved with. All SPI agents have to be trained as EMTs. When you hunt monsters and supernatural criminals for a living—especially if you were human—it wasn't a matter of if but *when* you or your partner or team member would need serious medical attention quick.

Liz Foster was another of SPI's commandos by way of the Marines. She was tall, but considering her background, she wasn't nearly as muscular as you'd expect a former Marine to be. But like a lot of other things about Liz, that was deceptive, and many a monster had died with a really surprised look on its face. She was human, but supernaturally quick, and she made each and every one of her strikes count.

Her favorite weapon was anything she could lay hands on, but she had a soft spot for flamethrowers. In our grendel-hunting excursion into New York's abandoned subway tunnels, she'd gotten plenty of opportunity to put her favorite toy to lethal use. Considering where we were going, flamethrowers weren't welcome.

We made quite the entrance into the main branch of the New York Public Library. We weren't here to bust ghosts, just collect a permanently dead vampire. Fortunately, this time, the majority of the NYPD who were on the scene were those in the know. The head librarian was a gnome with a very convincing height glamour. She knew who to call. Calvin and Liz were carrying openly: guns at their hips, more exotic weapons under their light jackets. As we came in the front doors, I saw that the NYPD had done their job and had set up barriers to keep curious library patrons from getting photos of anything newsworthy. The crowd showed zero interest in me and Ian, instead aiming their phones and flashes in the direction of Calvin and Liz, our heavily armed twin walls of muscle.

My partner gave an exasperated sigh.

"Hey, not one word," I told him. "Protected is good."

"I never said it wasn't."

There was a uniform posted to direct us to where Bela Báthory had been found.

Barring our way to the body was a police photographer working over something laid out on a large sheet of plastic.

"This is the clue I was referring to," Moreau told us. "It's a flag that was used to cover Bela Báthory's corpse. Dr. Van Daal said it was centuries old from the look of it, a museum-quality piece. She is having photos sent to Amelia Chandler and Conor Delaney, to get it identified as quickly as possible."

The flag was a stunning example of ancient weaving.

It was silk; at least that was the only fabric I could equate with the shimmering cloth at our feet. Woven through the bright threads of every color of the rainbow were fine threads of gold and silver. The Celtic knot designs were so intricate, that if it was meant to represent an animal or object, I couldn't detect it. It was large, at least six by four foot.

"Do you recognize it?" Moreau asked Ian.

"Other than it being beautiful, no."

"Not even vaguely familiar?"

"No."

"Good," I said. "Don't touch it."

"Not going to. At least not in public."

We proceeded to where the main action was.

Bela Báthory was laid out on a reading table like he was lying in state for a public viewing.

Oh boy, was he ever.

This was my first ever sight of a buck-naked, dead vampire that'd been eaten by ghouls.

"We meet again." Dr. Anika Van Daal looked from Ian and me to our sizable (and not just in numbers) entourage, one eyebrow raised inquisitively.

Ian sighed. "It's complicated."

"Isn't it always?" Dr. Van Daal turned her attention to Moreau. "Alain, always lovely to see you. I take it your presence here is due to political necessity considering the identity of the deceased?"

"Partially," Moreau said.

He didn't clarify what the other part was, but I thought Dr. Van Daal got the message that it also was complicated. From the looks of things, she had more than enough complexity to deal with. Van Daal's assistant was an elf, the rest of her team were humans. Van Daal knew what had done this; the others were just trying to ignore what had been done, and judging from the pasty faces of most of them, they weren't succeeding.

Bela Báthory's head was being photographed.

A good ten feet away from his body.

Interesting.

And so much for what had killed him permanently. Nothing got up once you severed its spinal cord.

"There's a good story there," Calvin muttered.

"There is indeed," Van Daal said. "The head was still attached to the body when it was found, but apparently the spinal cord had been severed, so the skin of the neck was all that was holding the head onto the body. When we shifted the body to continue our examination . . ."

She didn't say more and she didn't need to. I wondered with the morbid cop humor that I'd picked up from our NYPD friends if the head had bounced when it'd hit the floor. Probably. I was sure the more jaded investigators had found it funny; the newer folks had probably danged near lost their lunch. Van Daal's elven assistant was bagging the head, to preserve evidence, but mainly to keep the uninitiated from seeing Báthory's incisors.

Anika Van Daal stepped away from the body, giving us an unobstructed view of the deceased. My cola and cruller stirred uneasily in my stomach.

Moreau hadn't exaggerated. Bela Báthory had been eaten.

Ghoul teeth were pointed for tearing through flesh and muscle, unlike human dental work which only had incisors for puncturing, and even those weren't sharp on most people. The teeth that had done this weren't human, but the radius of the bites were.

Like I said, ghouls.

The human NYPD contingent in attendance were leaning more toward denial.

I didn't blame them in the least. I'd rather not know what had done this, either—and I especially didn't like what it meant.

The attack on the *Persephone* and Bela Báthory's abduction and permanent death were most definitely connected to the robberies.

And now all of it was connected to Ian.

Van Daal was talking to Moreau. "Thankfully for the librarian who found him, he'd been covered to the neck with what you saw on your way in. It wouldn't have been the first time they've discovered a homeless person sleeping in the stacks or on an out-of-the-way reading table. When the librarian tried to wake him up and Báthory's half-eaten arm fell out from under the flag and over the side of the table, the poor man realized that Mr. Báthory wasn't with us anymore."

I couldn't have agreed more. He'd been dead—well, undead—to begin with, meaning his corpse was easier to look at than the bank guards.

There was no blood.

The surveillance footage of the second robbery had shown a bloodbath. Those men had died from shock and blood loss.

There was no blood and no sign of bleeding on Bela Báthory's corpse.

It'd been three days since he'd been taken. From the dried and almost papery condition of his skin, he hadn't fed or been allowed to feed. The corpse's bloodless state could be explained by it being killed and the blood drained elsewhere.

I'd never seen the insides of a centuries-old vampire—either fed or starved. To me, Bela Báthory's exposed parts looked more like beef jerky than anything else.

Dang. I'd really liked beef jerky. Now it was off my snack food list.

A sick and twisted corner of my mind wondered if ghouls had a particular affinity for vampire jerky. That was a question I could go the rest of my life without knowing the answer to.

I'd never been one for getting closer to a dead body than I had to, especially a naked one, but what I saw didn't belong on a ghoul-eaten corpse.

"Permission to get a closer look at something, Dr. Van Daal?"

"Of course, Agent Fraser. What is it?"

"These." I indicated a set of puncture wounds, six of them, set in an offset arc. I had seen them before, but I . . . I stopped. I did recognize them. I'd seen these claws and the webbed hand they'd been attached to tear the throat out of a crewman on the *Persephone*.

"Creatures from the Black Lagoon," I murmured. "Though now known as Fomorians."

Dr. Van Daal gave me a quizzical glance. "I beg your pardon?"

Ian studied the claw marks over my shoulder. "You're sure?"

"As close as I could be without becoming fish food." I winced. "That wasn't the best way I could have said that." Ian's frown told me he'd already made the connection.

"What happened still isn't, wasn't, and never will be Rake's fault," I added.

"I didn't say that."

"You didn't need to."

"I found salt crusts around some of the wounds, as well as these." Van Daal held up a sealed glass tube; its contents were shaped like fingernails, but were green, silver, and black.

Ian squinted. "What the—?"

"Scales," I said. "I know what made these." I told Dr. Van Daal about the things that had taken Bela Báthory from his yacht.

She nodded as if I'd confirmed a theory for her. "There are also numerous puncture wounds on the body that correlate to claw-tipped, webbed fingers. The depth indicates extreme pressure. As best as I can tell outside of a lab, these wounds happened at the same time as the bites."

I felt sick. "The Fomorians held Báthory down while the ghouls ate him."

"I counted at least four pairs of hands," Van Daal said.

Moreau spoke. "A vampire of his age would have put up more of a fight than any number of mortal creatures could have held out against."

Ian's jaw hardened. "But it only took four of those lizard things to hold him down."

That image was chilling. I knew what a centuries-old vampire was capable of strength-wise. I'd seen Alain Moreau rip the wing off of an ancient Grecian harpy. Everything about him was as hard as granite, and even more impervious to damage.

Báthory had been fighting for his survival, and it had taken only four of those things to hold him down—while their ghoul friends ate him.

I'd be revisiting that horror in a future nightmare.

17

WE were leaving the library when Ian's phone rang and he yanked it out of its holster.

"Byrne," he snapped.

I couldn't understand the words, but whoever was on the other end of that call was yelling, screaming even.

Ian gave me a sharp glance and picked up the pace.

What the hell?

"Mr. Winthrop, calm down and for God's sake, be quiet. They'll hear—"

The bank vice president.

"We're five minutes away," Ian told him. "No, do *not* hide in the vault. They can . . . Mr. Winthrop?"

Ian swore and jumped into the Suburban; the rest of us piled in behind him.

"Gotham Bank," he told Yasha. "Step on it."

"What is—" I started.

"The ghouls are back."

*   *   *

Moreau had called it in, and an NYPD cruiser was already on the scene, and clued-in officers were inside the bank.

Yasha pulled up in front, and Ian almost waited until he'd stopped before jumping out, with Moreau, Calvin, and Liz right behind him. I didn't want my partner going in without me, but I was neither a vampire nor a commando. I was a mere mortal who didn't want her face to have a close encounter with asphalt. Yasha jumped the curb with the Suburban just as I was about to get out, and I'd barely missed becoming a pancake. He slammed it into park, cut the engine, and was right behind me. The cops probably didn't have silver-infused bullets in their guns, but we did. And Yasha was wearing his long jacket, which hid about the only thing guaranteed to put down a ghoul—a machete.

Take their head and pretty much anything would stay down for good.

Once out of the Suburban, I almost caught up with Ian and the others. My legs were shorter than theirs, but I had the adrenaline to make up for it.

I felt the portal's pulse as soon as I crossed the bank's threshold. I felt it, but I couldn't tell what direction it was coming from. Except for us and the cops, the bank was empty. Odd that they'd still be closed after two days. Yes, there'd been a robbery, and yes, there'd been a murder, but this was a bank in Midtown Manhattan.

Richard Winthrop had told Ian he was locking himself in the vault. Either the call—or Winthrop—had been cut off before Ian could tell him not to go into the vault because that was how the ghouls had gotten in last time. Portals were equal-opportunity doorways—they could go anywhere at any time.

The portal didn't matter; at least it wasn't my first priority.

Ian was. Winthrop had told him he was going to the vault, so that's where my partner had gone.

"Follow me," I told Yasha.

I had my gun out, held low and ready, with every nerve, every sense wide open and on high alert.

None of this felt right.

A hollow boom vibrated the marble beneath our feet.

The vault. The vault closing. Winthrop was supposed to already be in the vault. That's what he'd told Ian. What if—

"Shit!" I spat, and charged through the lobby.

Yasha, bless him, didn't ask questions, just hefted his Desert Eagle in one hand and a machete in the other to back me up.

I slid to a stop on the marble floor in front of the massive fire doors, doors that had been open when we'd been here before. Doors that were now closed against Moreau, and an enraged Calvin and Liz.

Ian was on the other side. He'd only been a few steps ahead of us and had just stepped into a trap. Once he'd sprung that trap, it'd slammed shut, locking any hope of help outside.

That wasn't stopping Alain Moreau. He had actually gotten the tips of his fingers in the seam between the two doors, and I heard the metal groan.

Calvin ran to the security desk, and after some frantic searching at a control panel, found the right button and the doors slowly began to open. Moreau and Liz didn't wait. As soon as they had a slot big enough to squeeze through, they were inside. Yasha, Calvin, and I were right behind them.

The two cops who had been the first to arrive were sprawled on the floor in front of the now-closed vault door, their heads turned at impossible angles.

Whatever Ian had been lured into had already happened.

Screw quiet.

"Ian!"

Nothing.

There was nothing down here except the vault and the four small offices for clients to open their safe deposit boxes. All of the doors were open. Calvin and Liz checked them.

Empty.

We turned to the vault door.

Even with Moreau's strength and Yasha at full werewolf, we weren't getting inside. If there was a portal in there, Ian could already be gone.

The monitor behind the security desk flickered to life, showing the inside of the vault, and a scene from a nightmare.

Ian and Richard Winthrop were backed into a corner. My partner stood protectively in front of the banker, using his body as a shield between Winthrop and six ghouls.

The ghouls didn't make any move to attack. They didn't need to; they had Ian cornered. All they had to do was wait for their getaway portal—and their leader.

Winthrop shifted behind Ian—and blurred, becoming taller.

No.

"Ian!" I screamed in warning as the ghoul loomed behind him.

Everything seemed to move in slow motion. Ian sensing the ghoul and turning—both too late.

The ghoul wanted to see shock and then despair in Ian's eyes.

My partner didn't give him what he wanted.

He attacked.

He was trapped, he was outnumbered, rescue was impossible, but he was not going down without a fight.

Until one of the ghouls sprayed a green mist in his face, and my partner was out before he hit the floor.

The ghoul looked directly at the camera, flipped a switch on the wall next to the door, and watched with a smile as his ghouls carried an unconscious Ian through the portal. His smooth and otherworldly voice filled the room. "Checkmate, Agent Byrne." Then he looked directly at the camera. "And Agent Fraser." He started to step through the portal, but paused and turned back toward the camera. "I am certain you have many colorful and imaginative names for me, especially now, but for future reference, you may call me Janus."

The ghoul quickly followed his henchmen through the portal and closed it behind them. Yasha was standing at my side. I heard him inhale what had to have been half the air in the room. Even though I knew what was coming next and how loud it would be, I made no move to cover my ears. I wanted to hear it. As a human, I couldn't produce a sound even remotely close, so I stood silently, tears pooling in my eyes, and let Yasha's bone-chilling howl of desolation, anguish, and rage express what I couldn't, as I continued to stare at the security monitor showing a now-empty vault.

I tore my eyes away from the monitor, rage building to a level I knew I couldn't contain without losing what little control I had.

"Where is Winthrop?" I growled. "He called us into a trap. I want him." I didn't specify what I wanted him for and I didn't need to. I'd probably have to fight Yasha to get my hands on the little weasel first, but at the moment, I thought I'd win.

"Gone," Moreau said without expression.

I couldn't believe what I was hearing. "He called us and ran away?"

Moreau shook his head. "Gone as in dead. They ate him. What's left is in his office. I've called Dr. Van Daal to examine the remains for clues."

The ghoul had to be one happy monster right now. No, Janus. He'd said his name was Janus. He'd gotten what he'd come for in the robbery two nights ago, and he'd taken Ian, who he'd been wanting for years.

Yeah, Janus was one happy psycho.

I didn't even know where to start, but I would do everything in my power to wipe that smirk off his shapeshifting face, him off the earth, and get my partner back. I took out my phone, and tapped the name of the only woman I knew who could possibly help.

"Who?" Yasha asked.

"Kitty."

18

KITTY Poertner could open and close portals. Size didn't matter. She could operate a small portal that crossed meters or miles. I'd seen her close a portal to Hell itself. She'd had some help from Rake on that one, but Kitty had done all the heavy lifting herself.

Kitty was the best, and right now, the best was what we needed.

For over a thousand years, Kitty's family had been the supernatural world's doorkeepers, or to be more exact, portalkeepers. Her specialty was stabilizing and closing dimensional rifts.

Hellpits, thankfully, didn't open that often, so Kitty had a day job. She was a baker, the owner of Kitty's Confections on Bleecker Street in the West Village, and could bake an angel food cake that was reputed to have made actual angels weep. But as a baker and a witch, Kitty had a ton of bad karma to live down. Kitty's great-great-great-grandmother had lived in Germany's Black Forest and had made Hannibal Lecter look like a cannibalism amateur. She'd chow down on adults in a pinch, but she preferred children. She lured them in with sweets, most notably gingerbread.

Yep, she was *that* witch.

A cannibalistic child abductor was a heavy load on a family tree.

Moreau had offered to send a car for Kitty, but she'd refused, saying that she could get here faster by taking the subway. I didn't argue with her. We had a problem that had to be solved before she got here.

We needed to get into a locked vault.

Richard Winthrop was dead. Janus had taken his key card and had probably tortured the banker to get the keypad code. Though being a gutless weasel, Winthrop had probably just given it to him. And in yet another taunt from Janus, we could see on the monitor that the key card was on the table in the center of the vault.

Gotham Bank's president had one, but she wasn't here. She'd been on vacation in Bali when the robbery had happened, and was in the process of flying back. She was due back early this evening, doing us absolutely zero good.

And for the sprinkles on top, the bank's head of security was the one who'd died of a heart attack while being eaten the night of the robbery. His key card hadn't been found.

I glanced back at the monitor showing an empty vault and a key card on the table. When we finally got inside, we'd probably find the guard's key card underneath the vice president's.

It was like Janus had checked out of a hotel. Just leave your key card in the room. Most hotel guests just take the toiletries and maybe the towels. Janus had taken Ian. I had news for him—unlike the Ritz, SPI wasn't about to chalk that up to the cost of doing business.

Since it was obvious that no one was in the vault, the

NYPD was content to wait for the bank president's flight to land this evening.

I wasn't content and I certainly wasn't willing to wait. Every minute that passed allowed signs of that portal to fade, reducing the chances that Kitty could either reopen it or at least determine where it led. That portal was our only hope right now of tracking Ian—and saving him from the most horrible death imaginable.

"Who the hell is Janus?" I asked Moreau.

"I know the name as belonging to the Roman god of beginnings and ends, of time and transitions—and of doorways and passages both for this world and other universes."

"Portals."

Moreau nodded. "Janus is traditionally depicted as having two faces since he looks to both the future and past."

"I've got news, he has more than two faces."

"It may be a name that amuses him to use, or he may be connected in some way to the person in antiquity whom the Romans viewed as that god."

"A Roman god kidnapped Ian?"

"I suspect it is merely a name that he uses." Moreau was texting. "Though I will have our archivists compile a report with all that they have on the Roman god, or any individual in our database who is using or has used the name."

We smelled Kitty before we saw her, and Yasha's stomach growled in response to the scent of sugar and vanilla. Though the scent probably came from the shopping bag she carried.

She set it on the desk, took out the top box, opened it, and pushed it toward us.

Lemon-blueberry scones. Otherwise known as wedge-shaped bites of heaven itself.

"Eat," she told us. Her tone said she wasn't taking no for an answer; and to tell you the truth, I didn't want to give her one.

Yasha and I gratefully fell to. Even Alain Moreau looked like he was regretting his liquid diet.

"You need to keep your strength up," Kitty told us both. She glanced at the vault door. "Still don't have it open." She didn't ask it as a question. The vault couldn't be more inaccessible. She gave the bag with its boxed goodies to the one NYPD detective in the room. "I'm sure your officers would appreciate not having to miss lunch. It's just doughnuts and cookies, but—"

The detective took the bag. "You're an angel of mercy, ma'am. Thank you."

Kitty waited until he was gone. "Portals aren't all I can open," she said with a mischievous wink.

I danged near choked on my scone.

"I have an uncle who used his powers for profit," Kitty explained. "He's doing five to ten in Sing Sing."

"And you bribe police with doughnuts to go away," Yasha said, smiling.

Kitty shrugged. "Cliché, but whatever works. Personally, I prefer baking to burglary."

"Using your powers for good and not evil," I noted. "And we're grateful that you do." I finished the first scone. "Choking a ghoul to death will take energy." I started to reach for another then stopped, the scone I'd wolfed down now sitting like a rock in my stomach. Kitty's comfort food wasn't providing much by way of comfort.

Kitty Poertner opening a bank vault involved her standing directly in front of it, staring intently at the control panel, and munching thoughtfully on an iced gingerbread man cookie— beginning with the head.

Closing a portal to Hell had done wonders for Kitty's confidence—that and accepting the fact that she wasn't her cannibalistic three-greats grandma and never would be. In celebration of that psychological breakthrough, last

Christmas, Kitty had baked and built not just a gingerbread house, but an entire Victorian gingerbread village for her shop's front window.

The cops were going to be back any second, and Kitty was still in her own little world. I didn't want to interrupt any serious magical working, but time wasn't on our side.

"Kitty, can you—"

Click, whirl, and the massive vault door began to open. Dang.

Yasha and Moreau pushed the door the rest of the way open, as Kitty and I slipped inside.

I stopped at the table where Janus had left Winthrop's key card. Yep, there was another one directly underneath, the card belonging to the head security guard. Janus had gotten everything he wanted from the Gotham Bank, and didn't need keys to the vault anymore.

Kitty was standing in front of the wall where the portal had been. It'd been nearly an hour since Ian had been dragged unconscious through it.

I could barely sense it now. Hopefully, Kitty was getting more from it.

"Well?" I asked quietly.

"The first portal, the one from two nights ago, was somewhere else in the bank?"

"Yes." I didn't know where she was going with this.

Kitty nodded as if that was the response she expected. "This portal was intended for a one-time use."

I knew where she was going now, and I didn't like it.

"It's not like a pair of doors off a hallway. After they're closed, the hallway still exists. This was a temporary connection. This portal, the exit portal, and the hall, if you will, that connected them were one unit. When they went through this portal and out the other side, he collapsed everything behind him."

"There's no way to track where he's taken Ian?"

"None."

I wanted to cry, scream, and kick whatever was closest.

That wouldn't bring Ian back, and if I was going to do serious damage to a ghoul in the near future, I couldn't have any broken bones.

I knew what I had to do—calm down and think. I took a breath and exhaled with as much control as I could.

"So it wouldn't have made any difference if we'd gotten in here right after they took Ian."

"No," Kitty replied.

That didn't make me feel any better, but it did take some of the pain out of the guilt.

On the floor, right in front of the wall where the portal had been, was Ian's pendant. The chain was broken. I squatted to pick it up. It was wet. Not with blood from where it'd been torn from Ian's neck, but with water.

Kitty was casting a shadow across it.

"Kitty, take a step back," I told her.

She did, and I saw.

The floor was definitely wet. A puddle of wet. I quickly glanced around. There were wet footprints on the side of the vault where the ghouls had stood when they'd cornered Ian.

Yasha started to come closer.

I quickly held up a hand. "Stop. They left footprints."

Alain Moreau was just outside the vault, keeping anyone, namely the cops, from interrupting us.

"What kind of footprints?" he asked.

I knelt next to the closest puddle, bent over, and sniffed the water.

Salty, with an underlying, ripe organic smell.

I knew that scent.

Three days ago, I'd gone for an unwilling swim in the stuff, and had managed to swallow some of it.

River water. Hudson River water, to be exact.

"Sir, we need a sample of this water."

Yasha frowned in confusion. "Why would ghouls have wet feet?"

"Because I don't think they were ghouls."

"I don't understand."

I jumped up and dashed out of the vault to the security desk. "Sir, I need this recording sent to HQ, to Kenji," I told Moreau.

"What is it?"

"The connection between Báthory's kidnapping and the robberies." I jerked my head in the direction of the vault. "I'd bet my life the lab report on the water from those footprints will come back as coming from the Hudson River."

"You can smell it?"

"I took a bath in it the other night. I've got a couple more talents past seeing through wards and shields." I gave him a fierce little grin. "I've got nearly a hound-dog quality sniffer. It's river water, all right. And those ghouls were wearing glamours."

My manager didn't look convinced.

"When we get this surveillance footage back to Kenji, I'll be able to show you. I can see through glamours in person. No problem. On TV, or in this case, surveillance recording, it's not easy for me, but I can do it. I was concentrating on Ian, and when who I thought was Richard Winthrop started morphing into the ghoul, my attention went to him. But after finding all those wet footprints in there, I realized that those ghouls looked fuzzy to me on camera. I thought it was just crappy equipment, but Ian was perfectly clear. They weren't."

Moreau stared nodding. "They weren't ghouls."

"No, sir, they weren't. Once Kenji works his magic on that recording, I should be able to get confirmation on my theory."

"Which is?"

I looked at Yasha. "That Ian was carried through that portal by the same things that kidnapped Bela Báthory."

Yasha looked over my shoulder at the monitor. "Like *Creature from the Black Lagoon*?"

I nodded. "Yeah, except these are real."

I didn't want to leave the bank. On some level, I felt like I was leaving Ian behind. But Ian wasn't there anymore, and his kidnappers weren't coming back. They'd gotten everything they wanted, including my partner.

And I was going to get him back.

19

BY the time we got back to headquarters, everyone had been told what had happened to Ian, and how it had happened— inside a locked bank vault with Ian trapped with six ghouls who weren't ghouls, with everyone who could have helped locked out, and the portal long gone by the time we got inside.

I still felt guilty. There was nothing logical about how I felt. I guess that was why feelings had nothing to do with logic. I knew it wasn't my fault, that there was nothing I could have done to prevent it, but Ian was my partner, and partners took care of one another.

I'd failed.

There it was.

My partner had been in the ultimate danger, and I'd been helpless, powerless to do anything about it. I could only imagine how Calvin and Liz must be feeling. Heck, they were his bodyguards. It'd been their assignment to protect Ian, and in their opinion, they'd failed, too. It didn't matter that there were several tons of steel and concrete between them and who they'd been guarding.

I stopped. It was exactly how Ian must have felt when that ghoul had killed his partner. Ian had been in the same room, but he'd been fighting for his own life against three ghouls. There was nothing he could have done. I knew that wasn't how Ian saw it. He was a big guy, a strong guy, trained to protect and defend—and kill. Yet he'd been powerless to stop what had been happening to his partner.

It was that helplessness that had been eating Ian alive since then.

Eating alive.

Jeez, Mac. Where did that come from? I bit my bottom lip and closed my eyes against the emotion again trying to force its way up past my tight throat.

This does Ian no good. This does Ian no good.

Those five words were quickly becoming my mantra. And until they didn't keep me from breaking down into a crying heap, I'd keep repeating them. Prayers I'd already said and would keep saying, but those five words were the dam that was keeping the waterworks at bay.

The faces of the agents in the bull pen were grim, and I was told "we'll get him back" by more than a few. I know they meant it to be reassuring, they weren't saying that I'd failed, but to me, it was like a punch to the gut.

We'll get him back. *We* will do it.

I was the one who lost him, and dammit, *I* was going to get him back. I was a seer, not a soldier, but I was not going to be left out of this when the time came. And the time would come, and soon. I gave a tight nod to each agent who spoke those words to me, and kept going straight to Kenji's desk.

We would get Ian back, and I hoped and prayed I was right about finding the clue we needed.

I walked quickly past my and Ian's desks, not wanting to see his empty chair. I willed myself not to look and made a beeline straight for the IT department and Kenji Hayashi. I knew the elf would be at his desk, or his command center as everyone else called it. Kenji was literally at the center of SPI's worldwide communications web. He was only a keystroke away from every agent at SPI New York, and another few clicks from every SPI agency office around the world. While each office had a chief technology agent—Kenji's official title—no one had anyone like him. He was what every other SPI CTA wanted to be when they grew up.

If anyone could clean up and enhance that video to show me what I needed to see, it would be Kenji. I slid into an empty chair next to where he was already working intently on the bank surveillance tape.

"Please tell me you can do something with that." I paused. "Was someone sitting here?"

The elf never looked away from his monitors. "I had it waiting for you, honey."

"Thank you." It came out shaky. I couldn't help it. "Just don't ask me if I'm all right, or I'm liable to completely lose it right here in front of everybody."

"Duly noted."

I had no idea what it was about being asked if you were all right that suddenly made you anything but all right.

"No one blames you," Kenji said, eyes still glued to his monitor, fingers a blur on the keyboard.

"They don't have to, because I do."

"Then let's see what I can do to help you push it aside and do something about it."

I couldn't help it; I leaned over and pecked him on the cheek. "Great plan."

Kenji had zoomed in on the five ghouls. "Those are some ugly bastards."

"Wait till you see what they really look like."

"Display case," Kenji said. "Fourth shelf, second from the right."

I looked and there it was—the Creature from the Black Lagoon.

"How many movie monsters turn out to be real?" I asked.

"Entirely too many of them."

Kenji did some rapid-fire mouse clicking and the image magnification and resolution changed at the same too-fast-for-me rate. I had to look away until it'd finished.

"Is that what you were expecting to see?" he asked me.

I opened my eyes, and leaned closer, though I didn't need to. I could see it just fine, and it was beautiful.

Waves of pixilation.

"High-five yourself, darlin'," I told him. "You did it."

Kenji grinned and held up his non-mouse hand. "How about you help?"

I returned his grin and the high five.

"Can you pull some stills from the Diamond Mart case?" I asked him.

A couple of months ago, there'd been a robbery at a Forty-seventh Street gem dealer, where trolls glamoured as three wealthy women had walked out with half a million dollars' worth of rare, colored diamonds. It was my first experience seeing glamoured supernaturals on surveillance cameras. In that case, the proof had turned out to be in the pixilation.

"Already done," Kenji told me. "Now let's download some of these pretty pictures to take to your meeting."

I had more than pixelated photos of Fomorians disguised as ghouls for show and tell. With Ian not here, it was my responsibility to make sure that Alain Moreau knew what we'd already found out. As the senior agent, Ian was responsible for sending reports to Moreau on any investigations we did together. More than once, I'd seen Ian putting together those reports at the last minute. Now, not only had he been kidnapped in the middle of the case, Ian was somehow critical to the villain's evil master plan.

That was a first. So was me making sure Moreau was up to speed on what we'd discovered.

I caught up with our manager outside of the conference room.

I broke into a jog to catch up. "Sir, a quick word."

"Yes, Agent Fraser?"

"I don't know if Ian had a chance to update you on our findings. Did he send you a report about meeting with some of the Hudson River's merfolk?"

"No."

"Uh, how about talking to one of Ambrus Báthory's chief bodyguards?"

His expression darkened. "Also, no."

Oh boy.

"Though it appears the two of you have been busy," he added.

"Yes, sir, we have."

"Perhaps you should tell me what you and Agent Byrne learned."

"Yes, sir."

I told him about the merfolk witnessing the kidnapping; that initially, Bela had been taken farther up the Hudson; and when the merfolk went to investigate, they discovered the pair of hydras guarding the passage upriver at Yonkers. Then I quickly summarized the meeting with Vlad Cervenka, his theory on why Bela had been taken, and his promise to try to get more information for us.

Moreau was silent for a few moments once I'd finished.

"I'm sorry about the delay, sir. Ian always does—"

Moreau raised his hand to stop me. "I am aware that **Agent Byrne** always does the reports for your joint investigations. What you learned would not have prevented his abduction. However, it could be invaluable to our impending discussion. I want you to include what you just told me in your presentation."

Presentation?

"Sir, I—"

"Ian's bloodwork came back from the lab."

Those words stopped my protest in its tracks. "What's wrong with Ian?"

"I didn't say anything was—"

"You didn't need to. What did that spearhead do to him?"

"We believe the readings Dr. Stephens is getting are due to the spearhead awakening something latent in Agent Byrne's physiology. Traits that his ancestors possessed, but that have decreased with each subsequent generation. Decreased, but still present. Touching that spearhead simply activated it."

"Activated what?"

"Contact with the spearhead didn't damage or injure Ian in any way. He's perfectly healthy—just different from what qualifies as healthy for humans."

"Are you saying Ian's not human anymore?"

"He's still human, only now he's something more."

20

ALAIN Moreau was running the meeting, but right now, I was doing the presenting.

It was one of the most difficult things I'd ever done.

Not only was my partner in the hands of his worst enemy, he wasn't entirely human anymore.

I did what I had to do: I pushed those thoughts out of my mind and put my full concentration into doing my job.

Finding Ian.

Our top agent having been kidnapped by our top suspect in two major cases was cause for all hands on deck.

Moreau was here, of course, along with Sandra Niles and Roy Benoit, the commanders of SPI's two quick-strike commando units. Since Moreau knew better than to even try to keep Yasha out of the loop now, our werewolf driver was there as well, leaning against the wall next to the door. There were plenty of seats, but either Yasha felt that precious seconds would be lost if he was sitting down when the call came in with Ian's location, or he didn't feel comfortable with all the department bigwigs. It was probably both.

Normally, I'd have felt the same way, but I'd just successfully connected the robberies to the kidnappings, both Ian and Bela Báthory's. I was a hound on a scent, and that scent had been literal when it came to those wet footprints in the vault. The lab had just confirmed that the scales found in the Gotham Bank vault were the same as those at the New York Public Library.

I now had the makings of a trail to follow, and no one—I didn't care how big their office was or how many people reported to them—was going to take me off of it.

My job wasn't to convince anyone in the room. Alain Moreau was convinced, and SPI wasn't a democracy; no voting would happen here.

What we were doing was more along the line of a think tank. Putting the facts as we knew them and theories as we perceived them together in an attempt to find Ian. At least that was my first priority. It was becoming apparent that Ian's kidnapping was only part of a much bigger picture. As little as I liked it—and I didn't—Ian's abduction was a piece in an increasingly large puzzle, and it might take fitting other pieces together first before we could determine where Ian was being held.

Amelia Chandler had heard back from her contact at the University of Dublin. He had positively identified the creatures from Noel Tierney's drawings of Ian's dreams as Fomorians. However, Amelia neither identified the artist as Noel or the source as Ian, because Moreau hadn't provided her with that information. Like my ability to see portals, that information was being kept on an as-needed-to-know basis. And for whatever reason, Alain Moreau didn't want SPI's best and brightest minds to know about Ian's reaction to the spearhead and his dreams as the source of the Fomorian connection. Moreau didn't know what it all meant, and anything he said would be mere speculation at this point. Mainly he and Vivienne Sagadraco kept their agents' secrets until they didn't need to be secret anymore.

Moreau had the most analytical mind of anyone I'd ever met. I trusted his discretion, and I also trusted him to be able to realize if that information would be useful in determining where Ian had been taken. That Ian's dreams had been triggered by his first encounter with Janus, and that he had left the spearhead specifically for Ian, told me that connection was going to be critical to not only determining Janus's interest in my partner but also finding and rescuing him. Yes, this meeting was a think tank, but Alain Moreau was a one-man brain trust.

"Agent Byrne's abductor has identified himself as Janus," Amelia Chandler was saying. "Our records have a few individuals with that name, or who use that alias. Unfortunately, they have all been eliminated as potential suspects. We believe he may be using the name due to his identification with some of the qualities of the Roman god Janus. We're examining these for clues as to this individual's true identity. Janus is considered a god of motion and transitions. Due to this double nature, he is symbolized with a two-headed image in coins, temples, etc. Our Janus could be relating this to his own multi-facial, shapeshifting nature. To the Romans, Janus represented time because he could see into the past with one face and the future with the other. Being the god of transitions, his visage was often found depicted over gates and doorways. This could also relate to this creature's mastery of portals and disguises."

She stepped aside from the podium, taking a small remote with her.

"This Janus's allies are the Fomorians, an ancient supernatural race in Irish mythology." Pictures of both Noel's drawings and book illustrations flashed on the screen behind her. The last one was the black lagoon creature. Logically, she kept that one up there since those were the ones we'd most likely encounter.

"Though like many mythological beings," she continued, "the Fomorians did exist, and as recent events have proven, they still do. In terms of power, they are in the demigod range. They are often portrayed as monsters or demons who come from under the sea. They are the enemies of the Tuatha Dé Danann, another real-life, Irish supernatural race with godlike powers. In the Second Battle of Magh Tuireadh, the Tuatha Dé Danann fought and defeated the Fomorians and drove them back into the sea. That was approximately four thousand years ago. They have not been seen or heard from since—until now."

Amelia had made no mention of the spearhead, and Harald Siggurson, SPI's bladed weapons expert, wasn't even in the meeting. I guess Moreau wasn't ready to take the spearhead public, even within SPI.

Moreau stepped forward. "Whenever a new or seldom-seen supernatural being is spotted anywhere in the world, SPI's procedure is to file a report so that the entire agency can be notified in case of an emerging pattern. That is precisely what we have here. During the past week, there have been sightings from our own people as well as by civilians of 'sea monsters.' Those sightings by civilians are seldom reported except on conspiracy, UFO/alien, and monster websites and chat rooms. However, we have agents who monitor those sites—"

"Poor bastards," Roy muttered.

"To separate actual encounters from overactive imaginations," Moreau continued. "There have been entirely too many actual encounters. Four days ago, a wave caused by a breaching kraken nearly swamped a cruise ship in the Bahamas. There was a storm in the area, so the media is blaming that for the wave. Last week, a fleet of Russian fishing trawlers vanished in the Sea of Okhotsk in the northwestern Pacific in calm waters and clear skies. Only one distress call was made which reported a creature several stories above the water, taking boats and breaking them in half. This report was intercepted by Eielson Air Force Base in Fairbanks, and fortunately was not obtained by the media. From the description, a kaiju is the assumed culprit."

"Kaiju?" someone asked.

"Like Godzilla," Roy replied.

"Two days ago, contact was lost with an American nuclear sub near the Mariana Trench in the southwestern Pacific," Moreau continued. "A pair of fishing boats from the Philippines reported multiple large waves in the immediate area. Again the seas were previously calm with no storms, and no report of seismic activity in the area. Sightings of large creatures of unknown origin were reported last night by a research vessel off the coast of Peru, and this morning from an oil platform in the North Sea close to Scotland."

"Agent Fraser had a personal kraken encounter three nights ago while a guest on Bela Báthory's yacht," Moreau said.

That earned me some looks.

I would have jumped in then to say I'd been on a date, but that date had been with Rake Danescu, who, to many here, didn't rate much higher than the ghoul-eaten nephew of a vampire crime lord. In any case, Alain didn't give me a chance.

"Agent Fraser, if you will tell everyone what you and Agent Byrne have learned."

I stood and, since Kenji had provided me with visual aids, went to the front of the room. The only good thing about giving a presentation was that holding the remote gave me something to do with my hands.

In addition to relaying what Ian and I had learned from the merfolk and the meeting with Vlad, I presented the evidence that connected Bela Báthory's kidnapping and murder to the bank robberies—and to Ian's abduction. But the information on Ian's role in all this was scattered all over the place, and I had yet to be able to see the pattern. I prayed someone else could see the picture in what few puzzle pieces we did have, though up the Hudson was looking like the most likely destination for Ian's Fomorian kidnappers.

"Hydras in Yonkers?" Sandra Niles was having a difficult time wrapping her head around that one. She wasn't the only one. "There haven't been any sightings, of hydras or a kraken, either by our own people or the public."

I resisted the urge to shrug, that wouldn't look very professional. "The merfolk hadn't been able to investigate further and the hydras were the reason they gave."

Sandra turned to Moreau. "Permission to arrange for a sonar scan of the area."

"Granted. Extend the search farther up the river."

"How far?"

"Until you find the next set of guards."

Roy Benoit leaned back in his chair. "If these Fomorians need to keep to salt water, the Hudson is only brackish up to Troy. If they can't be out of the water for very long, they can't get out that way. The only exit to the ocean is back out through New York Harbor. They've boxed themselves in, so they must have a good reason. Why the Hudson? And what's in those vampire safe deposit boxes that a bunch of sea monsters want? Most of all, why Ian?"

"This morning I received word that there have been similar robberies in several European cities," Moreau said. "Budapest was first, followed by Vienna, then Prague and Paris. The robbers were not seen on surveillance, and their mode of entry and exit was the same as we have had here: a portal."

"Safe deposit boxes belonging to old vampire families?" I asked.

Moreau nodded. "And as we are experiencing here, the victims have refused to cooperate with authorities, either SPI or mortal law enforcement. Some have even denied owning the boxes in question."

"Why the hell would they do that?" Roy asked. "If they put it in a bank, you'd think they'd want it back."

"Unknown. But if I had to hazard a guess, it would be that the contents were something so valuable to them that they couldn't risk keeping it close to them."

"Don't they trust their own people?"

Moreau gave us a half smile. "No, they don't. When the potential is there to live as long as vampires, those in power in these families could remain there for centuries. Even for a near-immortal, that is a long time to have to wait for a change in the ruling class."

Sandra snorted. "Like getting a crappy president and having to keep them for four centuries instead of just four years."

Another smile. "An accurate comparison. And the possibility is there with vampires for that individual to remain in power for even longer."

I sensed the warm weight of Ian's pendant beneath my shirt. I'd fixed the chain, and it was now hanging around my neck. I knew where I needed to go next, and who I was going to ask to get me there.

I had one stop to make first.

*   *   *

I told Alain Moreau where I was going, what I would be doing, and who would be going with me. I didn't know if I'd be able to use Ian's pendant to contact the merfolk, but I wouldn't know until I tried. If it didn't work, maybe the mermaid would talk to me anyway. Ian had used some sort of telepathy with them. I hadn't been able to hear what was said, but I had a little telepathic talent myself. Mine was with dragons, but maybe I'd get lucky and there'd be some crossover there somewhere.

I didn't tell Rake what had happened with Ian over the phone; some things simply needed to be done in person. Not because Rake would be upset, but because I needed to see his reaction. I knew he and Ian didn't like each other, and I was the reason, or at least the main reason. Rake's reaction to Ian being kidnapped by ghouls who were actually Fomorians could be what was called a deal breaker. In fact, it was potentially the biggest deal breaker I could possibly think of.

Rake said he would meet me in one hour at the midtown marina where he kept his boat. That gave me a little time for an interoffice detour.

Jenny Greene worked in SPI's HR department, though technically it was HSR (Human and Supernatural Resources). Jenny looked human to everyone else, but I knew she was a river hag, though "water spirit" was the more politically correct term. River hags looked almost human anyway—that is if you took a human, made her skin the color of the Wicked Witch of the West, and exchanged dental work with a piranha. I always thought they had to live in a body of water. Turned out any size body would do, and I'd been told that SPI had a pool in the basement for its water-dwelling employees to use during breaks.

Jenny had relatives that lived on the Hudson River, *north* of Yonkers. Water spirits were seriously family oriented, almost as much as dryads. When your primary habitat was one river or one forest, you tended to be pretty tight with your relatives. If her family had seen anything out of the ordinary, like a kraken or hydras, Jenny would know about it. Rule number one in solving a case and getting a good story—talk to the locals.

Jenny met me at the door to the HSR department with a big hug and tears in her river green eyes. So much for if she'd heard what had happened to Ian.

"Oh, Makenna, I am so sorry to hear what happened to Ian. We'll get him back."

"Yes, *we* most certainly will. In fact, you just might be able to help."

"I'll do anything I can."

"Where exactly does your family live on the Hudson?"

"Near Croton Point Park."

"How far north of Yonkers is that?"

"About twenty-five miles. Why?"

"Upriver from Yonkers is where the Fomorians have been taking their prisoners."

Jenny blanched. "Fomorians?"

"You've heard of them?"

"My people came from the River Shannon in Ireland. I know the stories. That's what took Ian?"

"We're almost certain."

She flashed a fierce smile full of dainty fangs that'd always reminded me of pushpins. Teeth that were at odds with her perpetual uniform of sweater set, skirt, and pearls.

"I'll call my aunt Shirley. She's the family busybody. She's also a troll."

I blinked.

"Related by marriage, dear. My uncle Pat has always been

the adventuresome sort. No one was shocked in the least when he brought a troll home to dinner. He and Shirley moved to Bear Mountain to be near her people. That's about forty miles up the Hudson from Yonkers. Her family has lived under the Bear Mountain Bridge for close to two hundred and fifty years. No one gets past without being noticed."

21

I had good irons in the fire. Yasha was going to check in with Vlad for an update. Jenny was tapping her family network. I was about to try to get an audience with the local merqueen.

But first, I needed to tell Rake that Ian had been kidnapped, and I was going to do it without crying. I hadn't cried yet, and I didn't have time to do it now. You cried at funerals, not search and rescues—and that's what this was going to be. I was going to find my partner and bring him home—alive and whole. For now, Ian was still both. I just had a feeling in my gut that didn't have a thing to do with either wishful thinking or the cheeseburger I'd made myself eat before leaving headquarters. Like Kitty had said, I had to keep my strength up. Not eating was not an option.

Yasha was driving me to the marina. He did not like the fact that I'd be going out on the river alone with Rake. Apparently it didn't matter that I'd been seeing Rake for months without a chaperone, let alone a bodyguard. But I knew what

Yasha was feeling. When it came to Rake, Ian was the self-appointed big brother. With Ian gone . . . no, with Ian not here right now, Yasha was taking on that responsibility. Fortunately, he realized how important touching base again with Vlad was, or I'd have had one heck of an argument on my hands.

I was riding shotgun—Ian's usual spot in the front seat. I glanced over at Yasha's big hands on the wheel, hands that were now hairier than they should have been for this time of the month. The full moon wasn't for another two days, but as we'd discovered last year when we were racing the clock to keep the supernatural community in the tristate area alive—including Yasha—our werewolf friend had started going wolf a wee bit earlier than scheduled. Normal people broke out in hives when they got nervous; werewolves broke out in fur and fangs. That night, we'd all had to depend on Rake and his boat to get us to our destination to save our little corner of the world. Rake hadn't liked having a changing werewolf on his boat. I couldn't really blame him, especially since Yasha didn't like Rake.

We arrived at the marina. Rake was waiting, and I knew Yasha was going to stay right where he was until we were safely in the boat—though "safe" and "in the boat" was an oxymoron right now with a kraken lurking somewhere in the Hudson River. I didn't try to dissuade him; I understood and appreciated it.

"I've got my phone," I assured my big, and really hairy now, Russian friend. "And it's in a waterproof pouch. I promise I'll call if we're attacked."

"Have you—"

"Yes, I've taken my Dramamine."

We sat there in silence, looking at each other.

"Yasha?"

"*Da?*"

"We're going to get him back."

His big shoulders sagged a little. *"Da."* He took a breath, let it out, and set his jaw. *"Da*, and we will make those who took him pay."

"Damn straight." I leaned across the console and gave him a big hug and a kiss on his hairy cheek. I got out of the Suburban, closed the door, then turned back to Yasha and bared my teeth in a fierce grin. "And when we find out where he is, sharpen your claws, darlin', cause we're goin' huntin'."

"I would ask what was that all about," Rake began, "but I heard some of it. However, lacking context, I'm confused."

"You eavesdropped."

"I'm a goblin, it's instinct; and these ears aren't here just to look good."

I kept walking past him down the dock to where the sleek, black speedboat was tied. Rake had to jog a little to catch up. He knew something was wrong, but I didn't want to tell him until we were out on the water—or at least until Yasha was gone.

"We're burning daylight," I said. "I don't want to be out there after dark if I can help it."

"Understood." His tone told me that was all he understood, but he knew me well enough to know when to push it and when to back off. This was the latter.

What I'd rehearsed in the Suburban on the way here had sounded so good in my head: calm, professional, and it even included questions for Rake that might point us in the right direction. Now, motoring slowly out of the slip and into the river with the sun casting a glow over the water, my head emptied and my eyes filled.

Aw jeez. Not now. I don't want to do this.

I was sitting in my favorite seat near the bow. Rake was at the wheel several feet behind me. The motor provided just enough noise to block any sound. I could cry quietly, get it out, get it over with, and then the wind would dry my eyes and face, or I could blame my red eyes on the wind and pollen.

It could work.

My tear ducts didn't care whether it would work or not, they were going into full production, and they were going to do it now.

I bit my bottom lip, and let it go.

I tried to be quiet, and I tried harder to stay perfectly still, but apparently trying and succeeding were two entirely different things.

The boat settled in the water as the engine was cut, and I heard the rattle of the anchor going over the side as Rake took me in his arms and held me.

I needed that, but I did *not* need that.

Crying turned into racking sobs.

Rake simply held me tighter.

Just when I thought I was finished . . . I wasn't. I had no clue where my tear ducts were getting all that water from. Apparently I had a lot of pent-up emotion. I finally had to quit crying because I couldn't breathe.

Oh no, my nose was running. I wasn't letting Rake see that.

I frantically dug in my purse and came out with one of those little purse pack thingies of tissues. There were only two left. That wasn't even going to get me started.

"Please tell me you have Kleenex." I barely got the words out through my stuffy nose.

Like a magician pulling a rabbit from a hat, Rake produced a full box. He hadn't even moved. Dating a mage had its advantages.

"Thank you." I turned away from him and blew my nose. Eww. "Do you have a trash bag?"

Rake instantly produced one of those, too.

"High maintenance, aren't I?"

"I can manage."

Remaining turned into the glorious sunset, I blew my nose until it wouldn't blow anymore. Then I dried my hands, and as an afterthought, dug my little bottle of hand sanitizer out of the bottom of my purse. *That* I half turned and let Rake see me do.

I turned toward him with a sniff and apologetic smile. "The mystery's gone, huh?"

"Mystery is overrated," Rake said, pulling me back against his chest, resting his chin on the top of my head. I took a breath, my first good one since however long it'd been since the dam had broken.

Rake pulled back just enough to look down at my face. "Alain called earlier and told me about Ian. You don't need to tell me a thing."

And cue the waterworks, though thankfully, it was now only two tears. Probably the last two I had left. It was a wonder I hadn't shriveled up from dehydration. I tried to swallow, but even my spit was gone. All that water had to come from somewhere.

"I've got drinks," Rake said. "Though I will have to get up to get them."

I gave a single, raspy laugh. "I'm not going anywhere."

"Good."

Rake went to the bench seat at the rear of the boat, lifted up a portion of it and pulled a plastic bottle and a can out of the built-in cooler. "Water or ginger ale?"

"Yes."

"As my lady wants."

I popped the top on the ginger ale and went to take a big swig. I stopped myself just before I did.

"Go easy on that stuff," said Ian's voice in my head. *"You're gonna give yourself the hiccups."*

I closed my eyes and pressed my lips together.

"Are you—"

I raised my hand against Rake finishing *that* sentence. Those four little words were guaranteed to send any woman on the verge of tears right over the edge: "Are you all right?" I had work to do, a partner to save. My crying was done.

"I'm fine. Better than fine. Good." I looked up at Rake. "Thank you. I needed that. I didn't want to do it, but I needed it."

Normally, Rake would have done a mocking half bow and said something like: "Always a pleasure to be of service, my dearest Makenna" with a sly emphasis on "pleasure" and "service."

Not this time.

"I'm glad I was here to help," he said, his voice low and soft. "And I'm even more grateful and honored that you let me. It is I who should be thanking you."

That nearly made me misty again, but not in a bad way. I gave him a shaky smile. "You mean that."

"Every last word. I wouldn't have said it if I didn't mean it."

I was vulnerable; in fact, I don't think I'd ever been more vulnerable in my life. Rake had given me what I'd desperately needed, but he hadn't pushed, he hadn't done or said anything to take advantage of the situation. He'd simply been honest. For the first time since I'd met him, I believed what Rake had said, no questions, no doubts. It was a new feeling for me, and I liked it. I liked it a lot.

Rake was standing at the wheel; I was still sitting on the other side. Only the console was between us.

I could work with that.

I turned toward him, brought my legs up on the cushion, and rose up on my knees . . .

. . . and kissed Rake Danescu.

It was tentative, it was soft, and with the boat rolling beneath us, it was also kinda dangerous to our noses.

I felt like living dangerously.

Moments later, the rolling turned to pitching with the wake of a passing tour boat, and sure enough, I whapped my nose on Rake's chin.

"Ow."

"I've had better reactions," Rake said as I held my nose and hoped it wasn't bleeding. "Though all things considered, I'll take it."

I looked up to a big, and actually goofy, grin on Rake's face.

I felt a smile coming on. "Maybe we should put this off until there's terra firma under our feet."

"Not fun, but probably wise." His dark eyes twinkled. "I'm going to hold you to that, you know."

I met his gaze. "I know. And like yourself, I wouldn't have said it if I didn't mean it."

The wind had a chill, and I glanced to the horizon. The sun was farther down than was comfortable, considering what had happened the last time Rake and I were out on the Hudson after dark.

"We better get a move on," I said.

"Agreed."

Rake reeled in the anchor and got the boat back under way.

"I also talked to Alain about helping to find Ian," he said as we passed the Intrepid Sea, Air & Space Museum. "I have contacts that SPI does not."

He didn't need to elaborate on that. I knew what he meant. Being a goblin and a dark mage, and doing business outside of what mortal and supernatural law allowed, Rake

THE GHOUL VENDETTA 163

knew a whole other world existed within our own, with its own rules and justice. In his work for goblin intelligence, Rake spent a lot of time there with the locals. If the Fomorians were working with Janus, some of Rake's contacts had to know about it, maybe even know where they were and what they were up to. To do business there and make deals required a willingness to break the rules or at least bend them until they squealed.

It wasn't how SPI or Alain Moreau did business—at least until now.

"What did Moreau say?"

Rake grinned crookedly. "He is willing to accept any information that I might procure."

Late last year, Vivienne Sagadraco read Rake the riot act about keeping secrets that would get her people killed. Rake had been more forthcoming since then, though he still had plenty of secrets. Goblins hoarded them like gold, and Rake was a billionaire in more ways than one.

"Sounds like Moreau." I paused. "What have you found out?"

"The heads of the vampire families who have been robbed are raising the drawbridges, so to speak. They're not venturing out, and if you're not among their most trusted, you're being kicked outside the gates."

Crap. I wanted Ambrus Báthory to trust Vlad enough to keep him inside with him; but at the same time, if he was inside he might not be able to get information outside. Yasha would find out one way or the other.

"At the same time, they're mobilizing the troops, and it's not to protect the heads of the Houses. It looks more like they're forming retrieval teams. They're determined to get back what's theirs."

I nodded grimly. "Sounds like a plan I can get behind. I take it they don't have a target location yet?"

"No, but they've got every ear to the ground. If one family finds out, they all will, and when they do, that target is going to get crowded."

"Crowds are fine, just as long as we're part of it and get back what's ours, too."

22

THEY say there's nothing like a good cry. I say there's nothing like a good cry followed by a better kiss. I didn't know who "they" were, or if they'd ever had their partner stolen by an obsessive and sadistic ghoul and his sea monster allies, but my head was clear, I could think, and I was ready to do whatever was necessary to get Ian back. Not that I hadn't been ready before, but I now had an almost calm determination, and it felt good.

Our destination was the spot where Ian had contacted the merfolk two nights before. I was sitting next to Rake as he steered the boat upriver. The streets weren't Manhattan's only high-traffic area. On a warm evening, the Hudson had more than its fair share. So while Rake's boat had the speed to get us to the northernmost tip of Manhattan quickly, traffic slowed us down. On the upside, we could hear well enough to talk.

Now that my head was clear, I could think, and with thinking came questions. While very little about anything that had happened made sense, one thing made even less sense than the others.

"Why wait until now to take Ian?" I asked Rake. "It's been years since that night in the jewelry shop. If this thing is as old and as powerful as we believe, then why wait this long to finish what he started with Ian?"

"I don't mean to trivialize this, darling, but I have encountered more than my share of evil individuals, both mortal and immortal. Their schedules are usually quite full. Apparently villainy—when you truly commit to it—is time consuming."

"Okay, I can see where all that plotting, and scheming, and betraying could fill up your day, but the Fomorians in that vault took orders from him, meaning he also had more than a minor role in kidnapping Bela Báthory. He's already busy. To risk coming *back* to that bank, through the steel, concrete, and bespelled wall of a vault . . ." I let that hang there for a few seconds. "Kitty said it took some major league effort to open a portal there. And then he lured Ian in, even knowing that he'd likely arrive with plenty of backup. I'm just saying that if I were carrying out some evil master plan that was hundreds, maybe thousands of years in the making, I'd hold off on any personal vendetta until I'd taken care of the official business."

"That sounds reasonable," Rake conceded. "What's your theory?"

"That taking Ian was necessary to whatever this plan of his is." I paused. "Meaning Ian is still alive because Janus needs him." I resisted the urge to kick something, mainly because everything around me belonged to Rake and was outrageously expensive. "We really need to find out who this guy is. Do you know of any things that are thousands of years old and can change appearance like the rest of us change clothes?"

"On this world, the longest lived beings are dragons, and

while they can glamour and have been known to be fond of human flesh, they aren't known shapeshifters."

"How about your world?"

"Our dragons aren't as large as the ones here, and true immortality hasn't been attained. However, people have been known to live extremely long lives while under the influence of certain objects of power. There was a goblin who had lived over a thousand years, and would have lived longer had he not severely misbehaved and angered the wrong people, one of whom drained the life from his body, leaving him a dried husk. Good riddance."

When we got close to where Ian had made contact with the merpeople, Rake cut the engine and let the tide pull us in the rest of the way. Then he dropped two anchors, one at the bow, the second off the stern. I hoped neither hit any merfolk on the way down, but I imagined they had plenty of experience getting out of the way of falling anchors. Hopefully.

"Sorry," I whispered over the side.

I pulled the chain and pendant from under my shirt and over my head, then looked around for the best place to try to make contact.

Rake had the bench seat open at the back of the boat, and was rummaging around inside. He came up with some kind of floatation device on a stout rope.

He held it out to me. "Put this on."

"I'm not going swimming."

"I didn't say it'd be your idea."

I quickly stepped back from the side. "Good point. Just because the Fomorians seem to have gotten everything they wanted, doesn't mean they can't still be around here."

I wondered if merfolk and Fomorians were like dolphins and sharks. If you saw dolphins, there weren't any sharks nearby. Just because I didn't see any Fomorians didn't mean they weren't there, and the only way I'd know if the merfolk were nearby would be to call them—if they answered. I glanced down at the pendant. If it had just as much to do with the person doing the dipping as it did the pendant itself, we were screwed.

"So if a Fomorian or a kraken grabs me, you'll play tug-of-war with them."

Rake grinned in a flash of teeth. He held the rope in his now glowing hands. "I won't be playing. Plus, I've got a nasty surprise if they try to take what's mine."

I didn't quite know what to say to that. Under normal circumstances, I would have had a comeback ready to let fly. Right now I was concerned about free-range kraken and non-communicative merfolk. I turned my attention back to the water over the side of the boat—that is, after I'd put on Rake's life-jacket-on-a-rope.

Ian had never spoken after he'd submerged the pendant in the water, so I did the same. I'd never asked whether he mentally did anything to call them. Right now, I just hoped the pendant would enable me to speak mind-to-mind with a mermaid as it did with Ian. If not, we were pretty much screwed.

I decided to go with "I'm Ian's friend, he's in trouble, and I really need your help."

Minutes passed, and my arm was staring to go numb from lack of circulation. The way I was leaning over the side wasn't the most comfortable position, but I wanted to keep as much of me as possible inside the boat.

"How long has it been?" I asked Rake in a bare whisper.

He glanced down at his watch. "Five and a half minutes."

"That's all?" I let my shoulder sag. "It took Ian less than a minute." I had a thought. "Could merfolk be afraid of goblins?"

Rake gave me a flat look.

"Sorry, but there's a lot of people who have problems with fangs."

His dark eyes glittered. "Do you?" he asked playfully.

"They're teeth, I'm not afraid of teeth."

The corner of his mouth kicked up a little. "It's all in how you use them." Suddenly the smile vanished, and his eyes went to a point beyond my shoulder. "Tail fin, twenty yards."

By the time I turned, it was gone, but the ripples were still there. I went back to projecting my thought message and leaned out a little farther. I trusted Rake's goblin eyes to be able to distinguish a mermaid from a Creature from the Black Lagoon.

Less than a minute later, the same mermaid Ian had "spoken" with two nights ago surfaced just beyond where the pendant dipped into the water. She glanced past me at Rake, her dark eyes regarding him with steady suspicion.

"I'll be over there," he said.

I kept my eyes on the mermaid. "I don't know how to talk to you. Can you understand me?"

The mermaid's lips curved in a kind smile as she held up a webbed-fingered hand with a questioning expression. She wanted to touch my hand like she had done with Ian. I nodded once, and she drifted closer, placing her green hand over mine.

The contact was immediate, though not jarring or invasive. I recalled everything that had happened with and to Ian since the last time we'd come here.

The mermaid's eyes went wide, and the gills on either side of her throat fluttered as if her breathing had quickened. She let go of my hand and submerged with a splash, and even I could see the wake she left as she sped away.

I plopped down on the seat behind me. "That could've gone better."

"What did you say?" Rake asked.

"I showed her what happened to Ian with my memories, and that the same things that took Bela Báthory also took Ian." I looked out over the now calm water. There was no sign that the mermaid had ever been here, or was coming back.

"Either I scared her away, or she got the message. Either way, we need to wait."

Rake smiled and lifted a padded bag he'd brought on board with us. "Then it's a good thing I brought sandwiches for us." He unzipped the bag. "While we wait, we can eat."

Naturally, the mermaid returned when I had a mouthful of turkey on whole wheat. I nearly choked when her green-haired head popped up over the side. She held on to the side of the boat with one hand, and beckoned us with the other then pointed out toward the middle of the river.

I nodded to her as I hurriedly rewrapped my sandwich. "I think we've just received a royal summons."

Rake started the boat and we followed at a good clip. One thing about merfolk was similar to dolphins—their speed. The mermaid could swim as fast as a dolphin. She would breach the surface occasionally to allow Rake to see her, then dive and speed off again.

The last time, Queen Sirene had come to us. This time, we were being led to where she was. I wondered if the presence of the Fomorians had forced them to move to a safer location. If there was a hungry kraken swimming around my neighborhood, I'd make myself scarce. The mermaid led us around the northern point of Inwood Hill Park, under the Henry Hudson Bridge and into the Spuyten Duyvil Creek. It was definitely shallower here. Maybe the merfolk's reasoning was that a kraken couldn't fit here.

It was now fully dark.

Rake had to slow the boat, and the mermaid surfaced and indicated that we wait. Rake anchored and we did. I wanted to finish my sandwich, but I wasn't about to be caught with my mouth full when the queen arrived.

When she surfaced a few minutes later, she looked disheveled and her majesty was not amused. Hopefully that was directed at the cause of the dishevelment, and not at our visit.

I remembered that Ian had bowed his head before the queen had approached him. I did the same, but since this lady didn't know me from Adam's house cat, I left my head down a little longer. Hopefully that was considered merfolk good manners.

Sirene swam closer, but not close enough for contact.

"Narema told me of Ian's plight," she said.

"Oh, thank God, you can talk."

"Yes, I can speak as you do. It is not easy, but it is important that we understand each other since I assume that you will be taking my words back to others."

"Yes, I will."

"For our safety, we were forced to come here. I would usually lead my people to the open ocean, but it is blocked by more of the Old Ones."

"Fomorians?"

"That is a name I do not know."

"The kraken with many tentacles, hydra with many heads, and men with scales and webbed fingers and feet."

"Those are a few of the Old Ones."

"Few? There are more?"

"Many more, many larger."

That was not good news.

"Upriver is not safe. Our path to the ocean is blocked. We must remain here until the danger has gone. All sea creatures are frightened. The Old Ones that have not been seen in many generations are coming up from the deep places. Rather than feeding and then returning to the depths, they are remaining close to the surface, hunting with impunity."

"Impunity?"

"They are forbidden to swim the oceans' upper reaches. Some are even defiantly walking on land like the ones you have encountered."

"Forbidden by who?"

"The ancient gods who defeated them and drove them into the seas. The Old Ones were placed under a curse never to approach or roam the land again. That they were allowed to live was only by the gods' forbearance. The curse is eternal."

"Sounds like someone got tired of waiting," Rake noted.

"It appears it's been broken," I said. "Or at least cracked."

"Not yet," the queen said, "but the Old Ones are restless, joyously so. They sense their bondage is at last coming to an end."

I half turned to Rake. "Any experience extending supposedly eternal curses?"

"The one who could help has been taken," Sirene said.

I froze. "Excuse me?"

"The one who could help. Our friend Ian."

"How?"

Sirene indicated the pendant with a nod. "You carry the symbol of his ancestors' authority."

"His ancestors? Who?"

The queen of New York's merfolk seemed baffled as to why I was even asking that question. "The ancient gods, of course, the Tuatha Dé Danann—and the Old Ones, the Fomorians."

23

"IF Ian had known, he would have told me," I said. "But how could he not have known? You'd think knowing you were descended from Irish gods would've gotten passed down."

Rake steered the boat back out into the Hudson. "You'll have to ask Ian."

"And I plan to."

Sirene hadn't been able to tell us anything more, and she had never heard of anyone named Janus. Regardless, that one bombshell more than made the trip worthwhile.

My brain was officially boggled.

My partner was descended from both the Tuatha Dé Danann and the Fomorians. At least that was what Sirene believed, and it went a long way toward explaining why Ian could communicate telepathically with merfolk. It also provided a clue as to why the Fomorians would want to get their hands on Ian. It had something to do with breaking the curse that was keeping them exiled to the oceans. But figuring out how that connected to the contents of vampire safe deposit boxes and Janus was going to take more brain cells than I had right now.

I'd tried calling Alain Moreau, but I couldn't get a signal, and neither could Rake. Once back at the marina, that shouldn't be a problem. We needed to get a photo of the pendant to Amelia's Irish professor friend Conor Delaney.

I had my hand clenched around the pendant. The Hudson wasn't exactly what'd you'd call smooth this evening, and there was no way I was going to risk dropping it overboard. I held on to the side of the boat with my other hand. I'd already taken pictures of it from every angle with my phone and Rake's, and I had my phone in its waterproof pouch strapped by its cord to my wrist. I'd taken every precaution I could, but we couldn't get back to the marina quickly enough for me, though Rake was going as fast as he safely and legally could.

That a kraken wasn't presently terrorizing the Manhattan shoreline confirmed that Ian was still alive. The curse was still holding.

When Rake pulled the boat into his slip and tied it off, we tried calling Moreau again from the marina. I didn't want to risk being the only holder of information that could help us find Ian. A lot could happen between the marina and headquarters.

We both had a strong phone signal. While I called Moreau and told him what we'd learned from Sirene, Rake e-mailed the photos from his phone. Moreau listened to me without interjecting any theories of his own. When I'd finished, he told me to have Rake bring me directly back to headquarters—and to come in with me.

It sounded like my boss decided to accept the help of a dark mage. I was glad. If we were going to have to fight an ancient race of godlike sea monsters to get Ian back, we needed as many dirty tricks up our sleeves as we could get.

*　*　*

By the time Rake and I had arrived at headquarters, Moreau had texted me for us to meet him in his office.

My manager's office was even more imposing than Vivienne Sagadraco's, which was no small feat. Ms. Sagadraco's office had one glass wall that looked out over SPI headquarters' five-floor atrium and down into the agents' bull pen. There wasn't even a window to the atrium in Moreau's office, let alone a glass wall. I guess when a vampire wanted to make a room nap-time dark, he didn't fool around.

When Moreau had ushered me and Rake inside, he closed the door behind us, and even the door became a part of the wood paneling.

I had a thought I tried to ignore but it wouldn't go away, and neither would my heebie-jeebies. I wondered if Moreau liked all the carved wood paneling because it reminded him of coffin lids, because that was the spooky vibe it was giving me.

Other than that, his office was how one would imagine an office in an English gentlemen's club would look. Though I'd never say that out loud, considering that Alain Moreau was French.

There were more chairs than usual in his office.

Rake and I had no sooner arrived than there was another knock at the door.

Three doctors—one psychiatric, two academic.

Noel Tierney, along with historian/mythologist Amelia Chandler, and bladed weapons expert Harald Siggurson.

Moreau introduced Rake around, and none of them seemed in the least surprised to see one of our world's most notorious dark mages not only in SPI headquarters, but in what was looking like a high-level meeting in the acting director's office.

Rake gave no outward sign of unease, but then this was

Rake. Unease wasn't in his emotional repertoire. He was, however, curious and most definitely intrigued.

Alain Moreau noticed, but then this was Moreau, and he was a vampire. Whether a raised heart rate and quicker breathing from a human, or suppressed emotions from a goblin—nothing slipped past him.

"Lord Danescu, Madame Sagadraco believes that you are eminently trustworthy," he said. "I don't believe I would venture so far in my estimation. However, she has never been mistaken in her assessment of an individual's moral character. So in the interests of rescuing Ian Byrne, I am setting aside any personal reservations I have."

Rake slowly inclined his head, bowing as much as he was able from a chair. "Madame Sagadraco honors me." The goblin raised his head and his dark eyes met Alain Moreau's ice blue ones.

"We will need your help," Moreau continued. "Not only now, but in the rescue mission to come. This Janus is a master of portals, and we have witnessed the size and power of just a few of the Fomorians from around our world. I have no doubt Janus will have more than ample allies at his disposal to stop us from retrieving what he considers to be his."

"You're saying you'll need more than my help," Rake said quietly.

"I believe it would be prudent to be prepared."

"Understood. I will see what I can do and make arrangements."

Rake understood, I didn't, but neither man was forthcoming with more information. I wouldn't ask now, but I'd be cornering Rake later.

Moreau turned to our weapons expert. "Dr. Siggurson, you have a report on that spearhead?"

"That I do. I e-mailed you the technical details, but I assume that's not what you want me to say here."

"I do not."

"You want the good stuff." Siggurson appeared to be nearly as excited as Amelia Chandler had been yesterday.

Moreau nodded once.

"The spearhead is much older than it appears. While there are many intact Bronze Age weapons, I have never seen nor heard of a spearhead in this condition. It's mint. As if it were fresh from the battlefield, cleaned, and put away. It's quite possibly the most astonishing example of Early Bronze Age weaponry in existence." He smiled. "That being said, it's not Bronze Age—at least not *human* Bronze Age. Human hands did not make that spearhead. It has the scrollwork and detail of a ceremonial weapon, yet it's incredibly strong. The purity of the metal, and what initially appeared to be scrollwork up and down the length are in fact words, though not in any known language of the time. It's Tuatha Dé Danann."

"Has it been translated?" Moreau asked.

"Yes, I did it myself," said Amelia Chandler. "They're spells of strength for the wielder of the spear, and speed and accuracy for the spear itself." Chandler paused and slowly smiled. "And there at the base of the blade was the name of the man for whom it was forged, which in turn became the most well-known name of the spear."

I blinked. "It has more than one?"

"It has several. Luin Celtchair and Crimmall are two of the names which it acquired after its owner's death. But it is most often known simply as Lugh's Spear. It's the spear of Lugh Lámhfhada—or Lugh of the Long Arm as he was also known—and it's one of the most famous mythological weapons in the world." Siggurson was grinning like Christmas had come early this year. "As with many mythological weapons, it was presumed lost—or believed never to have existed to begin with."

I sat perfectly still. The spearhead knew Ian, and had

glowed all happy-like when Ian had picked it up—and Ian had recognized the spearhead.

"Amelia and I Skyped with Conor Delaney at the University of Dublin about Noel's sketches," Siggurson said. "It didn't take him long to positively identify the combatants as Tuatha Dé Danann and Fomorians. Conor was also able to identify one of the bodies, confirming these sketches that Noel made from Agent Byrne's dream are from the Second Battle of Magh Tuireadh."

I shot a concerned glance at Alain Moreau.

"Yes, I told them about Agent Byrne's dreams, and his reaction to the spearhead. They had to know in order to get the answers we needed."

While Siggurson and Moreau were talking, Noel Tierney was bringing up a series of images on his laptop screen. He nodded to Moreau, who pressed a button on a console at his desk, and a screen lowered from the ceiling. Noel connected his laptop to the projector on Moreau's credenza. Within seconds, we were looking at the scene Noel had recorded from inside Ian's dreaming mind. Much larger, and no longer restricted in size to a sheet of sketch paper, it was much more impressive—and terrifying.

"Along the bottom edge is the body of a giant of a man, with a single eye in the middle of his forehead," Amelia Chandler said. "As you can see, that eye has a spear driven through it, with a familiar spearhead. A hand is seen grasping the shaft of the spear as if to extract it." She half turned to where Noel sat with his laptop. "You do amazing work, Noel."

Dr. Tierney looked more than a little queasy, probably at the all-too-vivid memory of when he'd witnessed this particular scene in all its Technicolor gory.

"It was apparent to Conor that the point of view is from the wielder of that spear," Chandler continued. "We agreed that this is Lugh Lámhfhada of the Tuatha Dé, killing his grandfather Balor, king of the Fomorians. Balor's death broke the Fomorians and turned the tide of battle. The Tuatha Dé drove the Fomorians into the sea. They never returned."

"Until now," I said.

I got out of my chair and moved so I could see the screen better. "Noel, you said you believed that Ian's dreams were caused by a past-life regression that had been dormant until his first encounter with Janus."

"Either that or more likely, he's a direct descendant and what he experienced was the emergence of a genetic memory," Tierney said.

"Never heard of it."

"Memories which are passed down through generations, from ancestor to descendent. There is much about DNA—human and supernatural—which we don't know. The concept of genetic memory is considered too far-fetched for most scientists; however, I have seen it in a few of our agents. I believe you know Rolf Haagen, one of the commandos in our Oslo office."

"Let's see . . . descendant of legendary Norse hero Sigurd, who wrapped his fist around a live grenade and shoved his arm down a grendel's throat. How could I forget?"

Amelia looked horrified. "His arm?"

I gave a negligent wave. "It was bionic or something. His original arm up to the elbow was bitten off by a Finnish ice dragon. Rolf said he was due for an upgrade and didn't mind losing it. He's a bat-shit crazy Viking, but we like him."

"Rolf is one of our proven cases of genetic memory," Noel said. "His documented dreams expanded gradually into waking memories." He glanced at Alain Moreau and sighed. "Unfortunately, unless I can find some examples among the general population, I'll never be able to publish in a professional journal."

"It was triggered when Gram—a fine sword—came into his possession," Siggurson said.

"From what Rake and I heard tonight, my vote's in favor of a direct descendant with genetic memory." I then gave them a quick rundown of our meeting with the merfolk queen, and removed the pendant from beneath my shirt so everyone could see it. "Sirene said that this was the symbol of Ian's ancestors' authority, and by ancestors, she said she was referring to the Tuatha Dé Danann and her name for the Fomorians, the Old Ones." I paused. "So how can Ian be the descendant of a legendary Irish hero *and* a race of sea monsters?"

Noel smiled. "Actually, Lugh was an Irish demigod."

"Not all Fomorians were sea monsters," Amelia told me. "There were those who were, and the others were seen in their day as deformed, but some Fomorians were very beautiful. Lugh's mother, the Fomorian princess Eithne, was one of them. She was the daughter of Balor. There was a druid prophesy that said Balor would be killed by his own grandson. So Balor locked Eithne away in a tower with twelve women to care for and guard her—and also to keep her from learning that men even existed."

I snorted. "Good luck with that."

Amelia grinned. "Cian of the Tuatha Dé Dannan found a way into that tower. He had a cow that gave so much milk that everyone wanted to own her. Balor tricked Cian into giving him the cow. Cian wanted revenge, so he had himself transported by magic to the top of Eithne's tower and seduced her. She gave birth to three boys, two of whom Balor succeeded in having drowned. The third, Lugh, was saved and fostered until he was grown. In time, Lugh joined his father's people, the Tuatha Dé Danann, who, in time, met the Fomorians in battle."

"And Lugh kills his grandad with a spear through the eye."

Amelia nodded. "An eye that could incinerate anything

in its sight. Until Lugh killed Balor, the battle had been going badly for the Tuatha Dé Danann."

"Okay, let me see if I've got this straight. The Fomorians are trying to come back. The Tuatha Dé Danann were responsible for exiling them to begin with. Four thousand years of keeping them that way isn't too shabby. Why don't we get them to help now?"

"Because they no longer exist," Amelia said, "at least not on our world. When it grew apparent to the Tuatha Dé that mankind was arising as the dominant force in this world, they were said to have either gone under the ground or returned to the world from which they came."

"So the bad guys are still here, but the good guys went home and left us with the mess. Lovely." I glanced back at the projection of one of Noel's sketches. Then I froze and went closer to the screen to see better.

Rake sat up straighter. "What is it?"

All getting closer to the screen got me was a blurred image. "Noel, where's the original for this?"

"I don't have them with me."

Crap.

"But it's a very high-quality scan," he added. "Would looking at it on-screen help?"

I crossed the room and knelt next to Noel's chair.

"What are you trying to see?" he asked. "I can increase the—"

"That." I pointed to the left edge of the screen. All that was visible was half a face; the edge of the paper had cut off the rest.

Noel hit the magnification a couple of times, but it didn't get any clearer. At least, the drawing wasn't clearer, but with a mixture of excitement and dread, I knew what I was seeing. How I'd missed it until now I didn't know.

"I couldn't see that one very well," Noel was saying. "The face was blurry. All I could get were the eyes."

"Eyes I've seen in person twice, and that was twice too many," I murmured. "And don't feel bad about not seeing the face; he didn't want you to. He didn't want anyone to see what he looked like. I'm not even sure he knows anymore."

Rake had stood and was next to the screen, staring intently at the projection. "Janus?"

"The very one."

"The uniform is Fomorian," Amelia said.

"And he's close to his king's dead body," I noted. "Relative? Guard? Would your friend Conor know who he is?"

Amelia got out her phone and began typing. "He has the files. We can definitely ask."

"It might help him ID the guy if you tell him that he's been stalking Lugh's descendant for years, and for some reason decided now was the time to snatch him for payback."

"I'm hopeful that Lord Danescu can help us discover the nature of that payback." Moreau stood. "The staff in our Archives is waiting for us now."

24

I didn't want to say anything in Moreau's office. My question was personal, for Rake's pointy ears only.

Amelia was waiting for a call or e-mail back from Conor Delaney. Noel and Harald Siggurson had already left. Moreau needed to make a quick call, so Rake and I waited outside of his office.

"What was all that with Moreau about SPI wanting your help, but probably needing *more* than your help?" I asked.

"I know people," was all Rake said.

"Uh-huh. What kind of people?"

"People from my world who have fought things like these Fomorians before." He gave a crooked smile that was rather chilling. "They're very good at it."

"Then they're more than welcome to join the party."

"I didn't think you'd disapprove."

We stood in silence for a moment as I tried to find a way to say what I needed to say before Moreau came out.

Just spit it out, Mac.

"This is going to be dangerous."

"Most assuredly," Rake agreed.

"I don't want you to feel obligated to help rescue Ian because of me."

"I don't."

I frowned in confusion. "I don't know how to take that. You don't like Ian."

"I never said that."

"You never had to."

"Ian has never even bothered to hide how he feels about me—because of you." Rake thought for a moment. "And even not because of you. On this world or my own, humans have a deep-seated distrust of goblins."

One corner of my lips quirked upward. "And goblins would *never* give anyone reason to distrust them."

"We pride ourselves on being at least one step ahead of everyone around us—whether human or goblin. Intellectual and strategic competitiveness is probably in our DNA, no genetic memory needed. We're encouraged to be that way before we can walk. It's astonishing how much plotting—and damage—goblin toddlers can do in a playroom. They can barely even speak. Some of my nieces and nephews are truly impressive—and, quite frankly, frightening."

"You're attempting to distract me with interesting goblin facts."

Rake's dark eyes sparkled. "Is it working?"

"Yes, but I haven't forgotten the subject that you're avoiding."

His smile was slow and wicked. "Have I ever told you what a splendid goblin you would have made?"

"No, you haven't. Another nice try. The topic is Ian, and why you're willing to risk your life to help him."

"He is a good man, a brave man, and a fine warrior, and your world would be much less safe without him."

"Whoa. When goblins decide to stop beatin' around the bush, they don't fool around."

Now it was Rake's turn for a confused frown. "I don't understand either of those quaint yet charming sayings, but I take it that you believe my reason."

"Yeah, I do."

"Why?"

"Because I know bullshit when I hear it." I paused and lowered my voice to a whisper. "And I know you." I stood on tiptoes and wrapped my arms around his neck. Then I placed a light kiss on his earlobe. Rake's breath caught and a shiver coursed the length of his body.

"Thank you," I said simply. "Again."

And he knew I meant it.

I had been here before. Dark wood shelves, dim lighting, cool temperature, and closely monitored humidity to ensure maximum book comfort. People who had to be in here for any length of time usually brought a sweater or jacket with them. I was a mountain girl. I thought it was perfect.

SPI's library and the books it contained had always reminded me of something out of a monastery—or a Harry Potter book.

Rake walked next to me, his sharp eyes taking in everything and missing nothing. Even though he was wearing a guest badge and was being escorted by Alain Moreau, the goblin dark mage was getting more than his fair share of looks of every kind, ranging from tongue-hanging lust to suspicion to barely restrained animosity. What could I say? Rake was a well-rounded guy.

"Very impressive," he murmured.

Most of the books in the main stacks had already been converted to digital, but there were some that would only reveal their secrets off the printed page. Scanning them into a digital format would render that content meaningless. They were bespelled books. Like most things that were considered of the supernatural, SPI had a department for that. It was a small department, with very specialized members. We didn't need a code broken on a thousand-year-old manuscript every day, but the last time we had, we'd been in a bit of a hurry, to say the least.

The mages of the SPI Archives had been superheroes that day.

I nodded in agreement with Rake's opinion, but said nothing. Moreau hadn't said why he'd brought Rake this far. He hadn't gotten Rake just any guest badge. The one clipped to his jacket pocket would give him access to any department as long as he was accompanied by either Moreau or Vivienne Sagadraco herself. I didn't know what was going on and neither did Rake, but we were about to find out.

Moreau strode straight through the library to a door against the far wall.

Oh boy.

The door looked like any other in the library, but only select SPI agents had seen what lay beyond.

The Archives.

There were several places in the SPI headquarters complex that you couldn't get into without additional security clearance. The Archives was one of them. Even if you needed to see a book that was there for a case you were working on, you weren't necessarily going to get inside. I'd never been involved in a case that warranted me coming down here. And if you were working on such a case, you'd better have a good reason with the authorization of at least two director-level department heads, and a sealed letter in hand from either Vivienne Sagadraco or Alain Moreau detailing your reasons for needing access. Even then chances were slim that you'd be given direct access.

Either the research would be done for you, or there was a room with a viewing stand on one side of a protective glass wall, where the manuscript would be placed. The agent in a room on the other side would communicate with the archivist that accompanied the manuscript for things such as page turning. Mere mortal mitts and breath wouldn't be allowed to sully what might very well be the only remaining copy of a manuscript, or one that was thousands of years old.

Any book or reference material on the supernatural that had been published in the last century was in SPI's library, and most of it was available on the agency intranet. Everything older than a hundred years was in the Archives, which was protected with the ferocity of a mama grizzly defending her cubs. The books, scrolls, and even stone slabs of the Archives dated back thousands of years. The majority of its staff spent all their time cataloging, copying, and digitally converting SPI's vast collection, so that when information was needed, it could be accessed with a few keystrokes or mouse clicks. The rest of the Archive staffers were among the world's most skilled in manuscript restoration and preservation.

Regardless of the dire circumstances, I couldn't help but experience a thrill at getting to go inside the Archives. I'd have to remember everything so I could tell Ian about it when we got him back. I smiled slightly. Though as SPI's resident superagent, I was sure Ian had been inside before, probably more than once.

Moreau scanned his badge, his thumbprint, and his retina.

Dang.

There were several clicks as not one, but three locks disengaged.

Dang again.

Moreau opened the door, went inside, and we followed him into a small office. The ogre wearing a SPI security uniform certainly wasn't small; in fact, it wasn't the room that was tiny, it was the ogre who made it look that way.

"Director Moreau." The ogre's voice sounded like rocks grinding in a concrete mixer.

"How are you today, William?"

William?

"Just fine, sir." William's small, yellow eyes scanned me and Rake. "You will need to sign for your guests, sir."

Moreau looked up from the tablet and smiled. "Already taken care of."

"Thank you, sir. Director Wellesley is expecting you." William pushed a button behind his desk, the door on the wall in front of us opened, and we were inside.

My first thought was that SPI was manufacturing biological weapons.

We were on an enclosed catwalk overlooking a place that was whiter and more pristine than our labs. Some of the staff were in lab coats. Others, who were working on a manuscript or scroll inside what looked like Plexiglas rooms with actual air locks, were wearing honest-to-God clean room suits complete with respirators.

I finally couldn't contain myself any longer. "This is unspeakably cool."

"Yes, Agent Fraser, it is," Moreau agreed.

"I must agree," Rake murmured.

"All areas except the one we will be using," Moreau said, "are strictly temperature and humidity controlled, and utterly dust-free."

He led us the full length of the Archive lab through a pair of sliding doors and into what appeared to be an observation room. An opaque window that was the length and height of a whiteboard was on one wall, with a long desk beneath. The window looked like the one that had separated the small conference room from Ian's infirmary room.

Moreau saw my glance. "Yes, there's a switch on the other side, that renders the window clear. When the requested manuscript has been brought up from the vault and is ready for study, the window is cleared."

"What manuscript have you requested?" Rake asked. "And why have I, of all people, been allowed into SPI's inner sanctum sanctorum?"

"Because, Lord Danescu, the words on a page cannot always be seen with the eyes."

"A bespelled manuscript."

"That is correct."

"Don't you have mages for that kind of thing?"

"We do, but they have been unsuccessful."

"And what makes you think I'll have any better luck?"

"It is a curse, written and cast by an inhuman dark sorcerer."

"And it takes one to know one."

"I'm hopeful that is the case. Agent Byrne's life may depend on it."

25

"WE have one of the original copies of a book known as *Lebor Gabála Érenn*," Moreau said, "or as it's known in English, *The Book of Invasions*. It chronicles the history of Ireland from the creation of the world to the Middle Ages. Most of what we know about the Tuatha Dé Danann comes from the *LGE*, as it is known in academic circles. It's one of the most influential records of early Irish literature, poems, and sagas. In the eleventh century, an unidentified scholar compiled them all into a single work written in Middle Irish, a form of Irish Gaelic used from approximately A.D. 900 to 1200. There's no mention of a curse on the Fomorians, how it was placed, or how it might be broken. However, we also have in our possession some of the original records of the Second Battle of Magh Tuireadh and its aftermath, which formed the source material for the eleventh-century author. Again, there is no mention of a curse—at least nothing that is visible to the untrained eye. We had our best mage cryptanalyst—who also happens to be a druid—review the folio, and he found the curse. Unfortunately, it is hidden by a spell and guarded by a particularly destructive ward."

"Meaning if the spell is broken to read the curse, the folio will self-destruct?" I asked.

"He believes that would be the result," Moreau replied. "He cannot coax the words from the page without breaking the ward, and he is uncertain of his ability to dismantle it, as he believes it to have been created by a sorcerer of demigod-level strength and skill. Our senior Archive staff strongly suspect that what's hidden there will reveal why the Fomorians took Ian and what they plan to do with him—or at least provide us with a strong clue."

"A curse created by a god?" There was a faint note of mockery in Rake's voice. "And you believe I can break his ward?"

"They were beings beyond the men of their time," Moreau replied coolly. "That does not make them gods; it merely makes them a great annoyance to those of us in the present time."

Rake laughed. "Good to know I'm not SPI's only pain in the ass."

In less than a minute, the window slid open, revealing a glass-walled room and the gleaming white laboratory beyond. On the other side of the glass wall, a single sheet of parchment lay on an angled Plexiglas stand that was enclosed in a glass box like you'd see in a museum.

The door to our room opened and a woman swept in, an entourage in her wake. Though people that short generally didn't sweep, and two guys in lab coats did not an entourage make, but the sheer force of the woman's presence made her seem as tall as Yasha, and multiplied her two assistants. Elizabeth Wellesley was the director, though I'd heard her called both director and dominatrix.

Moreau handled the introductions. "Agent Fraser, Lord Danescu, this is Elizabeth Wellesley, our chief archivist."

Wellesley nodded, but no hand was extended for shaking. No surprise there. Alarms probably went off in the staff restroom if someone didn't wash their hands.

"I have heard of Lord Danescu."

My presence was ignored altogether. My feelings weren't hurt.

Rake spared one glance for the curse under glass. "Begging your pardon, Director Wellesley, but you must be joking."

"I assure you, Lord Danescu, this is not a joking matter."

"Not the matter," Rake said, "the *manner*. It is no wonder your mages could not read the curse." He gestured at the window separating us from the folio enclosed in its protective case. "Not one, but three layers of glass. The case itself, and this." He rapped sharply on the window with a knuckle for emphasis, making the white-coated archivists jump. "An additional two layers. It's a wonder your mages could read the words written on the page, let alone a curse embedded in it." Rake paused. "Unless your mages were given direct access, and I will not be."

"Our chief cryptanalyst mage was given direct access," Wellesley said, her words cold and crisp. "He was unable to break the code."

Rake peered down at the folio through the three layers of offending glass. "Then he may not have hit it hard enough."

"I am aware of your questionable methods."

"Are methods questionable that yield results?"

The chief archivist turned to Moreau. "I cannot allow one of our folios to be subjected to potentially destructive magic."

"A piece of paper versus your top agent's life," Rake pointed out. "I'm really not seeing a comparison—and I would sincerely hope you do not, either."

I stepped between Rake and Director Wellesley. I'd had

it with the bickering, and Ian didn't have the time. "Rake, can you read that curse?"

"Yes."

"You're positive?"

"Without a doubt."

I looked hard into his eyes. There was no sign of cockiness or pride, just calm self-assurance and a certainty in his skill. "I'll take that as a yes."

I turned to the Elizabeth Wellesley. "And you're saying that you're unwilling to risk that folio even though Rake is certain he can break the ward that's concealing that curse?"

Unlike Rake, Elizabeth Wellesley hesitated. "It is one of the oldest documents in our possession. There are no copies; it is the only one known to exist."

I stayed calm, but it wasn't easy. "So is Ian."

"My apologies, Director Wellesley," Moreau said. "I must agree with Agent Fraser. Regardless of the age, rarity, and value of a document, I value our agents more—and I am certain Madame Sagadraco would fully agree. Open the case, remove the folio, and give Lord Danescu full access."

Every white-coated or clean room suited archivist in the lab below stopped what they were doing and stared in horrified but enthralled wonder as Rake reached into the case and removed the folio with his bare hands. If that room hadn't been soundproof, I was sure we'd have also heard gasps and possibly a few distressed whimpers.

To Rake's credit, he had washed and sterilized his hands in accordance with Archive protocol, and he handled the page with the care usually reserved for a bottle of nitroglycerine, but that didn't change the fact that he was touching it with his bare fingers.

He raised it to the light—apparently another no-no, judging from the cringe of the white-coat to his right—and smiled in grim satisfaction. I didn't know whether that satisfaction was at the archivist's reaction or at having seen what he expected to see on the folio page, but I suspected it was a little of both.

Elizabeth Wellesley and her assistants were in the room with Rake. Moreau and I remained in the observation room. The speakers were on to allow us to hear each other.

"I can assure you that I will remember everything that I read," Rake was saying.

"Can you read Middle Irish?" Wellesley asked him.

"No, but I don't need to. I will remember, and immediately write it down so that your eminently qualified linguists may translate it for us. I will, however, need paper and a pen or pencil readily at hand. Normally I would use my phone to type what I see, but my phone lacks Middle Irish characters. Speed is important; I can't hesitate while searching for a close approximation."

Wellesley glanced at one of her assistants, and he scurried to obey, probably glad to be the heck out of there, if only for a few minutes.

Rake changed the angle of the folio to the light and squinted. "By the way, Chief Archivist Wellesley, what happens in this room when there's a fire?"

"The room fills with a gas that will instantly extinguish the fire."

Rake raised a brow, but never paused in his study. "And concerning those of us who require oxygen?"

"The gas dissipates quickly enough not to have prolonged effect on mortal respiration." She didn't sound thrilled that it wouldn't, at least not where Rake was concerned.

"Prolonged effect," Rake mused. "So you take the oxygen out of the room to protect the paper, but your staff is expected to . . . I don't know, hold their breath?"

Rake was annoying her, he knew it, and he was enjoying it. I was starting to see a pattern here. I could also tell Moreau was thinking about stepping in, but that was all he did. Perhaps Rake wasn't the only one who had an issue with the chief archivist's priorities.

The assistant returned with a notepad and pen, put them on the table in front of Rake, and hightailed it back to the door.

"Is that a reaction you can override?" Rake asked with complete politeness. "Because I can assure you that this folio will burst into flames. The sorcerer who wrote it was apparently quite the showman—and pyromaniac. No doubt he wanted to be there when it was attempted. He probably wouldn't have bothered with the fail-safe if he knew it wasn't going to be read for four thousand years. Where's the fun in sending something up in flames if you're not going to be there to enjoy it?" He thought for a moment. "Will the door lock automatically, as well?"

"No, it will not."

"Oh good, then we won't be trapped like rats in a sadistic experiment." He smiled cheerfully. "I'm ready when you are."

"Would you like a respirator?" Moreau asked him, when Wellesley didn't make the offer.

"While I sincerely appreciate the offer, there cannot be anything between me and the page. I'm quite proficient at breath holding. I've dealt with nasty wards before; and since I'm still here and in one piece, I've always been successful and I do not anticipate that today will be an exception." He turned to the chief archivist. "There is no need for either you or your assistants to remain in here with me. I can assure you this page will burn, and when the gas is deployed, there is need for only one rat in the room."

Wellesley sent her assistants out of the room—much to their relief—but she remained inside with Rake.

"You wish to stay?" he asked her.

"I wish you weren't going to destroy an irreplaceable document, but as there is no other alternative, I feel I must remain until the end."

"Very well. You may want to stand by the door. While I don't anticipate a large fireball, better safe than scorched."

Rake carefully put the folio on the reading stand in front of him, and rolled up his sleeves to nearly his elbows.

He spread his hands the width of the folio apart, his long fingers framing the bottom of the page that presumably contained the curse. A soft red light started in the center of his palms, slowly spreading outward until his hands were glowing from wrist to fingertip. He stood perfectly still, his dark eyes intent on the page.

In response, the bottom of the folio began to glow, and through the clear reading stand, I could just make out the outlines of lettering, about a quarter of the page worth. The glow was golden—the gold of a newborn flame.

The letters appeared as fire.

In less than a second, the entire page exploded off the stand in a ball of flame, followed by a loud hiss as the room filled with gas. However, the fireball never left the area between Rake's spread fingers and the small shield he'd used to contain it. Within two seconds, the paper turned to ash, Rake released the spell, and the folio's ashes floated featherlike to the floor.

The room was still full of gas, but Rake didn't budge. He picked up the notepad and pen and began writing nearly as fast as Noel Tierney had sketched the scenes from Ian's dream.

At last Wellesley was forced by airless necessity to open the door to let more air in. Only then did Rake leave and come back into our observation room—not that he was competitive or stubborn or anything.

"Do you read Middle Irish, Chief Archivist Wellesley?" he asked her.

"I do."

With a flourish, Rake presented her with the notepad.

Wellesley took one look, her lips compressed into a thin, angry line. "This isn't Middle Irish, Lord Danescu."

Rake looked down at it from over her shoulder. "It isn't?"

"No, it isn't."

"Then the hidden text wasn't written in Middle Irish, because this is what I saw."

Alain Morcau took the pad from Wellesley, glanced at it, picked up the phone on the table, and keyed in a four-key internal number. "We need you in the Archives. Immediately." He disconnected from that call, and pressed a single key. "William, please let Amelia Chandler in when she arrives."

In less than five minutes, Amelia Chandler was scanning the page, her brow furrowed. "I'd rather not speak these first four lines out loud. I believe they're a curse, and a highly potent one at that. Perhaps since I'm not a mage, and I would be speaking the words in translation, it wouldn't activate the curse, but—"

"It's better not to take that chance," Rake said.

"Exactly." Amelia winced. "Especially since it apparently banished an entire race of godlike beings. However, these shorter stanzas say how long the curse will remain, and the conditions under which it could be broken."

Morcau sat back against the desk. "Read those, please."

With these words and my will,
this ban shall stand
and those condemned to swim the seas
shall not walk the land
as long as these three eternal be
the land holds fast to its locks

the veil stands strong
and the scion of Lámhfhada lives.

"And I thought goblins held on to grudges for a long time," Rake murmured.

"Ian's the scion of Lugh Lámhfhada," I said, feeling more than a little sick. "Three things must happen before that curse is broken—and killing Ian is one of them." I took a breath and forced my mind away from that. "What about the two lines above that? How does the land's locks hold fast, and a veil stand strong?"

"The veil could refer to the veil between the worlds and dimensions," Moreau said. "Tomorrow night is the summer solstice, when the veils are the thinnest and passage between the worlds, dimensions, and realms of the living and dead require the least effort."

"But what about land locks?"

Silence.

That wasn't what I—or Ian—needed to hear.

26

"DO you truly enjoy being a pain in the ass?" I asked Rake once we were out of the Archive and library.

"Yes, I do. Especially when my being so thwarts unwarranted rules, bureaucracy, or wanton stupidity."

We were in the hall waiting for the others. Amelia Chandler came out, saw us, and made a beeline.

"I've got more on that not so-mystery man in Noel's drawing," she told us. "According to Conor, the uniform marks this Janus as a member of King Balor's personal guard—and the symbol engraved over the heart on his armor indicates that he was their captain."

"That thing doesn't have a heart," I told her.

Rake barked a laugh. "An underling who screwed up, and he's been trying to make up for it ever since."

"Is Janus his real name?" I asked her.

"Conor doesn't know. But he did say that all of Balor's bodyguards had to be sorcerers—and the captain of the guard had to be the best of them all."

"Anything about him being a shapeshifter?"

"Nothing. At least not yet." Amelia reached out and put her hand on my arm. "We're going to keep digging, and we're not going to stop."

I swallowed the lump in my throat. "Thank you."

She glanced down at her watch. "It's nearly midnight. When was the last time you slept?"

I had to think about that one for a minute. "Actually, I'm not sure. It's been a *really* long day."

"And tomorrow is going to be the same," she said. "You've done all you can right now. We're making great progress, and you're not going to do Ian any good if you're too tired to think straight."

I knew all of those things were true. We were close to finding where Janus had taken Ian, and I couldn't be on the verge of exhaustion when it happened.

"You're right. But I'm not going home. I'll sleep here." I managed an anemic laugh. "I've slept here so often; it feels like a second home. I actually keep a weekend bag here now."

Moreau's voice came from behind us. "I just got a call from Ambrus Báthory."

I turned to see a rare satisfied smile on my manager's face.

"He wants to meet."

As cliché as it was, a vampire mafia don had made us an offer we couldn't refuse.

Ambrus Báthory said he would tell us what was in his and the other vampire families' safe deposit boxes.

Even better, the proposed meeting location couldn't have been safer.

St. Patrick's Cathedral.

It was a myth about vampires not being able to go into

churches. They could go there; they just wouldn't be comfortable when they did. Another myth was the whole garlic thing. Vampires didn't like an overabundance of garlic for the same reason as humans. It stank. It stank on the breath, in sweat, and I'd heard that it ruined the taste of perfectly good blood. Even Italian vampires didn't like garlic.

And of course, Ambrus Báthory wanted to meet now.

Sleep would have to wait. I insisted on going.

Those going inside the cathedral included me, Moreau, Rake, Yasha, and Sandra Niles, the commander of one of our two commando teams. The rest of Sandra's team was outside the cathedral covering all exits. It was a good thing it was almost two in the morning. While New York was the city that never sleeps, at least most of it was dozing right now. Only an occasional cab or late-night partier cruised by. Commandos were experts at concealment, but it was a heck of a lot easier now than during daylight and regular business hours. Sandra had been told that Báthory likewise had people stationed in, on, and around the cathedral. That was expected, but that knowledge didn't make me feel warm and fuzzy about our impending meeting, but at least I was breathing better.

Yasha was with me because he wasn't about to let me go anywhere without him. Moreau didn't mind, especially when Yasha told him that his friend Vlad Cervenka was responsible for nudging his temporary employer into cooperating. I would have to be sure to tell Ian how his best friend had come through for him by networking behind the scenes.

New York churches—or most churches anywhere nowadays—weren't unlocked at night. It didn't say nice things for us as a species, and made you wonder why God continued to put up with us. Ambrus Báthory had said that the front doors would be unlocked, and they were. For some reason, that wasn't as reassuring as it should have been.

The head of House Báthory was waiting for us seated on one of the ornate chairs near the church's altar. Again, it was something that should have made me feel better, but did the exact opposite.

What did make me feel better was seeing Vlad Cervenka standing at Báthory's right shoulder.

At least one of Báthory's people was on our side.

I hoped.

Ambrus Báthory remained seated when we reached the front of the church.

He was a big man, or he had been in life. Now he was what my grandma Fraser would have called "gone to seed." What had probably once been muscle had gone to fat. According to the file we had on him, Ambrus Báthory had been born in 1297. Humans during that time who may have been considered tall then, were short now. Báthory was dressed like a successful banker, the fleshy fingers of one hand resting on the carved handle of an ebony cane. Our file referenced an attack from a rival family in 1623 that had left him near permanent death with his right leg shattered. Vampires would eventually heal from nearly any injury, but there was no guarantee that the injury would heal right, especially considering what passed for medical knowledge in the early sixteen hundreds.

His skin was pale and looked soft, though with vampires, every aspect of their appearance was deceiving. I had no doubt Báthory could break me in half with that seemingly flabby arm and never have to rise from his chair—which looked more like a throne with him seated in it. The chair was facing the front pew, indicating that we were to sit there.

Moreau handled the introductions. No one made any move to shake hands, or any move at all, for that matter.

"Forgive me for not rising." Báthory's voice was smooth and cultured, which was at odds with his overripe and corrupt appearance. He inclined his head toward the pew. "Please, be seated."

I didn't know what the proper etiquette for dealing with a vampire don was, and right now I was too creeped out to care.

Alain Moreau solved that dilemma for all of us. "No, thank you, Monsieur Báthory. We would prefer to stand."

One side of Báthory's fleshy lips curved slightly. It could have been a smile, or an annoyed twitch. "There is no need to fear me."

"Not fear, Monsieur Báthory. Prudence." Moreau graciously inclined his head to the ancient vampire. "I aspire to have a life as long as your own."

Again, his lips twitched, this time in pain as he shifted his leg. "Be careful what you ask for, my boy, you just may get it."

"You said you had information for us, Monsieur Báthory," Moreau said pointedly.

The old vampire kept his eyes on Moreau. "My nephew was kidnapped to extract information from him."

"What kind of information?" Moreau asked.

"The location of my family's First Relics."

Moreau froze.

My manager obviously knew what First Relics were, and from his reaction, it was bad.

I gave Moreau a questioning look. Báthory saw.

"Each vampire family can trace their ancestry back to a single individual; the first of our family, if you will. The First Relics are the physical remains, the bones, of the First Father or First Mother of a vampire family."

Rake spoke. "I take it these remains have more than a symbolic or ritualistic importance?"

"Merely the source of our power and longevity."

I knew that the more powerful the vampire, the stronger

the fledgling. The strength was in the blood passed from the elder to the younger. If blood strengthened new vampires, the bones of the family's ancestor . . .

I made a face before I could stop myself.

Báthory smiled in a twist of fleshy lips. "Yes, Agent Fraser. We ingest the bones of our ultimate ancestor—at least myself and my chosen heir do. We take a small segment of bone, reduce it to dust, and mix it with the blood of a powerful . . . donor, shall we say."

"And without the . . ." I was thinking "ancestor smoothie," but I wasn't about to say it.

"Our strength fails, along with our power and influence over our families—and our enemies."

"Vampire civil war," Moreau stated.

Báthory's nod was more of a royal inclining of his head. "Chaos both inside our families and out. A ruthless struggle for power among the strongest of our kind. The elixir the family rulers consume is all that stands between peace and open slaughter and lawlessness."

"And this will affect humans?"

"Our laws, Agent Fraser, stipulate that we conceal ourselves from mortals. There are many among our kind who grow weary of living in mankind's shadows. They want to take and to rule what they believe to be theirs by right of being a supreme predator. Their ultimate goal would be to make enough fledglings to subdue and subjugate the entire human race."

Moreau was right. This was bad.

Then I did the math, and it was even worse.

"Your First Relics were in that safe deposit box," I said.

"Correct, Miss Fraser. The First Relics of the Báthorys and those of the strongest families in this part of the world. I keep some in my compound for easier access. For the rest, I and others have trusted the security of mortal and immortal banks. This is the first time that trust has been violated."

"So Janus has stolen your ancestor's remains. What can he do with them?"

"They possess great power to those who have the knowledge to access it."

"Mages."

"More powerful than mages," Rake said quietly. All eyes were on him. "It would take a near godlike power."

"It would," Báthory agreed.

"The same level of power that it would take to control a kraken," Rake added. "And if this Janus and those who are working with him can control a kraken without a power boost, what can they do with the remains of the most powerful vampires who ever walked?"

No one answered that question. No one wanted to.

Janus needed power, a lot of it.

He also needed Ian.

Now he had both.

This was why Ambrus Báthory had asked us here, why he had risked leaving the safety of his heavily guarded Long Island fortress.

Báthory's hard eyes were watchful. "I understand that one of your agents, Ian Byrne, was abducted by the same creature who took my relics."

"He was," Moreau said.

"Do you know why?"

"The creature responsible calls himself Janus. At least that is one of his aliases. He is a known shapeshifter. He first encountered Agent Byrne several years ago when he was still with the NYPD. His partner was killed; Agent Byrne escaped. Janus has hunted him ever since."

Not a lie, yet not the truth.

Báthory huffed a laugh. "The one that got away."

"Essentially."

"This Janus has gone to much trouble to regain escaped

prey. From time to time a meal gets away. If this being is as ancient as you say . . ." Báthory shook his head slowly. "One does not attain great age to become obsessed with mere prey."

I felt a growl growing in my throat.

Báthory noticed. "My apologies, Agent Fraser. Agent Byrne was your partner—"

"*Is* my partner."

"Perhaps. This creature has slaughtered and fed off of my nephew. I do not understand why Bela would be killed, and a mere mortal—"

"Mr. Báthory," I said quietly. "Do you really need to finish that sentence? I realize that the long-lived have little regard for us *mere mortals*; however, myself and those here with me do not share your lack of regard. That being said, we are at as much of a loss to fathom Janus's motives as yourself. You said you had information for us, information that would help us find Janus—and my partner. Stopping whatever it is that Janus has set into motion is a goal we can all agree on, is it not?"

The vampire don's lips curled into a fleshy smile, as he looked over my head to where Rake stood behind me.

"An intriguing mortal, Lord Danescu. I had wondered what you could see in her. I believe I understand."

I clenched my teeth. "And I believe I'm right here. Or is a mortal, regardless of how intriguing, not worthy of regard or speaking directly to?"

Ambrus Báthory leaned forward and the chair's dark wood creaked ominously. "I am regarding you now, Miss Fraser."

Yes, he was.

"I chose to deliver this information personally," he said, his voice low, "at great danger to myself and my family. It is information that I did not want to disclose, again for the safety of my family. My property has been stolen, and one way or another, I will have it back in my possession. Failure in this is not an option."

"I agree with you that failure is not an option. You want your property; I want my partner."

"Wouldn't the relics be safer in your own compound?" Rake asked.

"Unfortunately, the vast majority of the danger to my rule comes from within my own family," Báthory said. "The same is true of any of the older families. A takeover by outsiders is rarely attempted due not only to the danger, but the difficulty. Some of my worst enemies are my own fledglings."

Talk about biting the hand that feeds you—or in this case, that made you.

There were younger, powerful, and ambitious vampires in every family who would've loved to have known if the head of their family was losing his or her strength.

"We want our property returned," the vampire continued. "However, our resources in certain areas are lacking, areas where your organization is abundantly qualified."

"You propose an alliance," Moreau said.

"A temporary sharing of information and resources for our mutual benefit."

"What benefit is there to us?"

Báthory kept his dark eyes on Moreau, raising his left hand toward the equally dark-suited vampire standing to the left of his "throne." The vampire placed a manila envelope in his master's waiting hand. Báthory gave it to Moreau, his gaze unwavering.

"This is everything we know about the creature you know as Janus," Báthory said. "Before his present career as a bank robber, he was a tomb robber. Late last year, he stole the First Relics of two of the oldest families in Europe. My contacts there traced him to London, and from there to New York."

Alain Moreau frowned. "Did he have business in London or meet with anyone?"

"Not that my contacts were able to determine. However, also inside is a short list of contacts this Janus has here in the city, as well as the location of two known residences."

"We appreciate your forthrightness, and your invaluable assistance," Moreau assured him. "One of SPI's missions is to keep the peace between supernatural factions. It is in no one's interest to have the vampire families at war—either within a House or between more than one. You have my word that we will do everything in our power to retrieve the Houses' First Relics."

27

"POKING the dragon in his borrowed den," Rake teased. "You live dangerously."

I bristled. "I'm not going to stand there while *anyone* talks about Ian as if he's dead. He's not dead now, and he's not going to be that way for a long time."

We were back where we had left the Suburban. With a wave and a word from Rake, it appeared before us, and Yasha let out a heaving sigh of relief. Rake had hidden it with a ward, and guarded it with a spell.

"Batman wishes he could do that," I said.

"Batman has a cooler ride to hide," Rake muttered.

Rake said it, but at least he had the sense to lower his voice before he did. Yasha didn't put up with any insults to what he considered to be his partner. Yasha hadn't liked Rake doing any hocus-pocus on his precious Suburban, but he'd felt better going into the cathedral with his automotive partner safely concealed.

Rake leaned closer and kept his voice low. "Would you

be as fierce standing up for me?" He wasn't teasing now. Actually, he sounded a little hopeful.

"I have been."

Rake wasn't expecting that. "In front of who?"

"People who don't trust you." I gave him a half smile. "Yet."

"How many?"

I patted his cheek. "Darlin', how about I take the Fifth on that?"

We got in the Suburban and I checked my e-mail. I frowned in confusion. I had one from a name I didn't recognize in the NYPD. It was a legitimate NYPD e-mail address, so I opened it.

Ian's friend in Evidence. Randall Torres. He'd heard what had happened to Ian, so he forwarded the JPGs of the jewelry stolen by Janus and his ghouls in the string of robberies nearly six years ago to me.

I opened the photos in rapid succession.

All of the pieces had one thing in common: a large center stone. Only a few had been diamonds; most were semiprecious stones. I had a flashback to the Dragon Eggs—all diamonds, all cursed.

"I wonder if these are cursed," I murmured.

"I beg your pardon?" Moreau asked from the front passenger seat.

I told him my and Ian's theory about the stones Janus had stolen when Ian had first encountered him.

"Janus had been spotted at the Metropolitan Museum during the Mythos gala," I said. "Ms. Sagadraco felt that he may have been one of those behind the theft of the Dragon Eggs. If he was looking for a power boost then, maybe he'd started his collection a couple of years ago with these robberies. I'll forward the e-mail and photos to Kenji and have him run them through our cursed gem database."

Rake raised a brow. "You have a cursed gem database?"

"After what happened with the Dragon Eggs, and what nearly happened with us? Heck yes, we have a database."

I forwarded the e-mail to Kenji and flagged it as important. Unfortunately, there wasn't a "life or death" designation, but I could and did text him to let him know what was coming and what we thought it might be.

Rake considered it. "Cursed gems to help break a curse. Sounds logical enough."

"If they're anything like little Dragon Eggs, it's probably the power boost he's after, especially if he also has these First Relics." I leaned forward to Alain Moreau in the front seat. "Sir, do they really drink . . ."

"I'm afraid so, Agent Fraser. There's not anything the heads of these families wouldn't do to stay in power."

"Though the Dragon Eggs were merely the batteries for the ley lines that ran under North Brother Island . . ." I stopped and thought and slowly looked at Rake.

He was looking at me. "Are you thinking what I'm thinking?"

"I'm too tired to take over the world, but if you're thinking ley lines, and wondering where up the Hudson River do they intersect, then yes, I'm thinking what you're thinking."

"Agent Fraser?"

I looked in the rearview mirror at my manager's pale blue eyes looking back at me, the skin at the corners of his eyes crinkled with a smile.

"I remembered a minor fact about ley lines that I learned from the encounter with them last year," he said. "They derive their power by unlocking the power of the land."

I smiled back. And there was the answer to the last piece of the puzzle.

*   *   *

By the time we'd arrived at headquarters, Kenji had been a very busy boy, and every ley line that crossed the Hudson or anywhere nearby had been mapped on the big screen at his desk. Rake and Yasha were right behind me as we hurried through the bull pen. The elf computer guru's hair was standing up at angles that suggested someone had been gotten out of bed. By the intensity with which Kenji was working, he hadn't minded.

"I woke you up," I said. "I'm sorry. But that means you were asleep, which also makes me jealous."

Kenji grinned. "I think I just might be able to help with that—the you-getting-some-sleep part. After you hear what I have to say, you just might be feeling relaxed enough for a nap. I think I've found our boy, Ian."

"You *what*?" I nearly jumped out of my seat and kept jumping. "Who needs sleep? Not me."

Moreau arrived and was studying the elf's handiwork on screen.

"I'll put this on the monitor wall, sir," Kenji said. "Then everyone can see."

The far wall of the IT department flickered to life and a satellite map of the Hudson River Valley came into view. Overlaying the map were bright green, blue, and red lines.

"Okay, there are your ley lines. Greenies are weak, blues can pack a punch, but I think the Fomorians wouldn't want to bother with anything except the red ones." Kenji hit a couple of keys, and the green, then the blue lines faded away, leaving only the strong ley lines in red. "Fomorians need water, so we can eliminate those that aren't on the Hudson." A few more key clicks, and most of the red lines faded.

"That's still entirely too many lines," I noted.

"Agreed," Kenji said. "That's when I called Amelia Chandler for some local folklore. Hauntings, spirits, places of power." His fingers flew over the keys, leaving only two ley lines that intersected over the Hudson River, but almost on shore.

"Lady and gentlemen, may I present Pollepel Island, a place ancient Native Americans wouldn't be caught dead on at night because of evil spirits, an island at the northern edge of the maybe-not-mythological realm of the Heer of Dunderberg— the king of Thunder Mountain, also called the Storm King. Coincidentally, Storm King Mountain is directly across from Pollepel. The island also happens to have the ruins of an actual Scottish castle, likewise reputed to be haunted. I think our swamp men would feel right at home there." He sat back with a flourish. "Ta-da."

"I would say 'I could kiss you,' but I think I'll just go ahead and do it." I did, and threw in as much of a bone-crushing hug as I was capable of.

"All in a night's work. And by the way, there's more. Those gem JPGs?"

"Yes."

"The little guys are cursed."

I gave a little fist pump. "Knew it!"

"A few had been cut down from larger stones, but judging from what had happened to the owners, it didn't decrease their bad mojo one bit. It was hardly surprising they all ended up for sale. Their owners—or the surviving relatives—wanted to get those things as far away as possible."

Kenji got rid of the ley lines on the map and clicked in until we could clearly see the island and the surrounding area.

"Pollepel Island is about fifty miles north of here," he told us, "and is six miles north of West Point, to give you a closer reference. Back when our little patch of home was known as the colonies, Dutch seafarers going up and down the Hudson believed that the river was haunted in a fifteen-mile stretch from Dunderberg Mountain to Pollepel. When he was feeling particularly insulted by trespassers, the Heer of Dunderberg—aka the Storm King—would send his storm ship manned by his goblin minions—"

"Excuse me?" Rake interrupted. *"Minions?"*

Kenji spread his hands and grinned. "Hey, just relaying the local lore. The *minions* would wreak havoc on that stretch of the river. So down through the centuries, anything bad that happened on Pollepel and the surrounding area was the doing of the Storm King."

Kenji zeroed in on the satellite photo of Pollepel Island.

"Short story in a nutshell, Pollepel is a rocky island of a little less than seven acres about a thousand feet from the eastern shore of the Hudson. And if we move in a little closer, we can see the ruins of Bannerman Castle. Interesting guy, Francis Bannerman. Born in Scotland in 1851. His family immigrated to the States when he was three. He was a Brooklyn boy with a wide entrepreneurial streak. When he was fourteen, he founded a military surplus company, and as he grew, so did his business. He went from collecting and selling scrap he found in the harbor to buying full ships at Navy auctions. It's said that about half of those cannons in town squares around the country were bought from Bannerman. He outgrew his business in the city and his son was canoeing on the Hudson one day and saw Pollepel Island. Bannerman bought it in 1900 and soon after started building the castle and a summer house for his family." Kenji scrolled down through some information he had on another monitor. "Let's see . . . he died in 1918. Two years later, two hundred pounds of munitions exploded and destroyed a goodly chunk of the castle . . . In 1950, a storm sunk the island's ferryboat."

I grinned. "Probably those pesky goblin minions."

"In 1957, the last superintendent retired, and the island

was left vacant for the next three decades. It was sold to the state in 1967, and a very suspicious fire in 1969 destroyed much of what the explosion had left standing . . . However, there's now a Bannerman Castle Trust that's working to preserve what's left. Oh cool. It says here they give tours May through October."

Rake smiled and stood up straight from where he'd bent to get a better look at the summary. "Hmm, they need money; we need to get on that island. I think I'm about to make a substantial donation."

28

TOMORROW—well, tonight since it was closing in on three in the morning—would be the summer solstice; and at midnight, the veils between the worlds would be at their thinnest, and the power of the earth's ley lines would be most easily accessed. It'd also be a full moon.

Rake would arrange a tour of Pollepel Island and Bannerman's Castle for in the morning. I would be going with him, along with Kylie, our portal expert Kitty Poertner, commando team leader Roy, and of course, Yasha.

Alain Moreau would be standing by once Kitty and I confirmed the presence of a portal on the island to arrange what would be needed to go and get Ian before midnight.

There was one thing I could do over the next few hours that would greatly improve my chances of surviving a confrontation with Janus, his kraken keeper, or any of his Fomorians.

Sleep.

With Kenji's news and a plan for rescuing Ian quickly

coming together, my appetite came back with a vengeance. So before trying to get a few hours of sleep, or at least rest, I headed down to the cafeteria to fuel up. Rake went home to contact his goblin allies for some extra muscle when the time came to go in. My job was to get my head back in the game by having it spend some quality time on a pillow. I felt in my gut that Ian was on Pollepel Island, and with that knowledge, I could sleep.

I had thought it'd take me a while to wind down my thoughts enough to fall asleep. I was wrong. All it took was my head being on a pillow long enough to make a dent—approximately one point three seconds. And once asleep, I'd slept so hard that I woke up in a tiny pool of drool, and nearly overslept for Alain Moreau's eight a.m. briefing.

Kenji plopped down next to me in the big conference room. "Whoa, you slept hard."

I quickly swiped the back of my hand over the corner of my mouth. No drool there.

He flashed a crooked grin. "Pillow prints embedded in the side of your face."

We were assembling in the meeting room just off the bull pen. There were folding chairs stacked against the wall just inside the door. If you wanted to sit down, you grabbed one on the way in. Most of the agents chose to stand. We all knew why we were here. We didn't want to sit down; we wanted our orders so we could get this show on the road.

While we didn't believe Janus would sacrifice Ian until the full moon reached its zenith tonight, I wanted him safe and off Pollepel Island. Now.

Yasha would be listening to the meeting via the speaker system down in the motor pool. As soon as the boss dismissed us, Yasha would have the engine on and ready to go.

Alain Moreau stepped up to the front of the room, a map of Manhattan and the other boroughs projected on a screen behind them. There were a lot of red dots on that map. It'd been my experience that many red dots had never been anything but bad.

"You all have heard what happened yesterday. One of our own, Ian Byrne, has been taken captive by the Fomorians. Until a few hours ago, we thought Janus's desire for revenge against Agent Byrne stemmed from an incident a few years ago when Agent Byrne—then Detective Byrne of the NYPD—put an end to a string of robberies by Janus and his accomplices. We now know Ian has been targeted because he is the last of his line. A line that dates back thousands of years to Lugh Lámh-fhada, a king of the Tuatha Dé Danann, a supernatural race considered heroes and deities by the ancient Celtic people, and a bloodline that leads to Ian."

The assembled agents murmured. They knew Ian was the best of them all. He had their admiration and respect. Everyone liked Ian, and if a job went to Hades in a handbasket there was no one they'd trust more to have their backs. Knowing your coworker was a monster-killing badass was one thing. Being told he was the direct descendant of a Celtic god was something else entirely. These people knew their mythology; you had to in our line of work. They'd experienced firsthand just how real those so-called mythological critters were.

So when Alain Moreau said Ian was the last descendant of a line that began with Celtic gods and heroes, we believed it.

The murmuring ended with a single prolonged and impressed whistle.

"Ian's ancestor, Lugh, killed Balor, the last Fomorian king. The Fomorians were driven into the sea. As the last of Lugh's direct line, Ian's death is the last element in a chain reaction that will release the Fomorians from their exile.

Janus was the captain of Balor's personal guard tasked with finding Lugh Lámhfhada's descendant and sacrificing him so that the Fomorians could once again emerge from the oceans and walk the earth."

No impressed murmurs or whistles followed *that* pronouncement.

"Tonight is the summer solstice, when the veils between our world and others are at their thinnest. We believe the ritual will be conducted on Pollepel Island at Bannerman Castle, a place of power where two of the major ley lines on the East Coast intersect. To further power the ritual, Janus has collected objects of power to fuel his rite. To rescue Agent Byrne will require all of our teams."

Roy raised his hand.

"Commander Benoit?"

"Sir, I've been up to Bannerman. It's not a big place, and the castle is a ruin. There's not many places where they could be keeping Ian, let alone have some high-and-mighty ritual, and not have us be able to pick them off like opossums on pavement."

"Pollepel Island is a place of power and supernatural activity," Moreau said. "The ley lines that intersect beneath it are only part of its allure to the Fomorians. They have chosen not only the place but also the time, to take maximum advantage of all of that power. You could be standing next to the altar and never see or hear what is happening. Janus is a master of portal and dimensional manipulation. We could be dealing with an opening into an established dimension or even a world, or a pocket dimension of Janus's creation. The dimension where Agent Byrne is being held could very well be separate from where the ritual will be worked. We must not only rescue Agent Byrne, but also recover the artifacts stolen from those safe deposit boxes. Those are the keys that will release the Fomorians. Our mages have theorized that if Agent Byrne's blood comes in contact with the artifacts it will be too late—for Ian, and to prevent the Fomorians from returning."

Silence.

"We have commando teams flying in from Toronto and Chicago to be on duty here to deal with any issue that may arise in the city. They will be paired with drivers and guides who know the areas they'll be working." He paused. "I want our two teams on Pollepel Island. It's one of our own who is in the worst kind of danger. I know you will do everything that can possibly be done to secure his freedom and preserve his life. Ian has endured much these past few days, and I want the faces of his rescuers to be those of his friends."

After Alain Moreau dismissed the agents, he asked that Roy and Sandra remain. That was when he told them about getting assistance from Rake and his dark mage friends— though from the reaction that news received, a more accurate description would be "dropped a bomb." Ian wasn't the only one at SPI who distrusted Rake Danescu, and that was putting it mildly.

Our commando teams were professionals and professionals wouldn't dispute an order, but that didn't mean that they would like it. It would be up to Roy and Sandra to brief their teams and smooth over any problems.

"This is about necessity, Commanders. Not camaraderie."

In other words, they didn't have to like it, they simply had to do it.

Sandra gave a terse nod. And after blowing his breath out his nose like an angry bull, Roy did the same.

"I trust Rake," I told them both. "At least for this." I glanced at Moreau. "Should I tell them about my new skill set?"

He nodded once.

"I can see portals and detect dimensions."

Roy whistled.

"How?" Sandra asked me.

"Good question. I wish I knew. But there's no doubt that I've got the skill. Kitty Poertner has agreed to go with us. If it's like Mr. Moreau says and Janus has Ian in a pocket dimension, I can detect it, but I don't have the skills to get in. Kitty does."

My phone beeped with an incoming text.

"It's Rake," I told them. "That was fast. I guess if you throw enough money around, time is no object. He has a tour of Pollepel Island set up for us at eleven o'clock."

Moreau spoke. "Commander Niles, I need you to remain here and prepare both teams. Commander Benoit, since you've been to Pollepel Island before, you are to accompany Agent Fraser and Miss Poertner, and get the lay of the land from a tactical standpoint. Hopefully, Agent Fraser will be able to locate the portal."

"Kylie is going, too," I told him. "She has some kind of supernatural/dryad bond with Ian. They're, uh, seeing each other, in case you didn't know."

"I was aware."

Oh. Awkward. "And so is Yasha."

That got a raised eyebrow. "Seeing Agent O'Hara?"

Really awkward. "Going with us. With Ian not here right now, Yasha has kind of taken over as my shadow."

"The full moon is tonight. Monsieur Kazakov might be too—"

"He's going in his SPI-approved disguise," I said.

Moreau sighed. "Very well."

29

OLDER werewolves could change when they wanted to, but all werewolves, regardless of age, changed on the night of the full moon. Werewolves at SPI automatically got three days a month off: the day before, the day of, and the day after a full moon. But for those occasions when the moon was full, a werewolf agent was needed, and chances were high that the public might accidentally get a glimpse, SPI's Research and Development department had come up with a disguise for "that time of the month." Mood swings, cravings, anger, and irritability—trust me, you ain't seen cranky until you've seen a werewolf trying to force down their natural inclinations during a full moon.

I didn't understand how it worked, but it involved a little science, a lot of magic, and worked on the same principle as a goblin being able to walk down Broadway while looking just as human as anyone else.

The disguise R&D settled on? A German shepherd. Readily accepted the world over as police and military dogs. Pair a K-9 with a SPI commando in a flak vest or body armor, and your average New Yorker wouldn't bat an eye.

Where we were going, a dog would look right at home. The Hudson Highlands. Home of Storm King State Park and Pollepel Island. Storm King was known for its hiking and hunting. Today and tonight, our plan was to extend the hunting to Pollepel—first for Ian, then for every Fomorian that tried to stop us.

Since time was not on our side, Rake had a helicopter to take us to the Hudson Highlands. There, he had rented an SUV to meet the Bannerman Castle Trust representatives for the trip to the island.

By nine o'clock, we were at the West 30th Street Heliport about to board Rake's Sikorsky. I'd flown in it before and while the ride was a smooth, sometimes the air wasn't. Today, I wasn't about to take any chances. I popped a Dramamine. I could get dizzy from standing up too fast. Traveling by air, water, or the backseat of a car couldn't be done without my little orange-flavored, chewable buddies. Since coming to work for SPI, I carried three meds at all times: Dramamine, Tums, and Vicks. Tums were for those times when something I saw or smelled didn't agree with what I'd eaten. The Vicks was to smear under my nose to help me not smell it in the first place.

For today's trip, Kitty had said she'd take care of the food. To complete our disguise, we were taking a picnic lunch to Pollepel. Considering what we had planned for this evening, not eating during the day was not an option. Kitty had brought pastries, bread, and one of those carryout boxes of coffee from her bakery, and then she'd popped over to Murray's a couple of doors down for cheese and lunch meat. The helicopter would be stocked with drinks.

In accordance with New York's leash laws, Yasha was wearing one; I was holding the end. The Russian werewolf/German shepherd was sitting on the tarmac on his haunches.

Rake just looked at Yasha. Yasha stared right back.

"There's a 'no pet' clause in the car rental contract," Rake told me, never taking his eyes from Yasha.

"His human form or that form—either way, right now he's gonna shed." I patted Rake on the arm. "We'll vacuum. And if the rental place raises a stink, well darn, you won't get your deposit back. You can afford it."

"It's not the rental agency's stink I'm concerned about."

Yasha didn't growl. He simply peeled his upper lip away from his canines.

Rake did the same thing back at him.

I was tempted to smack both of them with a rolled-up newspaper.

The flight to the Hudson Highlands was blessedly uneventful.

Rake didn't suggest that Yasha fly cargo, and Yasha didn't pee on Rake's fancy hiking boots. It was about all I was hoping for at this point.

I was hoping for a better experience on Pollepel Island than we'd had on our previous jaunt to another of New York's river islands.

North Brother Island in the East River was twenty acres of pure unconditional spookiness located between the Bronx and Riker's Island, the cozy home of the New York City Department of Correction main jail complex. Riverside Hospital had operated here until 1963, when it was closed to the public, the island abandoned and officially declared off-limits to the public.

North Brother Island had been home to the hospital, Typhoid Mary, a tuberculosis pavilion, and a heroin addict treatment center. And of architectural interest, the hospital's chapel that had been located next to the island's dock had been converted into the morgue for easily getting dead bodies off the island for burial on nearby Hart Island.

Pollepel Island only had a haunted Scottish castle and possibly a kraken lurking offshore.

Piece of cake.

The Range Rover that Rake had rented was very new and very nice. It had been delivered to the county airport where we'd landed. I kept Yasha out of sight until the rental agency guy had gone.

I glanced inside and winced. The leather seats were soft as a baby's butt. Yasha's claws would punch holes all in it.

"Okay, we need a pad or— "

"Got it." Kylie tossed the picnic blanket Kitty had brought back into the third-row seat.

Behind the third row of seats were Kitty's picnic supplies. Beneath those in a cargo compartment were what most day-trippers wouldn't be bringing with them—guns, knives, and enough ammo to start our own little war, which was exactly what we would do if that's what it took to get Ian back. Those were concealed under a Rake-constructed glamour to hide them from any potentially prying law enforcement or ranger eyes.

Soon we were headed north to the small marina where we'd meet up with our guides.

Rake was driving, I was in the front passenger seat. Behind us were Kylie and Roy; Kitty, who was nearly as small as Kylie, was sharing the third-row seat with Yasha. He hadn't stopped squirming since we'd left Manhattan fifty miles ago. Though someone as large as Yasha didn't squirm so much as shift, and the Range Rover shifted with him. Yasha would shift; Rake would sigh. Just because he understood the reason for it didn't mean he wanted to put up with it. I had to admit, it wasn't exactly soothing to have a massive Russian almost werewolf disguised as a huge German shepherd in the backseat. We'd suffer in silence. At least I would. Rake's sighs were turning to snarls. Yasha wasn't the only creature with fangs in the car. Rake and I both knew Yasha was worried sick about Ian, but I wasn't sure if he'd ever been in a moving vehicle that he wasn't driving. At least in four-legged form, Yasha couldn't be a backseat driver. Though he could grumble—and grumble he did—until Kitty pulled his front half over into her lap and started rubbing his ears. Grumbles promptly turned to a prolonged groan. *That* would keep Yasha happy for a while.

Before we arrived at the marina, Kitty continued my education in all things portal, and made sure that Kylie had realistic expectations of what we could find—and would not find.

"There is a possibility," she said, "a remote one, but still a possibility, that Janus will not have opened the portal on Pollepel yet. If he was concerned about it being located, or is simply cautious, he could keep it closed until he needs to set up the ritual. At that point, he'll have to come out onto the island itself. If he needs the power boost that the intersecting ley lines will give him, he can't work his ritual while inside of his pocket dimension, even if it's directly over the ley lines. The ley lines' power can't pass through the island into a dimensional wall."

"Even if it's the summer solstice and all veils, dimensions, whatever are thinner?" I asked.

"Not even then. He must have direct contact with the land. He will have to come out before midnight."

Roy chuckled grimly. "And when he does, we'll be waiting with some firepower of our own."

"Even if he's hidden in a pocket dimension, won't he know we're there?" Kylie asked.

"Oh yes," Rake said.

That earned him scowls from everyone else in the vehicle.

"I'm not trying to be the bearer of bad news," he continued, "merely stating fact. A mage doesn't live as long as he has without knowing every trick in the book, and writing a lot of them himself. He'll know we're there. The question is, will he be cocky enough to think we can't do anything to stop him, or will he take action now?" He paused. "Which is why no one is to go anywhere alone. He already has Ian. We don't want him getting his hands on anyone else."

Rake didn't shoot a meaningful look at anybody, but I knew he meant me and Kitty. We were the portal finders. Rake would locate where the ley lines intersected, though I had a feeling that after my experience on North Brother Island I wouldn't be too shabby at that job myself. I had a feeling that my newfound portal-finding skills were due in part to my contact with those ley lines—and the seven cursed diamonds they'd activated.

But I wouldn't go off anywhere on my own. I had no intention of giving Janus any more than he already had.

"How are your goblin friends getting here?" I asked Rake.

"Same way Janus did. A portal. They have the coordinates. I'll let them know when we have confirmation that's where tonight's party will be."

"Party?"

"These people live for things like this. Hunting down sea monsters descended from gods is their idea of a fun night out."

30

I didn't know how much money Rake had donated to the Bannerman Castle Trust, but it must have been a lot.

The two representatives of the Bannerman Castle Trust were delighted to give their new patron and his friends a tour of the island and castle. When someone is donating that much, it was a given that they wanted to see what their investment would be used for.

It was a bright, sunny day. It didn't matter that it was a weekday, the Hudson River, and state parks around Pollepel Island would be full of people. We were getting there during the day, so we'd be ready to move when night came. The moment Kitty and I confirmed that there were one or more portals on Pollepel Island, we'd notify Alain Moreau, who would put things in motion there. The commando teams were packing and preparing now. All they were waiting on was a green light from us.

I didn't know how Moreau was planning to get two fully equipped commando teams here. The most efficient way would be by air. Black helicopters attracted attention anywhere, but especially in the skies around New York City. Then there was the issue of a staging area. I glanced over at Roy. As we approached the island, he had his tablet out, looking around, and then tapping away. That was Roy's job, and he was eminently qualified.

My job and Kitty's was to find that portal. Kylie was here to tap into her bond with Ian and, if possible, locate him. Until we did our jobs, Roy and Sandra's people couldn't do theirs.

I was carrying a weapon for Ian—Lugh's Spear. We didn't have any way of knowing if it would be needed, or if it would do any good, but Ian was Lugh's descendant, and the spear had already proven that it recognized him. Better to have it and not need it than to not have it and definitely need it. Lugh had killed Balor, broken the Fomorians, and forced them into the sea with this spear by his side, so I wasn't about to leave it in the lab.

I had the spearhead in a backpack. If the spear had liked Ian in the lab, I was hoping it'd work like a divining rod here. Stranger things happened in my life every day. It was all in how you defined strange. Most folk's strange was my ho-hum, daily routine.

The lab had put it in a padded silk pouch. For some reason, silk didn't block supernatural weapon vibes. I wanted it to react when I got close to Ian—portal or no portal—but at the same time, I didn't want to have to explain my backpack glowing, or possibly even worse, vibrating.

Yasha smelled Fomorians before we'd even set foot on the island.

I sat in the absolute center of the boat. This part of the Hudson River was deep enough to hide a kraken, and I had no desire to look over the side and see an eye the size of a VW Bug staring back at me.

We'd set up a signal for Yasha smelling Fomorians, ghouls, or Janus himself. During our last encounter with Janus under Times Square on New Year's Eve, Yasha had been in his werewolf form and had gotten a good snootful of what Janus smelled like.

One bark was for fish men. Two barks meant Janus.

As we crossed the river, it'd been nothing but single barks. Fortunately, there'd been plenty of them. That was good; that meant we were in the right place.

What I wanted most was a double.

I'd hoped to feel something the moment I set foot on the Pollepel Island dock.

I was disappointed.

Then again, none of us would have actual contact with the land itself until we reached the top of the stairway that the Trust had constructed to make the island more accessible to tour groups. Getting there was easy for me since I had Yasha pulling at his leash the entire way up. I didn't think he was sensing anything we couldn't; he knew Ian was here somewhere and wanted to find him now.

Rake was a multitasking master. He was talking with the Trust people, asking probing questions, while simultaneously probing with his magic. Fortunately, the rest of us didn't have to hide what we were doing. We were here to be curious and look around.

When Yasha and I reached the top of the stairs and set foot on the island, the ley lines' power vibrated up from the core of the island through the soles of my feet to the top of my head.

Yasha barked happily.

I reached down and patted his shoulder. "You said it, buddy." I looked down at Kylie, who wasn't far behind me, and grinned.

The dryad ran up the rest of the stairs. "Ley lines?"

"Oh yeah. Feels like there's a subway train running under here."

She squeezed my arm and took a shuddering breath. We were all wearing sunglasses, but I think Kylie might have been a little teary-eyed. I was blaming my misties on the pollen.

She started to pull away.

"We stay together, remember?"

Kylie stopped. "Dammit."

"I feel the same way, but we don't want to give Ian reason to yell at us later, because you know he will."

We moved aside to let the others pass. When Rake took his first step onto the island, I was watching for his reaction.

He gave our hosts a dazzling smile. "It's just as I imagined it would be."

Kylie and I resisted the urge to high-five.

It wasn't just us who Janus might go after if he felt we were getting too close. The three representatives of the Trust would be collateral damage. I couldn't see Janus not taking action just because there were a couple of innocent bystanders. To him, they'd be cannon fodder, or whatever ancient Irish warriors used to throw back at their enemies.

We stayed with our hosts throughout the initial tour. Then Rake did his job and started asking construction-type questions about the Trust's plans for the island if they had the funding to do everything they wanted to do. The dock and stairway had been built so that the island and castle could be opened to the public for guided tours. That had happened in the fall of 2003. The Trust's biggest—and most expensive—mission was to stabilize the castle and other island structures, including the house Bannerman had built as a summer residence for his family. The Trust hoped to restore the house and use it as a visitors' center. Once our guide started going into all the restoration details, that was all the distraction the rest of us needed. The Trust's representatives knew we were just friends along for the trip. We acted politely bored, so they gave us an equally polite warning to stay away from the parts of the castle walls that were only upright because they'd been braced.

We went off to explore.

We were all wearing hardhats and Yasha was on a leash. Me, Kylie, and Kitty walked Yasha around the island. Roy was nearby. Even in his human form, Yasha's sense of smell was keen, but in this form and this close to the full moon, anything living or undead that had been on this island in the past two days, the Russian would know about.

Especially if it was Ian.

As to sensing portals and ley lines, Kitty and I wouldn't get in each other's way. When a magic user was doing their thing, having another magic user in the immediate vicinity could interfere with concentration. But Kitty and I weren't working any magic, we were simply opening our senses to what was there.

The island appeared to be deserted.

But not every Fomorian could be contained in whatever pocket dimension Janus had created to house his prisoner. Even if that portal had been opened here for mere seconds, Yasha's sniffer would pick up their scent.

I'd wanted to douse myself with bug spray before setting foot on the island, but that would have interfered with Yasha's sense of smell. A couple of ticks and mosquito welts would be a small price to pay for Ian's survival. That didn't stop me from a serious bout of psychosomatic itching. I'd picked one tick off of myself already, so of course, now I felt like I was crawling with the things.

With a whine, Yasha sat back on his haunches and his rear foot pounded the ground as he tried to scratch under his left armpit, or whatever it was called on a dog. I'd have offered to help, but I had my own itches to contend with.

"Of the few portals I've experienced," I said to Kitty, "all of them have been on a wall: in an apartment, a parking garage, a wine cellar."

"It's easier to conjure them that way," she replied. "And considering what else this Janus has planned for tonight, my guess would be he'd opt for easy. Plus, from what you've told me, he's arrogant enough to believe he wouldn't need to make the extra effort."

A half dome of rock seemed to take up a fourth of the island or more. The top of it was as tall as the tallest wall of the castle.

Roy and I exchanged glances and we all started climbing.

As a team commander, Roy needed to get a look at the entire island for tactical purposes. He'd brought binoculars and a killer camera. The rest of us brought our portal-seeking or Ian-finding senses.

It was seriously windy up there.

Roy got a lot of what he needed. Yasha smelled the Fomorians in the water around the island.

All me, Kitty, and Kylie got was some seriously wind-tangled hair. What we could sense wasn't carried on wind currents.

Spread out below us was six acres of island. Immediately below us was the dock. Beyond that, on the other side of the island were the ruins of the castle. Tucked into the trees on a high point facing downriver was the Bannermans' summer residence. All had walls, even if those walls were propped up as was the case with the castle.

Any of them could contain a portal.

We needed to get into those buildings—buildings that were blocked off by posts and chains.

We ignored them; we had to. We didn't have time to do otherwise.

Rake and the Trust folks were still near the castle, which left us free and clear to explore the remains of the Bannermans' summer home. It was two stories tall and had been constructed with the same island stone that had been used to build the castle. The many windows were boarded up, the doors barred, and all access was roped off. We weren't about to let that stop us. Two towers flanked the main picture window that faced south toward West Point. The house continued behind these and included impressively curved walls filled with windows. If I had that kind of a view from my own private island, I'd have made the most of it, too. Though with the windows covered by black-painted plywood, I got the unsettling impression of a lot of eyes all staring at yours truly.

We made a circuit of the outside of the house. Neither Kitty nor I got any sense of a portal from any of the house's walls. The front door was unsurprisingly padlocked.

"I got this," Kitty said.

I smiled. "Oh yeah, our friendly neighborhood safecracker." I stood aside. "Be my guest."

Within seconds, there was a click and the door was open.

"Portal opener, baker, and safecracker," Roy noted. "I'm impressed."

I made sure my hardhat was as firmly on my head as possible, and stepped through to inside. In the front room, which had probably been the Bannermans' family room, was broken furniture and the remains of an old-fashioned pump organ. I'd remembered reading that Francis Bannerman's wife, Helen, had liked to play. I was surprised the family hadn't taken the organ when they'd moved out for good. Then again, the thing was huge and heavy.

Roy checked the next room before we went in, and then stepped back into the living room so he could keep an eye on us and watch for Rake and our hosts.

We passed through an arched doorway into what had been the kitchen. It was empty of furniture, at least intact furniture. In the corner of the room was a narrow opening in the wall with stairs that had been carved into the rock of the island, leading down to what I assumed would be a root cellar. Even across the room, I felt the cool, damp air coming up from below. Cool enough to almost use it as a refrigerator back when the Bannermans had occupied the house.

The Bannermans weren't here now; something else was. My senses immediately went on full alert. The only thing missing was a flashing neon sign over the opening that said "Evil Villain Lair." Just because I didn't sense a portal didn't mean there wasn't anything down there. Plenty of other senses with a vested interest in my self-preservation were telling me loud and clear not to go down there.

I had every intention of listening.

I glanced over at Kitty and Kylie. Both women were standing utterly still. Kylie was white as a sheet and her breathing had quickened.

So it wasn't just me.

With his hackles up, Yasha cautiously skirted the wall until he was beside the opening. His growl was so low it was more of a vibration in the air. No barking to signify either Fomorians or Janus, but growling was good enough for me. Yasha might not have known what was down there, but he didn't like it one bit. I tossed a questioning glance at Kitty.

The portalkeeper was frowning.

Kitty was the expert, I was the newbie, and we were both confused. There was something else we agreed on without the need to say one word—the need to get out of there. Now.

There was evil beneath this place, beneath this island, evil that was laid on thick enough to make our collective skin crawl. It could be Fomorians or it could be the evil spirits the local Indian tribes had been so afraid of. You didn't walk into a dark hole in the ground unless you were qualified to handle what you found—or what found you. Anyone other than a seasoned battle mage would be woefully—and fatally—unqualified.

We got the hell out.

31

"WHAT was that?" I asked when were safely back outside. While out here might not be any safer than in there, at least we had sunshine.

"It wasn't a portal," Kitty said.

With Roy's help, Kylie shakily lowered herself to a cracked stone bench. I squatted down to Kylie's eye level so she wouldn't have to move. "Did you sense Ian?"

She shook her head. "Ooh, bad idea," she breathed.

"Dizzy?"

"And then some."

It was definitely more than dizziness. The dryad looked like she was about to be sick.

"I don't know if what I sensed was Ian," Kylie panted, "the danger that Ian is in, or how Ian feels right now. It just hit really hard."

Kylie's voice was a bare whisper. She was so nauseated that even speaking was an effort.

While it could have been any of the above, it was probably the latter. Janus's ghouls had sprayed something in Ian's face to knock him out. And to prevent Ian from escaping, fighting, or putting up any kind of resistance, Janus was probably keeping him drugged and sick, and thereby helpless.

Something else Janus was going to pay for.

Kitty sat next to Kylie, her arm around the dryad's shoulders, helping to hold her upright. Yasha sat on the ground on her other side, leaning against her leg. Kitty was trying to keep moving to an absolute minimum, including breathing as smoothly as possible so as not to move the shoulder Kylie's head was resting against. I had been this sick before. It'd been on a plane. Too sick to live pretty much described it.

Dryad physiology was similar enough to humans, so I'd given her one of my Dramamine. It would take the edge off of the dizziness and nausea, but it would take time to work.

"Honey, we need to get you back to the dock," I told her. "Why don't you let Roy carry you? You don't need to be walking."

The dryad gave a huffing breath that was meant to be a laugh. "I don't think I could if I had to."

Yep, Janus would definitely be paying for that.

Roy bent and lifted Kylie into his arms as gently as possible, keeping her movement to a minimum. The little dryad laid her head against his chest and closed her eyes as Roy walked as smoothly as he could down the path back toward the dock.

We'd only been walking for a few minutes, when Rake came running toward us. He must have sensed that something was wrong. I jogged forward to meet him, so Kylie wouldn't hear what I was about to say.

"Janus must be keeping Ian drugged. Kylie sensed him and is sharing the sickness."

Rake glanced at the pale dryad curled in Roy's arms and his look was pure murder.

Yep, when Janus showed his faces tonight, there was a long line forming of people who wanted to bash in each and every one of those smarmy mugs.

One of the Trust representatives had caught up to Rake. The poor guy was gasping for air. He saw Kylie being carried and his eyes widened.

"Vertigo," I told him. "She gets it from time to time." I turned to Rake. "You about ready to go?"

"We'll be at the dock in ten minutes," Rake told our host. He took my hand. "Come back to the castle with me. There's something I want you to see."

What used to be the interior of Bannerman Castle was now open to the sky.

I didn't need to get any closer to know where those ley lines intersected—in the exact center of those towering, teetering walls. We were standing on the outside of those walls looking in. The outer ruins of the walls had been braced with some kind of telescoping metal poles to keep them upright. If or when they fell, more than likely they'd be falling in. That was the reason we were staying out. There were several arched doorways that had been part of the original structure. The doors were long gone, but we didn't need doors; we needed to see inside.

A gust of wind swept across the river, and I resisted the urge to back up, way up. A good storm wind could bring them down. But black magic strong enough to break a four-thousand-year-old curse and usher back a race of monsters?

There wouldn't be a brick left standing.

And Ian—and everyone who would be in there trying to rescue him—would be buried in the rubble.

"It's a miracle these walls are still standing," I noted with disgust.

"I felt the ley lines loud and clear, but I wanted a second opinion."

"You've got it."

"Did the spearhead react when Kylie did?"

"Not a peep. Tell you the truth, I'd forgotten that I'm even carrying the thing. Maybe it needs direct contact with Ian."

"Maybe," Rake said, but his attention was elsewhere. He was squinting at something past the weeds and briars, a lot of which was waist high on me.

"I didn't see that before," he murmured.

"What is it?"

Rake didn't answer. He quickly walked down a path that'd been cleared through the brambles, a path that ran parallel to the shortest of the castle walls, which was still at least a story and a half. Rake stopped when he got to an opening that let him see to the center, and whispered a curse.

I caught up with him and looked where he was looking.

My blood ran cold. I was glad we'd gone to the house earlier. If we'd come here instead, Kylie would have seen this.

This end of the island was covered with fallen stone from the collapsed section of the castle, with piles of stone scattered haphazardly around the ruins.

Not all of the stones had been left where they'd fallen. Some had been gathered and carried to the center of the ruins.

And stacked into an altar.

The trip from the island back to the marina was quiet.

Rake and I told Roy what we'd found. Rake had made a quick trip inside the walls to get a better look at that altar. The undergrowth around the altar had been very recently trampled by whoever or whatever had stacked those stones.

Before we'd boarded the boat, Roy had called Alain Moreau to report. By the time we pulled away from the island's dock, our commando teams were on their way.

Rake and Roy chatted with the Bannerman Castle Trust representatives in the front of the boat, while Kitty and I stayed with Kylie. The dryad was stretched out on one of the bench seats, Yasha at her side.

She was getting some of her color back as the Dramamine took effect. As far as the Trust people knew, Kylie was having a bout of vertigo. Which, considering how she felt, wasn't too far off the mark. As her head began to clear and she could think, Kylie believed that part of what she'd sensed had been Ian. It had only lasted for an instant, but it'd been long enough.

"Can you describe where he was?" I asked.

Kylie started to shake her head then groaned at the movement.

"That's okay, sweetie. You stay still. I'll take that as a no."

"It was dark and cold," she managed.

I sat back, fighting the urge to punch something. Ian was somewhere deep in the interior of that island.

Rake had in turn asked our hosts about tunnels on the island. Yes, they'd told him, there were tunnels and even some caves. And from what we'd sensed in the Bannermans' kitchen, one of the ways to access those tunnels was through their root cellar. Though Ian was too important to Janus to risk keeping him in one of the caves. Janus would have had a pocket dimension there. But with the ley lines intersecting in the castle ruins, Janus had to bring Ian to the surface tonight. And when he did, we would be waiting for him.

Even though Kitty and I hadn't found a portal to that pocket dimension, Kylie's experience had given us all the confirmation we needed that Ian was there.

And so had the altar.

Kylie hadn't seen that, and I wasn't going to tell her. Rake and I had agreed that was need-to-know information, and Kylie most definitely did not need to know. The people who needed to know did know, and they were on their way here to do something about it.

It was mid-afternoon, and the campers, hikers, boaters, picnickers, and general tree-loving city folk looking to get out of the city for a day were about to have a lot of heavily armed company.

32

SPI was having a company picnic.

Grilling wasn't allowed in Hudson Highlands State Park, which was located right across the river from the island, but that hadn't stopped our commando teams from enjoying one heck of a spread. Though it had to be the most solemn picnic in the history of this or any other state park.

The food had been cooked in the city— and brought here— by Bill and Nancy Garrison.

Bill and Nancy were the owners of the Full Moon, a slice of Southern hospitality down the street from SPI headquarters. It was a meat lover's paradise where the steaks were rare, the barbeque tangy, and the iced tea had enough sugar in it to make a spoon stand straight up.

Bill and Nancy were from the barbeque mecca that was my home state of North Carolina.

They were also werewolves, as were three of their staff who'd come with them—their office manager, the bartender, and Bill's assistant pit master. The bartender was still young as werewolves went, and was wearing warmup pants and long sleeves to hide his impending furriness. The rest were old and mature enough to hold it together at least until after dark.

Five werewolves hosting a picnic for mostly supernatural commandos a few hours shy of a full moon.

Yeah, that was probably a first for any state park, too.

Roy had wanted his and Sandra's teams here in plenty of time to go over how they were getting to the island, approaches to the castle ruins, and any opposition they were likely to encounter. I could think of one large opponent in particular, but Roy didn't seem too concerned about the kraken. Since he was in charge of this operation, I was glad he had a plan for dealing with or, more likely, avoiding it.

Gathering that many people in a state park called for a reason that'd be believable to anyone who might happen past. Food always worked. And considering what these people would be doing tonight, they needed a good meal before they did it. A few of the Hudson Highlands park rangers were elves. They had been contacted and told that we would be in the park tonight. It helped to have good friends in leafy places. Hiding nearly two dozen military types in plain sight was almost as difficult as hiding werewolves in broad daylight; yet right now, our people were doing both.

Alain Moreau was wearing jeans, a long-sleeved T-shirt, sunglasses, and an actual baseball cap. I almost didn't recognize him.

Even though Moreau was in the shade on the other side of the clearing our people had claimed for their own, I still lowered my voice because vampires had better hearing than even goblins. "How'd you talk him into letting you come up here?" I asked Bill and Nancy.

"Two of Roy's boys were having lunch when the call came in," Bill said. "We knew what had happened to Ian, and that the teams were waiting to hear where he was being held. We asked the boys where and they told us. They probably shouldn't have, but they didn't see the harm. When we called Alain, we didn't tell him how we found out, and we assured him we just wanted to help. We'll stay here with the vehicles to make sure they're here when y'all get back. Wouldn't be the first time an enemy tried to sabotage an exit."

"And since we were coming, we told Alain that we would bring food," Nancy said. "These boys and girls need to eat."

"Can't storm the castle on an empty stomach," I agreed. "Morcau didn't tell you to stay away?"

"He said he would prefer it if we did."

"And you told him you'd prefer to come."

"That's right."

Bill glanced out over the Hudson River and grinned. "I've always had me a taste for seafood."

"There's some exotic eatin' in there," I warned him. "And big."

"I've always been an adventuresome diner. Twice I brought in the biggest catch at the Big Rock Blue Marlin Tournament. My best was a six hundred pounder. I've always enjoyed a good fight."

It wasn't like Bill didn't know what a fight was. He'd been stationed down at Lejeune. Before he and Nancy had moved to New York, Bill had been a Marine master sergeant, and Nancy's dad had been his CO—a dad who raised his kids like Marines.

Nancy laid a hand on my arm. "Sweetheart, we consider Ian one of our own. If there was anything we could do to help, you know we're going to do it. And now I'm especially glad we're here so we can take care of Ian's girlfriend."

Nancy had immediately taken charge of Kylie, who was now asleep in a nest of blankets in the back of the Garrisons' Tahoe.

What could I say? I had to say something or well up with tears again. I swallowed. "Thank you. I know Ian will appreciate it. He won't like you putting yourselves anywhere near danger, but he'll appreciate that you're here and looking out for Kylie."

Nancy smiled and patted my arm.

Bill beamed. "And when he's back I'll grill him the biggest and best steak he's ever had in his life."

"In the meantime," Nancy said brightly. "Can I fix you a plate?"

SPI commando Calvin Miles was armed for Fomorian. He didn't have magic, but he had plenty of muscle—and heart. Yesterday morning, Alain Moreau had assigned Calvin and Liz to guard Ian, and Ian had been taken by the very creature they'd been tasked with protecting him from. I was Ian's partner, and I had felt the same sense of failure, but there was a big difference. I wasn't a commando; no one expected me to be able to protect Ian from anything, let alone a warrior mage from an ancient race of supernatural sea monsters. Heck, Ian had been assigned as my partner to protect *me*. No one expected me to run to anyone's rescue.

"It's our job to rescue, to protect," Calvin said quietly after he finished his third burger. "Me and Liz, we didn't do our job."

"There was a four-inch-thick fire door followed by a closed and locked bank vault between you and Ian," I reminded him.

"Doesn't matter."

"I suppose it also doesn't matter that the entire setup had been a trap to get Ian inside and keep everyone else outside, and that Janus had been planning this for years."

"No, it doesn't."

"And that the thing doing the planning is some kind of

supersorcerer, and was the right hand of the Irish god of blight and destruction."

"Nope, doesn't matter. We still failed." Then Calvin looked at me and smiled for the first time since Ian had been taken. "But we're gonna make up for it tonight."

A massive—and thankfully familiar—figure strolled out of the trees toward Alain Moreau. That he was instantly the target of every commando in the clearing didn't faze him in the least.

Vlad Cervenka.

"Stand down," Moreau called out. "He's a friendly."

"I don't know if I'd say that, Mr. Moreau," Vlad told him. "I do know that for tonight we have the same enemy."

For the time being, Yasha had dispensed with pretending to be a German shepherd, and came forward to shake his friend's hand.

"Let me guess," I said. "Ambrus Báthory has paid you to retrieve his First Relics."

"As did the heads of the Frontino, Ruthven, and Tepes families." The vampire shrugged. "If I'm collecting one box, what's a few more?"

"Does Mr. Báthory know about the others?"

Vlad shook his head. "And the others don't know about him. My business is my business. There is no reason to tell them."

I nodded in approval. "Get paid three times for doing the same job."

"More, actually." Vlad had a military-style duffel bag slung over one huge shoulder. "I intend to get all of them, contact the owners, and negotiate a fair recovery fee."

"Enterprising," Moreau said.

"I've never been opposed to extra income. Though I did

tell my clients that if they entrusted me to get their property back, I would recruit my usual expert help." He jerked his big blond head back toward the trees where he'd come from. "The heads of the families are familiar with the quality of our work. My team is staying out of the sun."

"Youngsters?" I asked.

Vlad grinned. "Just saving their strength for the job. They are conscientious workers."

Roy had wandered over and looked at the six-foot-eight vampire with approval. Then he glanced at Moreau. "Permission to share a little, sir?" The Cajun commander grinned. "Seeing that I think he and his friends are going in regardless of whether we want him to or not."

Moreau nodded. "Agreed. Though he knows about Janus taking Ian, just not the details."

"Then you know we're going in there to rescue one of our own," Roy said to Vlad. "Janus will be using those relics to boost this ritual he's doing, which involves him sacrificing our agent. Chances are the relics and our man will be in close proximity, meaning we're all heading for the same place."

"And you intend to kill anything that keeps you from getting there?" Vlad asked.

"That's the plan. I sure as hell don't think they're gonna step aside if we ask nicely."

The vampire's pale eyes glittered. "I was not going to ask."

Roy grinned. "A man after my own heart."

"I will be going in with my people," Moreau told Vlad. "We can increase our chances of success if we act together. Yasha Kazakov tells me that you are a man of honor, a man whose word, once given, is his bond."

"If you do not have honor, you are not a man."

"Wisely said. I propose an alliance. You and your friends help us retrieve our agent; we will assist you with the relics.

It is in everyone's best interests if all of the stolen relics are returned to their families. That is your intent, is it not?"

"It is." The vampire grinned. "Any day I can maintain my honor and make a profit is a good day."

The sun had gone down behind Storm King Mountain.

Our section of the park was empty, as had been confirmed by our park ranger friends.

Time to get ready to go.

"Makenna."

I stopped.

Alain Moreau's voice hadn't been loud. It didn't need to be. The entire conversation we were about to have had just been summed up by using my first name rather than "Agent Fraser." I'd heard the same on numerous occasions from my mom or Grandma Fraser when I'd been on my way out of the house to do something I had no business getting into. Though if it'd been Mom or Grandma Fraser, they'd have used "Makenna Anne" or "Makenna Anne Fraser."

Alain Moreau was about to strongly suggest that I stay on this side of the river tonight. Actually, it'd be more like an order. Though orders came from mere managers. Commands came from managers who were also vampires.

And I knew all of this from the sound of my name.

Vivienne Sagadraco could read my thoughts; and when she allowed me to, I could read hers. Alain Moreau had that vampire mind-reading thing going on. As a vampire—and me as a human—he could also influence my thoughts.

I knew he wouldn't do that.

"I have to go, sir," I said quietly. "Please don't ask me to stay away." I paused and gathered my nerve for what I had to say. It'd been running through my mind in a near-constant loop, but it was time to say it out loud. "If we can't get Ian back, and there was something I could have done to help, I'd never be able to forgive myself. At that point, I might as well be dead, too. Can you understand that?"

It was hard to read emotion on a vampire. It wasn't that they didn't have any; they had plenty. My theory was that when you didn't breathe, your facial muscles simply didn't move all that much.

Alain Moreau wasn't moving now.

I would rather it if he did.

"I understand," he finally said. "You understand that it is my job to keep my people from needless risk."

"This risk isn't needless, sir."

"I know. Not for someone who is qualified to take that risk. You're not qualified. You know this."

It took everything I had to keep my voice level and calm. "Yes, sir, I do know. I'll be with Rake. He's already tried to talk me out of it and knows that he can't. Our commandos don't need to watch out for me. I'd never jeopardize a mission by being a burden on our people. And I know I'm not qualified to go up against any of those Fomorians. What skills I do have probably won't be needed—but they might. If they are, and I'm not there to help . . . well, sir, like I said, I'd never forgive myself."

"I don't doubt your bravery, Makenna."

I half smiled. "I'm glad one of us thinks I'm being brave right now. Truth is, I'm scared to death of what's over there, and what's between us and what's over there; but I can't and won't let that stop me from doing what I know is right, what I know I have to do."

Moreau was looking over my left shoulder.

I half turned.

Rake stood in the shadows, leaning against a tree.

"I see you're not having any better luck," the goblin noted wryly.

"You expected me to?" Moreau asked.

"Not really." Rake pushed away from the tree with his shoulder, and walked over to us. "Though not due to any lack of persuasiveness on your part, but due to Makenna's determination."

I snorted. "At least you didn't call me stubborn."

"I was being diplomatic. I'll see to it that Makenna won't be involved in any ground fighting," he told Moreau, "and will be able to retreat quickly, if need be."

Rake and Moreau exchanged a look. The vampire almost smiled and nodded. "Very well."

I glanced back and forth between them. "*Ground* fighting? As opposed to what?"

33

RAKE led me, Roy, Sandra, and Moreau to a clearing the size of school baseball field.

It was empty, but Rake held up a hand and we all stopped on the edge of the tree line, waiting for what, I had no clue.

I didn't have to wait long for my clue—or to be nearly knocked to the ground by a sudden burst of wind and stink of sulfur as something massive blocked out the moon and soared overhead.

Dragon.

The last time a dragon had swooped that close over my head, it'd been Vivienne Sagadraco's dragon sister Tiamat nearly roasting and eviscerating me in the middle of Times Square on New Year's Eve.

No one else threw themselves to the ground, so I held still.

I did, however, duck my head when the next one came in for a landing.

"Where are they coming—"

"They're with us," Rake assured me with a fierce smile. "Janus isn't the only one who can play with portals." He walked a little way out into the clearing, turned and pointed up.

The night sky was dark, but a square of starless black was open in the sky just above the trees. It was about the length and height of a tractor trailer—just wide enough and tall enough to admit the dragons as they flew through the portal from wherever they'd come from.

In their dragon forms, Vivienne Sagadraco and her sister Tiamat were as tall as three-story buildings. The dragons and their riders that were coming through the portal at the rate of one every thirty seconds were smaller, but no less awe inspiring.

"Your transportation, Commanders," Rake said with a flourish. "As promised."

"I must admit," Sandra said. "They are impressive."

"We call them sentry dragons," Rake said with no small measure of pride. "Fire-breathing, nimble, and intelligent. They're used by the military and law enforcement back home."

I think my mouth had fallen open. "What the NYPD wouldn't give for some of those." Then my eyes widened to match my gaping mouth as I realized why Roy hadn't been concerned about getting over to the island without being attacked by the kraken.

"We're flying over on those." I didn't ask it as a question, more as a statement of disbelief.

"Yes, we are." Rake started across the clearing toward the line of eleven sentry dragons. Their armored goblin riders had dismounted, and the one who had been the first to come through the portal waved to Rake.

"Captain Calik Bakari," Rake told us by way of introduction as we got closer. "A friend, and one of the best dragon pilots you'll ever meet."

"And the others?" Sandra asked. "Are they police, or—"

"Rheskilian Royal Fighter Squadron," Rake replied. "Calik and his squad patrol the area off the coast of Davans Perch back home. Calik and I have known each other almost all our lives. They're similar to the Coast Guard here."

"And their commander approved this?" Roy asked.

Rake grinned. "That would be Calik; so yes, he did."

The goblin captain removed his helmet, revealing a boyishly handsome face with a cheerful smile—that is if anything with fangs could be described as cheerful.

"Based on what Rake said you needed done," Calik said, "I thought a quarter of my people would be sufficient. We can't exactly run off for a few hours and leave the coast unguarded right now."

Rake frowned. "Problems?"

"Probably. The Khrynsani found some new friends to play with. Off-world friends with their own army."

Rake started to ask another question, but Calik raised his hand. "Later. Come meet your transportation."

And with that, I got closer to a sentry dragon than I'd ever wanted to be.

Their bodies were the size of Clydesdales, each bat-like wing the width of a two-lane road. The eyes were saucer-sized with a slit pupil, and they contained way too much intelligence, an intelligence that seemed to be wondering what barbeque sauce would go best with me.

The sulfur smell came from the dragon's insides. The insides of his nostrils glowed orange with restrained flame. If he'd have sneezed, the goblin holding his reins would've been toast.

"They're nimble, and quick enough to fly and land pretty much anywhere they want to," Calik told us. "They're popular with our military and law enforcement in our larger cities."

"I can see why," Sandra said.

"You did say you had a way to get us over there," I admitted to Rake.

"Yes."

"This was it all the time."

"Yes."

"Why didn't you tell me?"

"Because I knew you wouldn't like it and it's the best option we have."

"If I survive this, we're gonna have a discussion about your forthrightness."

"You will survive, and I'll look forward to it."

"No, you won't," I muttered.

Rake's out of town friends were armored, but it wasn't like any armor that I had ever seen. Roy and Sandra coolly assessed the newcomers. They'd never seen their like before—at least not in our dimension.

The dragons and their riders were armored and equipped for getting Ian off of that island, and leaving no survivors after they'd done it. They were in black from head to toe, including boots that came up to mid thigh. Their armor was leather and matte black steel; they were wearing blades anywhere and everywhere they had room, and both men and women wore their long black hair pulled back in a single goblin battle braid. They were Death personified; that is, if Death wore really hot boots.

I had a feeling that once these goblins got within killing distance of Fomorians, things were going to get real ugly, real fast.

It would be beautiful.

Rake's eyes scanned the line of dragons and stopped when it got to one that was missing something very important—a rider. He smiled and hurried over. I ran to catch up.

"Uh, where's its pilot?" I asked.

Rake's smile broadened into a grin. "You're looking at him, lovely Makenna."

"Excuse me?"

"I'm going to the island. *We're* going to the island— unless you come to your senses between now and then."

"I won't."

"Then how could we possibly get to the island without transportation?"

Each dragon had a saddle that would carry two riders. We had twenty commandos; there were ten dragons. Two trips over for each dragon. We could have everyone on the island without kraken interference in less than five minutes.

Okay, this could work.

Rake must have seen on my face that he'd won me over.

"Not so fast, flyboy. Just how good are you on this thing?"

"Been flying sentries and their smaller cousins since I was a boy. I was raised in Davans Perch. Its cliffs overlook the Sea of Kenyon and are surrounded by mountains much like these." His dark eyes were sparkling with gleeful antic-ipation. "I'm good at many things." He lowered his voice. "I'm exceptional at a few. Flying sentry dragons is but one of them. Did you bring the extra flight armor?" Rake called back to Calik.

Calik sauntered over and glanced down at me with a toothy grin. "I did. And I think it'll fit her perfectly." He handed me what looked like a leather cat suit. "That's the base. Put that on and Rake can help you with the rest."

Oh boy.

Rake propelled me toward a rhododendron hedge with a hand at the small of my back. "You can change over there. If we're going to die in battle, we goblins believe in leaving behind a good-looking corpse."

34

IT took about half an hour, but when I'd gotten strapped and buckled into all the pieces and parts of the goblin flight suit, I was armored enough to help keep me alive. I had to admit, it was comfortable. If I couldn't actually be a badass, at least I could look like one. I didn't think it'd be enough to fool a Fomorian, but I could hope. As to armaments, bullets might or might not work against the types of Fomorians we found on the island. I had two guns on me, but while my shooting skills had improved a lot, that was on SPI's firing range, not in a combat situation. There was a whole world of difference, a world I wasn't qualified to participate in. My guns were strictly for defense; I'd leave the offense to the professionals.

In addition to my usual daggers, Sandra had pulled me aside to give me a present from Harald Siggurson—a leather scabbard for the spearhead. I had it strapped to my thigh like a dagger; and in a pinch, I could use it like one. Nothing happened when I touched it, and like on the island, it wasn't giving any indication that anything was going on, which made it worthless for anything but stabbing Fomorians. Though on the upside, at least it didn't mind that I wasn't Ian. I was carrying it now on the off chance that I could get it to Ian, and now that the spearhead had made Ian more than human, he could use it somehow. Of course, any of that was unlikely with Janus keeping Ian drugged and helpless, but I wasn't about to leave anything behind that might be of use.

I was as ready as I ever would be.

I went to find Rake.

Calik had to point him out to me. Even then, it was next to impossible to see the black-clad, gray-skinned goblin concealed in the trees next to the shoreline.

Only a thousand feet of the Hudson separated us from Pollepel Island—and Ian.

Twigs snapped and leaves crunched beneath my boots as I made my way down to the river's edge where Rake stood.

"I make more noise than a bull in a china shop." Even so, I kept my voice down.

"You're human," he said as if that explained everything. It did.

Rake was a goblin dark mage, a master of magic who moved with the stealth and intense focus of a panther on the prowl. I was still fumbling with my new magical skills, and my movement? See above regarding bull in china shop.

We were an odd couple, yet Rake kept insisting that we were a couple.

And I was kind of starting to believe him.

The reflection of the full moon on the river made it look more like twilight than full night. It'd make it easier for the humans in our group to see. However, it also made it easier for whatever guards Janus had posted on the island to see us, and who knows what lurked between us and the island.

I gazed out over the river.

Including what swam just beneath the surface.

There was no wind, so the river shouldn't have been moving like it was. Something was causing the surface to ripple and swirl. Just because we couldn't see it didn't mean it wasn't there.

Not only had Janus picked a castle, he'd found one with its own nature-made moat.

"Do Calik and his people know about the kraken?"

"They do."

"Good. Cause that'd suck to get snatched out of midair."

"It most certainly would."

"Though the Fomorians—and anybody else around here—will see dragons flying over the Hudson. You wouldn't happen to have a fix for that in your bag of tricks, would you?"

"As a matter of fact, mounted into the dragons' chest harnesses are ward stones that can put a veil around both dragons and riders."

"Nifty. What happens if or when we have to get off of the dragon?"

"Then we're on our own."

I looked back over at the island.

It had changed.

There was what looked like a halo around it, like the haze you'd see around the moon. It extended out into the river in all directions a couple of hundred feet, and even higher into the dark sky above the island itself.

"What is that? Can we get through it?"

"Oh yes. It's a gift from the Fomorians," Rake said. "I've been standing here watching it go up."

"I wouldn't call anything from a Fomorian a gift."

"This one is. That light makes the island look deserted, quiet."

"Too quiet."

Rake nodded. "Which is their intention. They don't want to attract attention. It's a shield that will make any mortal who looks at the island this night see what they expect to see; and even more important, hear only the normal sounds of the night."

"A soundproof battlefield," I noted with approval. "Just what the doctor ordered."

"Janus doesn't want his ritual disturbed."

I gazed at the haze with a tight smile. "You can't always get what you want. If you try sometimes, you just might find, you get what you deserve."

The highlands rose on both sides of the river. On the opposite bank, slightly downriver loomed Storm King Mountain. I tried to use the view to help ease my growing anxiety.

"These mountains remind me of home," I said.

"They do for me as well," Rake murmured from my side. "I've always thought it would be nice to have a weekend home here. The mountains near my home in Davans Perch are very similar to these." He was silent for a few seconds. "Is there anything I can do to convince you to stay here?"

"We've had this discussion."

"And there is time for us to have it once more."

"My answer's the same."

"Makenna, I—"

I reached down and took his hand. "I know how you feel."

"No, you don't." Rake moved closer, his breath soft against my cheek. "I don't want to lose you."

"You're not going—"

"I *can't* lose you."

That shut me up.

"I can't imagine my life now without you in it."

I searched Rake's dark gaze and saw something I'd never seen before—at least not on Rake.

Fear.

He wasn't afraid of what we were walking into or what we would have to face and fight once we got there. Rake Danescu was genuinely afraid of losing me. Goblins didn't admit vulnerability lightly, if at all.

"These things are an ancient race, Makenna. Some would say they are gods."

"I'm not one of them."

"Nor am I. But that does not change the fact that they have capabilities far beyond human."

"Are you saying I can't handle it?" I wasn't defensive, merely curious. I'd felt outclassed since my first day at SPI. Tonight would just be one more time that I felt out of my league. But I knew what Rake was implying—this time was different. This time death was a real possibility. I wasn't buying it. "So sea monster deities are more dangerous than Isidor Silvanus, Lucifer's lieutenant, and the hosts of Hell? Because we all came out of that one just fine."

"Luck runs out for all of us."

"Luck had nothing to do with that. It was determination, skill, and cunning. Well, you were skillful and cunning. I was just determined." I paused. "And I still am."

Rake sighed and raised my hand to his lips. "Very well."

"Just because I'm going doesn't mean I'm not worried about one very big thing," I admitted.

"Which is?"

"Janus knows we're here. He even went ahead and set up an altar. It's at the exact intersection of those ley lines and tonight's the summer solstice, so it's where and when he has to do his ritual." I wasn't about to say "sacrifice Ian." I was determined that it wasn't going to happen, so I had no intention of giving that act any acknowledgment or power by saying those words out loud. "Yet he's obviously confident that he can keep us from interrupting him. How?"

"We'll find out," Rake said.

"You don't seem concerned about what might be waiting for us."

"I would rather know everything my adversary had planned, but there are times when it simply isn't possible. I accept that, plan for every contingency that I can, and prepare to be flexible if it becomes necessary."

I just looked at him.

"You can't control everything, Makenna."

"That doesn't mean I'm going to stop trying."

He leaned forward and kissed me on top of my head. "And that's one of the reasons why I love you."

I froze. "What?"

He smiled ever so slightly. "I did say that word, didn't I?"

"Yes, you did." I paused. "Do you want to take it back?"

Rake pondered that for a moment. "No. No, I don't."

"I . . . I don't know what to say to that. Well, I do, but I don't think I'm ready to say it yet." I took a deep breath. "But I do feel a very strong need to do this."

I stepped in closer than we already were, stood on tiptoes, took his face in my hands, and kissed him.

Part of it was gratitude. Rake was risking his life to help save Ian. He didn't have to do it, but he was, and I knew I was a big part of the reason behind that. He cared what happed to Ian because he cared about me. No, he loved me. He had just said it. The rest of what I was feeling was something else, something more—maybe almost . . .

I'd intended to kiss him briefly and then pull away, as I'd done on the boat. It wasn't like we had much by way of privacy. However, at that moment of contact, with Rake's lips soft and pliable beneath mine, I suddenly didn't care who saw what we were doing. I wanted to do more; I needed to do more. I pressed my mouth insistently against his, the tip of my tongue exploring the smooth sharpness of his fangs. Rake shivered at the contact, and his breath came in a quick hiss as his arms wrapped around my waist and hips to pull me hard against him, deepening the kiss, devouring me.

"Rake?"

It was Calik.

Rake took his lips away from mine. He was panting. "Dammit."

"I'm sorry, but it's time."

Rake's eyes were midnight pools as he gazed down at me. "Not half as sorry as I am."

Calik made sure we heard him as he left to rejoin the others.

My breathing had taken on a ragged edge. "Rake, I . . ."

He lowered his lips to mine, stopping me from saying what I didn't know how to say—at least not yet.

"With a kiss like that, you don't have to say anything. I firmly believe that actions can speak much louder than words." He smiled slowly, his voice a husky whisper. "And that kiss, my beloved Makenna, was a shout."

35

THERE'S no good way to sneak onto a six-and-a-half-acre island.

Rake and I would be going over in the first wave and staying there. While some of our commandos were also mages, they didn't have the strength to fully conceal a dozen people from sight and sound on a narrow stretch of rocky beach. Rake did. The ward the Fomorians had put on the island kept us from being seen by anyone on the far shore. We needed something to keep the Fomorians from seeing us.

Roy Benoit had put his recon mission from this morning to good use. We didn't land on the island's new docks and stairs. The climb would have left us vulnerable to attack from above, plus we would have to climb all those flights of wooden stairs to get to the top. I remembered from this morning that they'd creaked. The other side of the island hadn't been suitable for a dock, but it was perfect for dragons dropping off passengers, with solid rock leading up to the Bannermans' house and the castle walls beyond. When the next wave of commandos arrived, Roy had told us we'd split up and approach the castle from two sides.

Since we hadn't found the portal, Kitty would be staying with the Garrisons and Kylie. If we did need her, she was a thirty-second dragon flight away.

Some of the dragons would be making one more trip for Yasha, Vlad and friends, and Alain Moreau, who was now dressed like our commandos. Once on the island, Yasha would go full werewolf. I knew that anything that tried to get between him and Ian would be torn to shreds. Vlad ground out his cigar against a boulder and carefully put it on the edge of a picnic table where he could pick it up again when he came back. Confident guy. Though if anyone could survive a battle with an ancient race of gods, it would be Vlad.

The moon was climbing higher in the sky.

An hour until midnight.

It was time to go.

Our dragon crouched as low to the ground as it could, but it was still like trying to mount a Clydesdale. Rake reached up, grabbed the saddle horn with one hand, put a foot in the mounting stirrup and vaulted into the saddle.

I stood there, staring stupidly. "Oh yeah, that's easy."

Rake leaned over and extended his hand down to me.

I would have asked if he was kidding, but I knew he wasn't. I got as close to the dragon as I could, and reached up as far as I could.

Rake bypassed my hand, gripped my forearm, and in one smooth move, swung me up into the saddle behind him. It happened too fast for me to get out a squeak, let alone a scream.

As soon as I had found out how we'd be getting to the island, I'd popped my second Dramamine of the day. I'd arrived here this morning in a helicopter. Now, I was about to fly across the Hudson on the back of an overgrown bat, and somehow I didn't think I was going to like it.

I was right.

I'd picked out a spot between Rake's shoulder blades to keep my eyes on for the trip over. I made the mistake of letting my curiosity get the better of me, and looked down. My logical mind knew we would be in the air for less than a minute, but my lizard brain was positive that I was going to fall off the sky dragon's back right into the kraken's gaping maw. My lower legs were strapped into the stirrup harness, so even if the dragon did a barrel roll and flew upside down, I still wouldn't fall off, though I was certain that if that happened, I'd be praying for a quick death. If by some miracle I made it intact to the other side, my flipping stomach would probably render me unable to do anything but throw up on the feet, fins, whatever of the first Fomorian that jumped out at me. My hands had a death grip on the back of Rake's half of the saddle. Fortunately, there were hand grips built in, or my fingernails would have surely made their own.

The landing was smooth, almost as smooth as Rake's helicopter, and without the noise or the having to duck under rotor blades. Though a helicopter couldn't get mad and roast you like a s'more.

Me, Rake, and Sandra and her team waited in silence for the dragons to return with Roy and his people. Rake concealed the team until then.

The moon provided enough light to see that what the ruins of Bannerman Castle didn't take up on the island, undergrowth did.

There was a path of sorts, from here to the house, that had been more or less tamped down by kayakers who came to see the island and explore the castle, meaning the way was mostly clear if you were only about a foot wide and walked single file. Off-trail were brambles and stone and brick from the decaying buildings. That the footing was uncertain would be putting it mildly. The relatively maintained trails that we had used this morning were at the top of the hill.

We knew where Janus would bring Ian. Getting to the castle ruins through whatever Janus had arranged for us would be the hard part.

SPI's commandos could and would move like wraiths in absolute silence because that was how they moved all the time, even though there was no point in tiptoeing when the bad guys knew we were here. Whether Janus had guards stationed to ensure we didn't make it to the castle in one piece was a question I wasn't in a hurry to have answered.

The feel of the ley lines running beneath the island had increased from a low thrum to an eager vibration as if the island itself was waking up.

It was.

In my opinion, the ancient Native Americans had had the right idea. This place was best avoided at night, especially a night when the veils between the worlds were thin, when monsters forbidden to walk the land came up from the depths.

It was way too quiet.

That right there told me we were not alone.

Silence was one of the warning signs that there was an apex predator in the area.

It was a warm summer night on an island in the middle of a river. The night should have been alive with crickets, frogs, cicadas, and night birds. Even the wind seemed to be in hiding. Nature recognized evil a lot better than the rest of us, but we didn't have the luxury of hiding until it passed.

The question now became where was the evil and what form would it take?

Janus knew we were here.

My skin felt like it was trying to crawl somewhere and hide. From the night I had first encountered him on an icy street in SoHo, to the abandoned subway tunnel under Times Square, Janus terrified me, and I hadn't even been the one he'd been stalking for years. Grandma Fraser had always said that the scariest thing I'd ever face in my life was the unknown. Regardless of what the unknown turned out to be, it'd never be as terrifying as what I would come up with in my own head. Sometimes it sucked to have a vivid imagination.

Janus's goal was to break the curse that had bound his people from taking and ruling what they believed to be rightfully theirs. Lugh Lámhfhada had killed Balor their king with a spear through his eye. With their king gone, the Fomorians had no chance of standing up to the army of the Tuatha Dé Danann. They'd been banished and had stayed that way for four thousand years. I wasn't buying that Janus was doing all of this out of loyalty to his dead king. That would take nobility. Janus was thirteen kinds of evil, but he wasn't noble, and I seriously doubt he ever had been. No, there was something else in it for him.

Power. The ultimate power.

I'd imagine after four thousand years of living in exile, the Fomorians would be grateful as all get-out to the one who freed them.

That was what Janus was counting on.

He wanted to be king.

And to be king, the first thing he had to do was kill Ian and break the curse on a race of sea monsters.

Behind us, the second wave of commandos landed.

Showtime.

The dragons went back to get Yasha, Vlad and friends, and Moreau.

Two mages on each team deployed a magical version of a camo shield in front of their teams as they moved. It wouldn't stop or deflect weapons, but it'd confuse the heck out of an opponent's aim.

Rake's job of concealment was done. Our job was now scouting and air support. We would be flying over the castle ruins and reporting back via headsets to Roy, Sandra, and Moreau. Calik and his squadron's job was to rain flaming destruction on any Fomorians who tried to stop them.

At least this time, I had a rock to stand on to get back into the dragon's saddle.

As far as we knew, Fomorians couldn't fly. Between that and our dragons' harness-mounted ward stones, we felt relatively safe flying over the castle ruins.

Rake banked our dragon over the edge of the island and toward the castle. Just because there wasn't any light coming from inside the castle ruins yet didn't mean no one was inside. The Fomorians were a race of ancient Irish gods/monsters. They'd been waiting for close to four thousand years for this night. They'd chosen this island. The only structure on the island that Janus would find worthy was the castle. Janus's ego alone wouldn't allow him to sacrifice Ian in a clear spot in a briar patch. He would have set the stage for his night of nights in the most dramatic setting he could find. It would need to be bathed in moonlight. Janus wouldn't be satisfied with anything but high-drama, Broadway-caliber lighting.

The light of the full moon illuminated the ruins of the castle walls, but its glow didn't make it to the ground inside. Having spent their exile in the ocean depths, maybe the Fomorians didn't need light—or couldn't tolerate it.

Fear twisted the pit of my stomach.

Or we were horribly wrong about Janus's plans.

Beyond the island, from the deepest part of the river, came a sound like the blowing of a massive horn. It sounded for several seconds then trailed off.

Our dragon jerked beneath us, and Rake pulled back on the reins and said something soothing in Goblin. It didn't work for me and the dragon wasn't buying it, either. Something was being called. It wasn't any of us calling it, so it had to be bad.

Another horn blew from downriver, and a third from upriver.

The other dragons were equally skittish; their pilots struggling to calm them or at least keep them under control. Rake had said sentry dragons were highly intelligent. That these highly intelligent animals wanted to leave told me more than I wanted to know about what was happening.

Rake and I looked all around us. We were at least a hundred feet above the highest point on the island. Nothing moved on the island below us, or in the river around us.

Until it did.

A slice of river in the direct beam of the moon bubbled and roiled as if a submarine was surfacing.

It was bigger and it was worse.

The kraken.

And it was surfacing just off the side of the island where we'd dropped off our commandos.

Rake swore and his hands blazed red with battle magic.

In the sky around us, the pilots who had magic at their beck and call called it, their hands glowing like Rake's. The dragons, including ours, gave what sounded like coughs which apparently pushed the fire up from their lungs—or wherever it came from—and got it ready for launching.

That night on the *Persephone*, I had only seen one or two of the kraken's tentacles. Never in my wildest nightmares did I think the entire beast would be nearly half the size of the island. We were in the air. I could only imagine what this thing looked like from the ground.

· I could see Rake speaking furiously into his headset. The

wind kept me from hearing him, but I wasn't the one who needed the warning.

The kraken reached out with one tentacle, then two, wrapping them around a tree and a boulder, and started pulling itself up on the island.

"Hold on!" Rake yelled over the sounds and flashes of gunfire from below as he put the dragon into a dive toward the beaching kraken.

The dragon knew what to do. When we got close enough, a column of fire blasted from its mouth, setting fire to the tentacle wrapped around the boulder. Other dragons followed suit until it looked like an aerial dogfight out of an old war movie. More tentacles were out of the water, and while launching what looked like a red laser from the palm of his hand, Rake had to bank sharply to avoid a tentacle that snapped like a fleshy whip to knock us out of the sky.

I held on for dear life.

Calik came out of nowhere—swooping close enough to part my hair—and set fire to the tentacle determined to turn me and Rake into fish food. Every time the kraken breached the surface with one of its many pieces and parts, a sky dragon would scorch it for him, her, whatever. The kraken would jerk the burned appendage below the river's surface, and soon the surface of the Hudson was steaming.

The dragons kept the kraken at bay while the commandos ran for the castle walls.

The horns sounded over the water again, and seams of light appeared beneath the surface, opening and disgorging Fomorians, then closing as another opened nearby, resulting in a tide of monsters emerging from the river on every side of the island.

Portals in the water.

I swore. They hadn't been on the island. No wonder we hadn't been able to find them. Janus was a master of portals;

he didn't need a wall as an anchor. He could and was opening portals anywhere. He didn't need to have troops here waiting for us. Once Janus had Ian, he knew we would come. All he had to do was wait until we were right where he wanted us, then open his portals all around us to release his army.

Like Ian in the bank vault, we had been set up.

The kraken was only a distraction.

We'd known there were Fomorians in the water, but assumed that because they were water monsters and the curse was still in place, that they had to stay there.

We were wrong.

Our commandos had the castle walls surrounded.

The Fomorian army emerging from the Hudson had them surrounded.

36

THESE weren't the misshapen mutants from legend with one arm, one leg, or one eye.

These were warriors that were equally at home on land as in the water. They were the things from the yacht and the bank vault. On the yacht, I'd only seen them for a few moments up close, and there hadn't been that many of them.

Now there were hundreds.

We were three dozen.

The Fomorians were armed with tridents and what looked like electrified nets. Bullets wouldn't kill them; at least mine hadn't.

They were here, they were swarming onto the island from the river and forcing our people toward the castle walls. That was where we needed to go, but we'd been planning to stage an attack inside the walls, not be ground to bits against them. The Fomorians were fearless, throwing themselves in front of our guns, a few drawing fire and absorbing bullets so that the many could get past them and, through breaches in the bricks, inside the castle walls.

Smaller creatures scuttled out of the water and over the rocks in waves. They looked like crabs, but they were the size of dogs. Two of our commandos who were closest opened fire, sending shells and crab legs flying, but more just came out of the water to take their place. Our people were being overrun.

The goblins sent their dragons into dives again and again, swooping from the skies, raining fiery death on the Fomorian warriors. One would ignite, be consumed in the dragons' seemingly inextinguishable fire, and fall away, only to have more rise out of the river to take its places.

They were legion.

We were dozens.

A blast of Fomorian magic knocked a goblin from her low-flying dragon, but she hung on to the saddle horn with one hand, and used the long, curved sword she clenched in the other to cleanly slice the offending Fomorian's head from its shoulders as she flew past. Payback thus delivered, she swung herself back into the saddle and banked her dragon around inside the castle walls for another approach.

Our people had fallen back inside the castle walls through an opening. Fomorians must bleed blue, because Alain Moreau was covered in it. Yasha and Vlad worked as a grisly team. Whatever appendage the Fomorians would use to strike at them, the Russian werewolf and Czech vampire would rip it off. Vlad was using one particularly sturdy severed arm to crack attackers' skulls open. Vlad's team mostly used their bare hands. The Czech vampire was right; his people did good work. However, none of it permanently stopped things that could apparently continue to function without brains.

Our teams were using the breach in the castle wall as a choke point.

There were hundreds of Fomorians on the island, but those hundreds had to come at our people a few at a time. The Fomorians could have collapsed the walls and crushed us, but they didn't, and the reason why finally made his appearance.

Light from an unknown source flared to life, illuminating the area inside the castle walls as bright as day. At the center, on the altar we'd seen this morning, was a sight I'd expected and dreaded.

An unconscious Ian was being bound hand and foot to the altar by four Fomorians. The clothes he'd been wearing when he'd been kidnapped were gone, replaced by the same garb worn by the Tuatha Dé Danann I'd seen in Noel's drawings from Ian's dreams—except for his chest, which had been left bare. An elaborately armored Janus loomed over Ian with a dagger, using its sharp tip to trace symbols of fire in the air over him. With each completed symbol, points of multi-colored lights scattered on the altar around Ian glowed brighter.

The stolen cursed gems.

Placed among the glittering gems were the white, yellow, and brown bones of the vampire families' First Relics—their ultimate and most powerful ancestors.

The Fomorians quickly stepped away from the altar. As soon as they were clear, a nearly transparent dome arched over Janus's head, its glowing nimbus enclosing Ian, the altar, and the objects of power surrounding him.

We hadn't seen Janus appear with Ian. The portal had to have opened right next to the altar. I hadn't sensed it this morning; I couldn't sense it now. The strength of the intersecting ley lines had completely hidden any sign of the portal. And now it was enclosed in the dome, and the dome's base was sunk into the bedrock of the island, feeding off of the power of two of the most powerful ley lines on the planet—fueled by the power of the earth itself.

Janus had solved the problem of how to sacrifice Ian over the ley line nexus, yet keep everyone out and make us watch helplessly. And when he was done, Janus could simply open his portal and escape the way he came in.

Janus hadn't tried to stop us from reaching the island. He wanted us here. He wanted an audience for his greatest triumph. Then he'd tell his Fomorians to obliterate us.

A gout of dragon fire grazed the top of the dome—and was reflected and shot back at the dragon who'd breathed it. The goblin pilot sent it into a dive, barely avoiding being immolated by its own fire. Janus was ignoring the chaos and destruction around him, the dragons' flames unable to reach him.

We had to land. I didn't know how we could get through that shield, but we couldn't do it from where we were.

I drew breath to make myself heard. "Rake, we—"

"Hold on," Rake shouted. "We're going in."

Going in meant dropping directly to the ground beneath us. All the Dramamine in the world couldn't stop the disorienting wave of nausea as my stomach felt like it met my throat. It probably had. Rake reached back and with two snaps had disengaged my leg harnesses. My dismount turned into falling off.

Rake's hands were glowing a red so dark they were almost black.

He'd seen the dragon's fire ricochet right back at him, he knew the consequences, and he wasn't suicidal.

I kept my mouth shut, got out of the way, and watched his back.

Rake released his spell and it engulfed the dome, the surface crackling and popping. At first it appeared to be eating its way through Janus's dome. Then the dome's glow flared, absorbed Rake's red spell, and became even stronger.

"Admirable effort, Lord Danescu," Janus said, his voice easily carrying over the sounds of battle. He glanced up at the reinforced dome above his head. "Please, feel free to continue. I welcome your assistance."

Janus's voice rang inside the confines of the castle walls. If you'd raised a horde of minions from the depths to do your bidding, you could spare a little magic to make sure they could hear you.

"And I do appreciate it when guests arrive on time," he continued. "I went to such trouble with the arrangements. A curse as ancient as this should not be broken without fanfare." His eyes glittered with unnatural light. "Though I believe the guest list is even more important than the decorations." Janus looked overhead at the sentry dragons. "I'm glad to see you gave careful consideration to your transportation here this evening. My control over my new subjects is tenuous so far as hunting is concerned. Keeping them from swarming your boat today was quite taxing."

So much for my paranoia crossing the river today being misplaced.

Janus glanced down at Ian. "I can't have the guest of honor sleeping through our celebration." He quickly passed the palm of his hand over Ian's face and my partner awoke with a start, struggling against his bonds.

I snarled. No way in hell was I just going to stand—

Rake grabbed my arm. "No."

Janus wanted to repeat history and have Ian conscious and completely aware so he would see his friends surrounded, forced to watch helplessly as they were devoured.

My partner may have been tied to an altar, but he was in full command of his faculties—and his vocabulary. If swearing could qualify as a curse, Janus and his army would never see the light of day again.

Janus ignored his captive. "Where is the little dryad who was here with you this morning?" he asked me and Rake.

We chose not to answer.

One of the Fomorians spoke to Janus in a guttural language.

"On shore being watched over by five werewolves and a portal witch," he cheerfully translated. "Take your brothers and the hydra to the shore and kill the werewolves," he told the Fomorian. "Bring the dryad and witch here. It is not quite midnight; we have time for amusement."

A rumbling shook the ground beneath my feet. Movement overhead caught my eye and I looked up. It wasn't the ground that had rumbled; it was the sky. A thick band of clouds came from behind Storm King Mountain on either side, roiling toward Pollepel Island.

"That's not natural," I said. "Did you put in an order for this—"

Rake shook his head. "That level of craft is beyond anyone I know."

For the first time, I saw an expression I'd never seen on Janus's many faces.

The beginnings of fear.

I felt a little surge of satisfaction—and hope. "Looks like Janus didn't invite them, either."

Whoever or whatever was coming, I just prayed they had picked a side, and ours was it.

Janus shouted commands in a language I didn't recognize, his magic magnifying his voice's volume until I had no choice but to press my palms over my ears or risk being deafened. Overhead, the sentry dragons shrieked in what sounded like pain. The effect on the Fomorian army was instantaneous. They broke off their attack on our commandos and rushed to meet the new arrivals, weapons at the ready. Within seconds, the clouds had fully surrounded the island, from the surface of the Hudson to beyond the top of the castle walls, completely hiding the island from view.

Many of the Fomorians panicked, broke off fighting, and

fled for the safety of the river. Those remaining began backing up in fear.

Janus roared an order that had halted the possible deserters in their tracks. Apparently they feared their boss more than what was coming from inside those clouds. For now.

The odds were getting more even.

Janus quickly turned his attention back to Ian and began chanting, his words quick and crisp. It wasn't midnight, but whatever was coming had lit a fire under Janus, making him rush to get the ritual done now.

Nothing could reach him.

Our time had run out.

The combined powers of the ley lines, the cursed gems, and the vampire families' First Relics were there to power more than the breaking of the Tuatha Dé Danann curse; they were there as fuel for a shield that even Rake's most powerful magic couldn't destroy.

Just as four thousand years ago, no one had been able to stop Balor from incinerating the Tuatha Dé Danann with his all-powerful, all-killing eye—until Lugh Lámhfhada had thrown his spear through it.

I didn't think. I knew what I had to do. It was Ian's last chance.

I snatched the spearhead from its scabbard and ran toward Janus's shield and that altar—and Ian.

Janus's chanting reached its peak as he raised his arms over his head, dagger held aloft, glowing red at his words. He must have heard or sensed movement from behind him. He turned, and when he saw that it was me, he smiled.

Ian's face blanched of any remaining color as he struggled against his bonds. "Mac, no!"

I had grasped the spearhead at the base, keeping the point tucked up against my palm and underside of my forearm. Janus only saw me sprinting toward him, presumably unarmed, a human woman running toward certain death in a desperate attempt to save her partner. Only at the last instant did I flip the spearhead in my hand, slicing in an uppercut into the shield. It vanished as if it had never existed, sending me sprawling in the rocky dirt to land at Janus's feet.

The Fomorian leader snatched me up by the back of the neck and I slashed out with the spearhead, slicing open his robe and cutting a thin line in his chest which smoked at the contact.

Janus dangled me at arm's length, careful not to touch the spearhead—or to let the spearhead touch him. I continued to slash at him with it, but Janus held me by the scruff of the neck like a kitten whose claws couldn't reach him.

Thunder and lightning boiled from the clouds. Seeing their leader occupied with me, the Fomorians around the altar and inside the castle walls fled in fear of what was coming. Calvin and Liz took advantage of Janus being turned away from Ian to quickly cut his bonds and drag him off the altar.

When Janus realized his prize had escaped, he pulled me against him, his forearm tight around my throat, cutting off my air. His other hand gripped my wrist, controlling it, turning the spearhead I clutched toward me. His power surged down through my hand, and I couldn't have dropped the spearhead if my life depended on it—and now it did.

"Surrender, Scion of Lámhfhada, or watch me cut her to pieces with your ancestor's own weapon."

The cloud surrounding the island split from the direction of Storm King Mountain and a glowing host of warriors, men and women, galloped across the river toward us, riding blazing white horses. The golden glow from them was so bright it hurt my eyes to look directly at them, but I wasn't about to look away. I knew what I was seeing—a supernatural race that the ancient Irish had worshiped as gods, a race that hadn't been seen by mortal eyes in thousands of years.

They were Noel Tierney's drawings brought to vibrantly colored life.

The Tuatha Dé Danann. I felt Janus call to the power of the ley lines to shield him.

Nothing.

He tried again, stepping back and dragging me with him so that his body touched the altar containing the gems and First Relics. There was a sputter of magic, but it fizzled when it tried to rise past the spearhead I clutched in my hand.

Janus snarled and flung me away from him.

I landed hard against jagged rock. I must have blacked out for a time. When I came to, Rake had covered me with his body, the Tuatha Dé Danann were inside the castle walls, and Janus was encased once again in a protective shield, which now was more like a prison.

"Those aren't the Storm King's minions," I managed.

"No, they are not." Rake wrapped his arms around me and stood.

"Where's the spearhead?" I asked.

"I've got it."

"Give it here and I'll cut the bastard out of his bubble again."

"Not so fast. We've got another problem."

Moreau quickly strode to where we were, half of his face blue with Fomorian blood. "The Fomorians are coming back."

An explosion came from the east wall as it came crashing down. Our people ran away from the walls to take up defensive positions around us. The kraken grabbed the still-standing sections of wall with its tentacles and tossed them aside like toy building blocks.

Calvin and Liz solemnly stepped between the approaching Fomorians and a still-unsteady-on-his-feet Ian. A growling Yasha and silent Vlad and his vampire mercenaries stood between us and the advancing horde.

Coming back? Why? Weren't they terrified of the Tuatha Dé Danann? Then I saw and understood. The Fomorians *were* terrified. They came back because they had no choice. The Tuatha Dé Danann's forces stood between the Fomorians and the water, their only hope of escape, an escape that had now been cut off. They had no choice but to fight for their lives.

Though no one was fighting right now. The settling stone and dust was the only sound. It was a standoff. The Tuatha Dé Danann stood with their backs to the water, facing the Fomorian forces, holding their weapons at the ready. The Fomorians near us stood ready to protect Janus should we make a move against him.

No one moved. The silence was absolute, and the threat of deadly violence hung heavily in the air.

"You have no power here," Janus was telling a tall, glowing figure standing just outside of his protective shield. The man's face glowed nearly as bright as his golden armor. He wore no helmet, his pale hair loose and flowing, a gem-encrusted circlet resting on his brow.

Ian stood by his side. I was relieved to see that my partner was not glowing.

"The Dark One speaks the truth. I cannot curse his army back into exile," the Tuatha Dé Danann's leader told Ian. "We are no longer of this world. We cannot curse a race who is."

"Then why are you—" Ian began.

Janus laughed. "I want to spill Lámhfhada blood myself, but I want my people free to ravage this world more." He raised his voice to a clarion shout with words I didn't understand.

"He calls to his warriors and cursed ones to kill Lámhfhada's heir." The Tuatha regarded Rake with eyes as bright as emeralds. "They may or may not heed his words. I am no longer of this world, so my voice has no power here. A mage of strength can speak the words and mend the curse. You have seen the words in fire and your power is great."

The curse on the folio in the SPI Archives. How did they know Rake had—

"Yes, I have seen the words," Rake said. "But I do not know how to speak them."

"With a touch, I can teach you."

"I am not of this world, either."

The bright warrior gazed down at me and smiled. "In choosing this brave one, you have chosen this world over the one of your birth. You know this."

I glanced sharply at Rake.

"And if I fail?" he asked.

"The Fomorians will spill the blood of our heir and your valiant companions. The fractured curse will be truly broken, and Janus and his legions will have the freedom to take this world."

Rake gave a weak smile. "No pressure." Then he handed me over to Alain Moreau and stood tall. "Teach me."

The Tuatha Dé Danann's leader laid his glowing hands on either side of Rake's head for only a few seconds. As soon as he released him, Rake began to speak, his voice magnified by the three remaining walls, projecting it toward the approaching Fomorians, the ancient language spilling from his lips, each word sending a shiver of power through him. As the final word passed his lips, a great cry went up from the island all around us as the curse did its work. Portals flashed like strobes as the Fomorians were pulled from where they stood, their bodies growing indistinct and glowing nearly as bright as the Tuatha Dé Danann as they were pulled like shooting stars from the island and through the underwater portals, banished back to where they'd come from.

Rake's dark eyes rolled back in his head and he collapsed

in a boneless heap to the ground. I wasn't fast enough to catch him, but Ian was.

A jagged line of darkness opened like a wound at the foot of the altar. What looked like stars gleamed from inside, but their color was wrong—or at least wrong for our world.

"Those greater than I await their chance," Janus told us. "They have begun to awaken. They will find you. I will be there to guide them, and this time, you will not escape."

Janus stepped through the portal and it closed behind him as if it had never existed.

And we were alone.

37

CALVIN went over with his med kit and squatted down to check on Rake. Apparently satisfied, he turned to Ian. "You hungry? I think we got some leftover burgers from the picnic."

Ian just stared at him. "Picnic?"

Rake didn't regain consciousness until we'd gotten him back to our picnic/staging area.

We'd folded down the seats in the Range Rover to made a bed, and I had his head in my lap.

"I don't understand why I passed out," Rake was saying. He was still groggy.

"Honey, I hate to be the one to break it to you, but that curse was originally cast by a god."

"Yes."

"You're not a god."

"I'm not?"

"No."

I glanced outside to where Kylie and Ian were having a

passionate reunion. "Eh, dating a god—or even a descendant of one—is overrated."

Rake smiled sleepily. "You think so?"

I kissed him softly on the lips. "I know so."

Moreau had contacted the Garrisons as soon as Janus had sent his warriors and the hydra to kill them and bring back Kylie and Kitty. The ladies and the werewolves had been ready for them. Kitty and Kylie weren't slouches in the weapons department; and as to the werewolves, let's just say that Bill and Nancy Garrison and their crew topped Bill's Big Rock Tournament catch weight, bagging a hydra and half a dozen Fomorians. The rest ran back to the river with their fins between their legs just in time to get sucked into those portals. I'd loved to have seen that, but Bill Garrison was a natural-born storyteller, so it had been almost like I was there. Janus's shield dome had protected him from more than us and the Tuatha Dé Danann. It had shielded him from Rake's repair of the fractured curse. He'd had just enough time to escape, and escape he had.

Once we'd been sure there weren't any more Fomorian stragglers hanging around, Moreau had contacted headquarters to let them know our mission had been a success.

Little had we known how much of a success it'd been.

When Janus had begun his ritual, the curse had cracked, and there'd been reports of undersea earthquakes, tsunami, and rogue waves around the world. These events were for the most part written off as seismic or weather-related incidents. Not so coincidentally, at the same time, there'd been sightings of various large sea monsters, kaiju, and kraken. These sightings had been either unconfirmed or explained by the weather or seismic phenomenon.

Vlad Cervenka stood off to the side, relighting his cigar, a duffel bag full of an assortment of ancient vampire bones at his feet. Janus had taken the relics out of their safe deposit boxes. That'd be some trick to get the right bones back to the right family. Maybe like Lugh's Spear, the bones would glow when their descendants picked them up. Maybe not. Alain Moreau walked over to him and shook his hand and began talking to the big Czech. I wondered if it was a job offer.

Rake had dozed for a few minutes, then he opened his eyes, his brow creased. "Calik?"

"Calik is fine," I assured him. "His squadron is fine; their dragons are fine. Also, they've gone home."

When Calik was sure their job was finished, he'd saluted us and led his Royal Fighter Squadron back through their portal.

"He said they couldn't stay here any longer than they had to," I added.

Rake woke up a little more. "There's a situation in the Seven Kingdoms," he said solemnly. "They're needed."

"I heard one of them mention an expedition."

Rake nodded, his dark eyes gazing at the stars through the Rover's moon roof.

"Do you need to go with them?" I asked quietly.

"No. If it doesn't go well, my people will need a place to go. I can do more good for them and their allies here."

"Are we about to have guests?" I asked.

"I hope it doesn't come to that."

"You called it 'the Seven Kingdoms.' You didn't call it 'home.'"

"I didn't, did I?"

"No, you didn't." I hesitated. "The Tuatha said you'd chosen this world—and me."

"He did—and I have." Rake's eyes went from the stars to my face. "Though that statement wasn't entirely accurate. My home is wherever you are."

I leaned down to kiss him, wondering how should I go

about introducing an incredibly hot and handsome goblin to my family?

Alain Moreau had wanted Ian to take a week off.

Ian took the weekend.

My partner got a standing ovation when he stepped off the elevator into the bull pen on Monday morning. SPI agents never let any opportunity go by to give our fellow agents a hard time.

Ian was a descendant of not one but two not-so-mythological Irish kings, so it was a given that his office chair would be decked out like a throne and have one of those Burger King paper crowns perched on the back. We'd even gotten him not one but two Ultimate Breakfast Platters (to satisfy even a king-sized appetite) and had them laid out on his desk on a silver platter.

Ian loved it.

A meeting with Noel Tierney in his professional capacity was a given when an agent had had a particularly tough mission. Kidnapped by a race of sea monster gods and nearly being sacrificed by their leader to bring about worldwide Armageddon certainly qualified. Then there was the not-insignificant life change that came with being the descendant of a legendary hero of Irish not-mythology.

We already knew one such SPI agent. Rolf Haagen in SPI's Norwegian office. Rolf's sword, that he'd described at the time as a family heirloom, had nearly killed Janus that New Year's Eve under Times Square. Ian had used it to cut into him like hot butter. On any other night, all of Midtown would have heard his screams. It turned out Rolf's family heirloom was one of those swords with a name.

Gram.

Rolf's ancestor had quite a name, too.

Sigurd.

At the time, I didn't know whether to be really impressed that we knew the descendant of a legendary Norse hero, or to be really worried for the safety and continued well-being of the Norse gods.

My partner had one up on Rolf Haagen. His ancestor *was* a god—or at least what the ancient Irish believed to be a god. Where the Tuatha Dé Danann had actually came from, no one knew. Ian didn't have a problem with that part of his lineage. It was knowing he had a Fomorian side that might wake him up at night. Noel could help with that. Ian had a stack of reading material to catch up on, and ancestors to research. Elizabeth Wellesley had promised to deliver everything SPI had to his tablet. I couldn't blame Ian; if my ancestors had been that cool/evil, I'd have wanted to know everything about them, too.

Like Rolf Haagen and Gram, there'd be times when the spear of Lugh would be needed. And as I had fortunately discovered, the spearhead didn't need to be attached to a shaft to do its thing. Though you couldn't exactly walk around town with a seven-foot spear; even jaded New Yorkers would have a problem with that. Probably. That didn't mean Ian wouldn't have access to the weapon of his ancestor. Ian could do the concealed-carry thing under his jacket. In fact, I had a feeling Ian's trusty machete was about to have some illustrious company.

For now, our Research and Development folks were studying the spearhead. They loved getting their hands on supernatural weapons for study. Our commandos had also gathered the tridents and nets that some of the Fomorians had left behind. Our lab people would be giddy with geeky joy for weeks.

Once again, Ian had asked that I come with him to see Noel. This time, it wasn't because he was nervous or didn't like the idea of seeing the agency shrink.

He told me that since I was his partner, this was a part

of who he was now, and I should be there. He'd wanted Kylie to come as well, but she and her entire department were swamped dealing with news that was coming out of the Hudson Highlands concerning strange sightings, sounds, and phenomena late last week.

"You aren't the first SPI agent to be descended from an ancient god, goddess, or hero," Noel was telling Ian. "In fact, you aren't even in the first dozen. I was going to suggest that you come to our next meeting."

"*Next* meeting?" I asked. "This is a regular thing?"

"Oh yes. We meet every month. The next one's here in New York."

"So it's like a support group?"

"We try to avoid using that kind of terminology."

I could see why. People talked about their feelings in support groups. I couldn't see a bunch of demigods and superheroes sitting in a circle with boxes of Kleenex talking about their feelings. But if they did, I'd love to be a fly on the wall.

Ian slowly raised an eyebrow. "So, what exactly goes on in these meetings?"

"We share and discuss the challenges that can come with having a famous bloodline—and some of the abilities that can manifest as a result."

I didn't think Ian heard anything past "share."

"It helps to accept and deal with them," Noel continued, "when you know that others are experiencing the same thing."

It took him a moment, but Ian slowly nodded in understanding and maybe even agreement.

Noel smiled, and I detected a wee bit of relief there. "However, boasting about your feats of daring and challenging each other to tests of strength is against the bylaws."

Ian just looked at him. "Bylaws for a support group?"

"For this bunch, it was needed. I moderate the sessions—

so I have my own set of challenges." Noel's smile faded. "And you certainly won't be the first in the group whose nemesis has threatened to return with new allies."

I remembered Janus's parting words. I imagined Ian was doing the same.

"Those greater than I await their chance," Janus had told us. *"They have begun to awaken. They will find you. I will be there to guide them, and this time, you will not escape."*

Ian smiled. "Bring it."

ABOUT THE AUTHOR

Lisa Shearin is the *New York Times* bestselling author of the Raine Benares novels, a comedic fantasy adventure series, as well as the SPI Files novels, an urban fantasy series best described as *Men in Black* with supernaturals instead of aliens. Lisa is a voracious collector of fountain pens, teapots, and teacups, both vintage and modern. She lives on a small farm in North Carolina with her husband, four spoiled-rotten retired racing greyhounds, and enough deer and woodland creatures to fill a Disney movie.

Visit her online at lisashearin.com, facebook.com /LisaShearinAuthor, and twitter.com/LisaShearin.